Futuris...

Love in another...
"Saranne Dawson's fut... ...ances hold readers
spellbound!"

—*Romantic Times*

MAGIC...

Connor made a sound low in his throat, and a soft sigh
escaped from Jillian's parted lips. It was a silent
acknowledgment that they stood at the edge of childhood
friendship, testing its outer limits.

And then their lips met slowly, so very tentatively, clinging
to the moment, trembling on the brink of the next.

It felt so very right—and so wrong. This was Connor, her
dearest friend. And this was Jillian, his little sister. And they
were both surrounded by very adult bodies that were urging
them on to a path that was exciting—and terrifying.

"Would you like me to sleep in here—on the floor?"
Connor asked.

In that brief space between his question and the
qualification, Jillian felt her body saying yes. But aloud, she
said, "No, I'll be fine."

Connor came back to her, kissed the top of her head lightly,
then said good night and slipped out the door.

For one brief moment, Jillian had glimpsed a magic that
was far beyond anything she and Connor had known in
childhood. And she wanted that magic....

On Wings of Love

Saranne Dawson

LOVE SPELL ◆ **NEW YORK CITY**

LOVE SPELL®

June 1994

Published by

Dorchester Publishing Co., Inc.
276 Fifth Avenue
New York, NY 10001

Printed in the United States of America.

Prologue

"You can't, Connor! I won't let you!"

Connor said nothing. Tears he refused to shed were stinging his eyes as he stared at the eleven-year-old girl who stood there, her huge blue eyes blazing and her small fists planted against her slim hips. She punctuated each word with a shake of her unruly black curls. Through the film of tears, he envisioned the woman she would become—the woman he'd never see.

"It's a great honor, Jillian. My mother says—"

"I don't care what she says! You can't leave! You belong to *me*!"

From the greater wisdom of his fourteen years, he understood she was really saying that they belonged to each other in some way that neither of them really understood.

Pain twisted like a knife in his gut. Three years

ago, when he was her age, he hadn't understood, either. But he was older now, and he knew that he'd made the right decision. If only it didn't hurt so much.

He smiled at her and reached out to take her hand, but she slapped it away.

"I have to go now, Jillian. They're waiting for me. I . . . I'll never forget you."

He turned away quickly and started back to the house, where they awaited him. When he reached the wide steps that led to the massive front door, he paused. She had turned her back on him. Her face was lifted to the heavens, and as he watched, she raised one arm and made a slow, circling motion with her hand. He looked up, too, and saw the dark shape silhouetted against the blue sky. The kera stopped its slow glide and seemed for a moment to hang motionless in midair, then began to dive toward her.

With that image burned into his brain, Connor went inside to greet his future.

Chapter One

Jillian climbed the precipitous rock face with all the ease of a lifetime spent in such pursuits. Three keras circled overhead briefly, acknowledging her presence with their piercing shrieks before flying off in search of food.

The nests were widely scattered along the ledges of the cliff, sometimes alone and sometimes in small groups, depending upon the space available. On each nest sat a kera, watching her with dark, intelligent eyes that left her only long enough to check on the buff-colored, fuzzy offspring gathered around them in the nest.

Jillian reached the first ledge and crouched beside a nest, talking softly to the great golden bird as she examined the nestlings with an expert eye. They were perhaps three or four days old, and all, she saw with great relief, appeared to be healthy. There was no sign of the disease that had claimed so many of them last year.

She dug into the pouch strapped to her waist and withdrew a treat, watched closely by the adult kera, who knew very well what was in that pouch. The treat was a piece of dried meat mixed with cornmeal and molasses. She'd begun making them years ago, after a greedy kera had stolen a molasses cake she was eating.

The huge bird plucked the treat neatly from between her fingers with its big, hooked beak, then made a low sound that was uncannily like a human chuckle. Jillian never failed to smile at that sound—but her smile was forever tinged with sadness. She'd known only one person who could truly imitate that sound.

She fed small treats to each of the nestlings, then moved on, repeating her routine at each of the two dozen nests. She found no diseased nestlings and had found none yesterday, either, when she'd visited the other rookery.

By the time she had made her way back down the treacherous cliff, Jillian was tired but happy. She removed the hobbles from her mare and set off across the hills, riding home into a blazing sun that was slowly sinking toward the far horizon.

It was going to be a good year. Her current class of trainees were coming along quite nicely and would be ready for their introductions to their new masters right on time, at summer's end. And perhaps with this year's group, she would actually be able to meet the ever growing demand.

Because so many nestlings had died last year, the list was long.

But then, the list was always long. A few others had attempted to breed keras in captivity, but the results were poor. Either there were no nestlings at all, or the birds died young. Only here, in the rocky cliffs at the edge of her family's land, did they breed well, returning there each spring from wherever they had been taken.

Keras had first appeared in the lands of the Lesai a little over a hundred years ago. No one knew their origins, but her ancestors who'd discovered them believed they were a crossbreed between the great falcons that had been used for hunting for many centuries and some unknown bird that had perhaps been blown off course while migrating.

Falcons were strong and intelligent, but the birds that came to be known as keras—a word in her language that meant alien or stranger—had proved to be much larger and stronger than falcons, as well as more intelligent.

At first, the keras, too, had been trained merely for hunting. But then Jillian's great-grandfather, whose fascination with the keras had been as strong as her own, had had an inspiration. And his vision had forever altered the lives of the Lesai.

He had turned over the management of the family's vast estates to his younger brothers and had devoted himself completely to training the birds as messengers. Under his patient tutelage, the keras were trained not just to travel from one designated place to another, but also to seek out their master wherever he happened to be.

The lands of the Lesai were vast and sprawling and in most places sparsely populated, with noble families like Jillian's often possessing tens of thousands of acres on which they grew crops or mined or logged. A kera, as it traveled from one estate to another, or within a given estate, could be depended upon to carry its message to its master directly.

Only in Lesai City was it impossible for a kera owner to receive a message directly. The birds simply didn't like crowded places, and so they flew instead to specially constructed towers on the outskirts. So intelligent were they that they could be commanded either to give over the message in the leather pouches that were strapped to their necks to the tower staff or simply to wait there until their master appeared.

Everyone was in awe of the magnificent golden birds with their seven-foot wingspans. A few people—mostly ignorant rural peasants—considered the keras to be the devil's messengers, but the vast majority of the populace treasured them. Possession of a kera was a mark of success among the growing merchant class and had long since become a requirement among the nobility. To kill one brought the death penalty— a penalty reserved in Lesai society only for the most heinous crimes.

Unfortunately, the kera's life span was not long, no more than ten to twelve years, so replacements were constantly needed. And when the birds knew their time had come, they invariably returned here to Talita to await death.

It was nearly dusk when Jillian reached the manor. After turning over her mare to a stableboy, she hurried to the great house, eager to bathe and fill her empty stomach. When she entered, she found her brother Jakeb conferring with their longtime housekeeper, Marra, at the rear of the large foyer. Both turned to her.

"There's no sign of disease this year," she said with a smile.

"Great news, Jillian," Jakeb said. "And after you've bathed and changed, I have some more good news for you."

Jillian started to ask what it was, then stopped. She loved Jakeb, but he was a man set in his formal ways, and it was clear that, whatever the news was, it would have to wait until she once again became a lady of the manor, instead of an ersatz stableboy. He deplored her rough clothes— especially her trousers—but he was practical enough to accept their necessity.

Marra, the housekeeper, smiled at her. "I'm very happy for you, Lady Jillian."

"Thank you, Marra." Jillian inclined her head politely. Marra had once been very dear to her, having raised her from birth since her own mother had died within days of Jillian's entry into the world. But then Marra had betrayed her—and in twenty years, Jillian had never forgiven that betrayal. To Jakeb's pleas that she grant Marra forgiveness, Jillian had stated, "Some things can *never* be forgiven."

Jillian climbed wearily up the wide stairs and

went to her suite, where she stripped off the dirty, sweaty clothing and slipped happily into the bath her maid quickly drew for her. She wondered what Jakeb's news was, reflecting wryly that what might be good news to him wasn't necessarily viewed with the same pleasure by her.

Jillian had two brothers, both of them some years older than she. They had spoiled her shamelessly from the day she was born—aided and abetted by their late father. Jakeb lived here and managed the family estate, Talita—the largest in the land—while Timor lived in the city, where he was a close adviser to their uncle, the ruler of the Lesai.

Most highborn women in their society married at eighteen or nineteen, and when Jillian had reached that age, her brothers had had several candidates in mind. But Jillian had refused to accept them, and at thirty-one, she remained unmarried.

Instead, she devoted herself to the keras—a devotion that had actually begun when Jillian had reached three—and her brothers had long since given up any hope that she would marry, even though her position was such that she could certainly still find a husband.

Jillian didn't want a husband. She didn't dislike men, but she disliked the demands of marriage and the inevitable children. Furthermore, she'd observed over the years that even the best men somehow became tyrants when a sweetheart became a wife.

These were the reasons she gave herself and

others, but the truth was that Jillian had never forgotten her love for a boy who'd been taken from her: Marra's son, Connor.

Jillian hadn't understood the pain then, but years later when she read a story that referred to two people as soul mates, she'd understood instantly that she and Connor had had a perfect love and a perfect understanding.

But Marra, Connor's widowed mother, had sent him off to the Kraaken, to live out his life on their secluded island. To Marra's mind, as to many others among the peasantry, it was a high honor for her son to be chosen for that mystical priesthood. But to Jillian, Marra's had been the worst sort of betrayal. And Connor had gone along with it, seduced, no doubt, by all the tales of Kraaken magic and immortality—tales Jillian regarded as being self-serving nonsense.

Jillian hated the Kraaken—and if *she* had possessed magic, she would have used it to destroy their island home long ago. The large island lay just off the coast of Lesai City, and seeing its gray, humped shape never failed to invoke a burning rage within her. Most of the other nobility distrusted the Kraaken; Jillian *hated* them.

She dressed in a simple blue gown the color of her eyes, then slipped over her head a thin gold chain with a gem-studded pendant in the shape of a kera, a gift her brothers had given her some years ago. Then she went down to join her brother, sister-in-law and their uncle, her mother's brother, who had moved into the great house following his wife's death a few years ago.

Tessa, her sister-in-law, greeted her with an expression of pleasure over the health of the nestlings. Jillian tolerated her sister-in-law, but she wasn't overly fond of her. Tessa came from a family of considerably less stature ("Barely nobility at all," one of Jillian's insufferable aunts had proclaimed), and apparently to make up for that, she had become unbearably stuffy and formal. What Jillian was prepared to tolerate in her brother was far less acceptable in this sister by marriage. The truth was that Jillian had liked Tessa a lot better before the other woman had become so enamored of her position.

Her uncle's greeting and pleasure over the news of the nestlings was far more real. He shared her love for the birds and helped as best he could, given the fact that he was somewhat crippled.

With very little prodding, Jillian launched into a description of her day and forgot all about Jakeb's news until the dessert course was being served.

"As I said earlier, Jillian, I have some news of interest to you. Timor included it in the pouch he sent me and asked that I pass it on to you, along with his greetings and his eagerness to see you.

"The news is a rumor he heard, and before he passed it on, he went himself to interview the ship's captain. The man is new to his command and to his route and hadn't been in our port before. He comes from Trantor, but his family's home is somewhere beyond there, near the desert.

"He told Timor that the people who live in the mountains beyond the desert have great birds

16

that they've trained—birds quite similar to keras, but larger. He'd actually seen them a few times himself, although not close up. Timor took him out to the tower and he says they're quite similar except for size."

Jillian had stopped eating the moment her brother mentioned the keras. She exchanged an excited look with her uncle. They all knew that she dreamed of one day finding the birds believed to have crossbred with falcons all those years ago. She had in fact made a journey to Trantor, as well as to some other distant places, hoping to find someone who could tell her of the birds' origins. But this was the first time she'd heard of anyone who'd seen such birds.

"Go there, Jillian," her uncle urged. "I can manage the training alone at this point and the nestlings won't be ready to begin their training until fall."

"Timor said that if you want to speak to the captain yourself, you should come to the city right away. He'll be sailing again in three days' time. Not that you require any urging, of course," Jakeb added with an indulgent smile.

The sun had barely risen the next morning when Jillian set out for the city, accompanied by two members of the family's personal guard. Both Jakeb and her uncle were up to see her off. Jakeb frowned, as he always did, when he saw her trousers and the absence of a sidesaddle.

"Don't worry, Jakeb," she smiled. "I won't forget to stop at the tower and change into something suitable, then ride into the city in a carriage."

She saw the guards just barely suppressing their amusement. Jakeb never failed to frown and she never failed to remind him that she knew how to be a lady when required.

Her uncle took her hand. "Godspeed, child. And may you find them this time. Don't worry about the training if you decide to journey across the sea."

"I won't, Uncle," she replied, squeezing his hand. "I know they're in good hands with you."

Then they were off, flying down the road from the house that led to the wider road through the family's lands that eventually joined the Great Southern Road into Lesai City. The morning was glorious and the horses were fresh, so Jillian let her mare run for a time as they passed through fields where peasants were already plowing the land for the spring planting.

If it had been Jakeb or Timor riding by, the peasants would have stopped their work and bowed or curtsied, but Jillian received a friendly wave, which she returned. She was, and always had been, much loved by the people on the huge estate. Tessa, her sister-in-law, visited them only when absolutely required to do so, but Jillian had been a regular guest in their homes since childhood.

It was midafternoon by the time they reached a high spot on the busy Great Southern and came into view of the two tall towers at the city's edge. Beyond it, the white palace shimmered on its hill at the center of the sprawling city.

The day was very clear and Jillian turned toward the sea that lapped at the city's door. Her gaze narrowed and her mouth became twisted with anger when she saw the faint dark smudge out where sea and sky met: the island of the Kraaken. It wasn't generally visible from this vantage point. One of the guards followed her gaze.

"There're rumors that the Kraaken are planning to start some trouble again," he told her. He got to the city far more frequently than she did.

She made a sound of disgust. "There's nothing new in that, Correy. I don't understand why my uncle tolerates them."

"Mayhap His Majesty fears them, as most folks do," the guard suggested.

"Nonsense! He told me himself that he doesn't believe in their magic—or their ridiculous claims of immortality. No one's ever seen their magic, and as far as their claims of immortality are concerned—well, that's a safe enough claim when they hide out on their island. Let's be on our way."

"You don't believe in those old stories about how they used their magic to aid us in battle then?" the guard asked as they set off again.

"I don't believe *any* old stories that are passed along by word of mouth," she stated. "They tend to stray far from the truth in the telling."

They reached the nearest tower less than an hour later. It was a tall white structure built of the same smooth stone that was the standard building material for all fine homes in the city. The tower had a sturdy base that tapered to a slender top, from which jutted an elaborate, two-tiered balcony.

Jillian could see several keras perched on the upper tier of the balcony, and as Jillian and the two guards rode toward it, one bird took off and dove toward her, then circled over her head, emitting its characteristic shriek.

She smiled and raised her hand, making the circling motion that the birds understood to be a greeting. The other birds on the tower joined the first one, so that her arrival at the tower was accompanied by a cacophony of cries.

When Jillian and the guards dismounted at the base of the tower, the birds swooped down, surrounding her. Jillian withdrew treats from her pouch and distributed them. The keras chuckled their thanks, then took off again.

The towermaster had been alerted to her arrival by the noisy birds and hurried out to greet her. In this place, Jillian was accorded even more respect than her uncle, the king.

"A too rare pleasure, milady," he said, bowing. "Will you stay for some refreshments or only to change for the city?"

"Only to change this time, Hektor, but thank you for the offer. Perhaps my men would like some refreshment while I transform myself into something acceptable to my brother."

She went off to the small cottage attached to the tower, where the towermaster's wife greeted her warmly and led her into a small bedroom to change. Since their children were grown and gone, they had given over this room to Jillian and kept a change of clothing there for her, so that she wouldn't have to carry anything with her. The rest of her city wardrobe was at her brother's home.

By the time she had changed into a gown and light cape, the carriage sent by her brother had arrived. A kera had been dispatched shortly before Jillian's own departure this morning to inform her brother of her arrival.

The towermaster came to see her off. "His Majesty is considering the construction of another tower—perhaps even two, milady," the man told her.

"I'm not surprised," she responded. "I told him several years ago that they should soon be building more. I just hope they also take my advice to build them farther out. These two will soon be useless, because the city will swallow them up."

He inquired about the nestlings and she told him they were all healthy this year, then issued her annual invitation to visit Talita during the summer to see the fledglings. He accepted as always.

She bade farewell to both the towermaster and to her guards, who would ride ahead into the city, leaving her in the care of Timor's servants on the carriage.

Soon, the noise of the city assaulted her ears. Jillian always found it disconcerting and wondered why anyone would choose to live amid such an unholy din. Even in the high-walled garden of her brother's home, the city was a steady, droning presence.

But most of the nobility lived here and visited

their estates only occasionally, entrusting them to the care of managers. Jillian's family had always been the exception. By tradition, the eldest brother made his home on the estate, a fact that Jillian knew irritated her sister-in-law. Jillian, of course, could have chosen to live in the city, but in fact she rarely even visited it, preferring the isolation of Talita and the company of her keras.

The carriage passed through an old and poor section of the city and Jillian saw to her satisfaction that the stinking and unhealthy open sewers here were finally being covered over with wooden planks. She had prevailed upon Timor to get something done about it, and when that hadn't produced results, she'd gone directly to her uncle, the king. Their Majesties were essentially good and well-intentioned people, but they lived in splendid isolation in their hilltop palace and rarely saw how the less fortunate lived.

She wondered if during this trip to the city, she might begin her campaign to have free schools opened for the poor. She smiled, envisioning the long-suffering look her uncle's face would have when she appeared at court with yet another demand. No doubt he was very happy that she chose to remain at Talita most of the time.

Although she wasn't aware of it as the carriage made its slow progress through the narrow streets of the old quarter, Jillian received many stares from passersby—attention attributable both to her beauty and to her reputation as the royal family's eccentric. She would have been surprised to learn how well-known she was in this city she so rarely visited, though it was doubtful that she would have much cared. Jillian paid scant attention either to her appearance or to her image in general. She was—and had always been—her own woman.

Timor's large home sat behind a high stone wall on a slight rise at one edge of the city, in a district reserved for the nobility. Beyond the handsome iron gates were several acres of well-tended grounds. The house itself was built of glistening white stone and topped with a red-tiled roof. Tall, mullioned windows set off the three-storied structure.

Jillian alighted from the carriage as the major-domo opened the massive, carved front door to welcome her with all the formality of his station. Then he ushered her into a small reception room and went to get her sister-in-law.

Timor's wife, Tabeetha, had been a childhood friend of Jillian's, and while those old bonds still existed, they'd been loosened by the different paths their lives had taken. Tabby's childhood enthusiasm and propensity for mischief had been tempered greatly by the life she now lived at court.

When Tabeetha came into the room, she was accompanied by her four-year-old daughter, Shula, who promptly forgot her manners and launched herself, squealing, into Jillian's arms. Jillian scooped up the little girl and swung her around, laughing. She had four nieces and nephews, but Shula was her favorite. Already, the girl was showing an affinity for the keras, and Jillian had hopes that she might one day come to work with her. But she was certain that her brother and sister-in-law had very different—and far more conventional—plans for Shula.

They walked out into the gardens, chatting about friends and relatives as they awaited Timor's arrival. This one was pregnant again; that one had lost a baby; another had scandalized the court with a very daring dress that Tabeetha feared might soon become the fashion.

Tabeetha herself had found a marvelous new dressmaker and wanted Jillian to visit her while she was in the city.

"Why?" Jillian countered. "I have no need of a closetful of dresses. And I'm quite satisfied with my present dressmaker. She makes wonderful trousers for me."

Tabeetha sighed. "Jillian, you never change. Even though you're well past marriage age, I know at least half-a-dozen men who would leap at the chance to offer for your hand if you gave them any encouragement."

"Several of them haven't needed any encouragement," Jillian observed dryly. "And I don't want a husband."

Tabeetha was silent for a moment. Then she said quietly, "It's still Connor, isn't it—even after all these years, and even though you know you could never have married him."

"Connor is dead," Jillian stated succinctly. "The Connor I knew died at the age of fourteen, when the accursed Kraaken came and took him."

"Speaking of the Kraaken," Tabeetha said, wisely changing the subject, "Timor has become rather concerned about them. There are rumors."

"Oh, what sort of rumors?" Jillian recalled that one of her guards had mentioned something.

"The story is that they're trying to stir up trouble between us and the Masani."

"It wouldn't surprise me," Jillian replied. The Masani lands were across the sea and the Lesai had battled with them off and on for centuries, although peace had reigned for many years now. According to the old stories, the Kraaken had aided the Lesai in the last war, providing magic that had made the Lesai victorious.

Those stories, however, came from the Lesai priests, who were known to be under the influence of the Kraaken, although not actually members of the reclusive Kraaken brotherhood.

"But how could they be stirring up trouble among the Masani?" Jillian asked. "Only the recruiters ever leave the island, and then only to come here."

"It seems that they've indicated an interest in recruiting from among the Masani as well."

"Really? Well, the Lesai navy controls the seas, so they can put a stop to that before it starts. And anyway, the Kraaken don't have ships large enough to carry them to Trantor." Trantor was the Masani port.

"Yes, but—" Tabeetha stopped and smiled. Shula dropped Jillian's hand and called, "Daddy! Aunt Jillie's here!"

Both women turned as Timor walked toward

them, trailed by his eight-year-old son, Evan. Timor was a handsome man who shared Jillian's black hair and deep blue eyes, but Jillian, who hadn't seen him for several months, thought that he was beginning to show his thirty-eight years. The lines were etched more deeply into his face and a slight paunch was evident even in his well-cut clothes.

Brother and sister embraced with all the affection of siblings who'd been close all their lives. Timor was younger than Jakeb by three years, though still seven years senior to Jillian.

Jillian then greeted her nephew, Evan, a devilish little boy whose pale blue eyes were always alight with mischief, much as his father's had once been.

"You've grown so tall," she exclaimed, holding him away from her.

"I'm the tallest in my class," he told her proudly. "And the best at kickball, too."

"It's a pity you aren't also the best at your studies," his father remarked ruefully.

"As if *you* were," Jillian grinned. "I can recall our father telling you once that his fondest hope was that you'd one day have a son just like you."

Timor laughed. "Trust you to remember that, Jillie. Tell me, how are the nestlings this year? Any sign of disease?"

"None. I may even be able to fill all of last year's orders. Now tell me about this captain. I'm eager to meet him."

"I've invited him to join us for breakfast tomorrow morning. I'm almost afraid to say it, Jillie, and get your hopes up, but it really sounds as though the birds he saw might be the ones you seek. He even suggested the possibility that a particularly violent storm could have carried them across the sea. He says that's been known to happen."

"Will you go after them?" Tabeetha asked.

"Oh, yes. Absolutely. Uncle Rood can handle the final part of training. He's become quite good with them. And the nestlings won't be ready to begin training until fall, so I have plenty of time."

Tabeetha shook her head, laughing. "You hide yourself out at Talita and rarely even venture into the city, but you don't hesitate to go off on a journey across the sea."

The captain was a tall craggy-faced man who spoke Lesai with a thick accent that required many questions and careful listening, but he confirmed what Timor had already told Jillian, and her excitement grew.

"They're about half again as big as your keras, milady," he said. "I never saw one up close, but as a sailor, I've learned to judge such things pretty well.

"The ones I saw were maybe a shade or two lighter than your keras, but still golden in color. I can't be sure about the shape of their heads or the color of their eyes, but I was told that they have green eyes the color of emeralds.

"I was just a boy when I saw them. My father came from a place on the far side of the great desert and he took me back there once. It was my uncle who told me that some of them had been tamed and trained by the hill tribes long ago. He even said there were old tales of the birds having magical powers, though he didn't believe that himself.

"I could see how some people might think that, though," Jillian observed. "They're so intelligent and that sound they make is very close to human. Even here, there are a few rural people who think they're the devil's agents."

The captain nodded. "When Lord Timor took me out to the tower and I saw one up close, I got this feeling that it knew what we were saying. It's something in their eyes."

"Do you know anything about this hill tribe?" Jillian asked. "Would they be friendly to outsiders?"

"Oh, they're friendly enough, I think. They keep pretty much to themselves, but they've always traded with the desert tribes."

"Do you have space on your ship to take me to Trantor, Captain?" she asked. "I understand that you're sailing soon."

"I am, milady, but my ship's small and I have no accommodations suitable for a lady."

"I think passage can be arranged on another ship, Jillian," Timor said. "I've already made some inquiries."

The captain took his leave after giving Jillian a map that showed the location of the hill tribe. As soon as he'd gone, Jillian asked her brother about the ship he'd mentioned.

"It's a large, new ship—one of Helza's fleet. The

captain is a seasoned veteran and a man Helza trusts completely." Helza was their cousin—not one of Jillian's favorites, but a highly respected businessman who owned good, sound ships and hired only the best men.

"When does it sail?"

"In two days' time," Timor told her. "But there is something I want to discuss with you."

"Oh?" Jillian caught a note of gravity in her brother's voice.

"Tabby said that she told you about the rumors that the Kraaken might be up to something?"

"Yes, she mentioned that."

"Two days ago, High Priest Jenner sent a message to court requesting ship's passage and an escort for one of their brothers so that he can begin recruiting from among the Masani. The Kraaken's purpose, according to Jenner, is to draw into their priesthood men from other lands, as a way of fostering peace among all peoples."

Jillian made a sound of disgust. "Do you believe that?"

"I don't—and neither does anyone else on the council. Even our uncle is doubtful, though his opinion is, of course, influenced by Aunt Twyla."

"Twyla has always been soft in the head where the Kraaken are concerned," Jillian grumbled.

"Well, you know how it is," Timor shrugged. "She credits the Kraaken with saving Sassy's life, and she's been championing them ever since."

"I'll give the Kraaken credit for one thing,"

Jillian replied. "They're certainly ready to take advantage of any opportunity."

Sasson, their cousin, was the crown prince, a sickly child who had once been declared to be near death by the palace physicians. The priest for the royal family had offered to seek the Kraaken's assistance, and when the boy recovered, the queen was convinced that Kraaken magic had saved his life.

"We cannot refuse Jenner's request," Timor went on, "but what we *can* do is see to it that this recruiter is kept under careful observation. And that's where *you* come in. We would like you to act as his escort."

"Me? An escort for a Kraaken? Have you lost your mind, Timor? Given half a chance, I'd toss him overboard."

"I'm sure you can restrain yourself," Timor replied dryly. "This could be very important, Jillie. Furthermore, if you determine that his *real* mission is to stir up trouble, then something will be done about the Kraaken. Not even Twyla would defend them then.

"You'll be traveling with a contingent of Royal Guards, of course, and they'll keep an eye on him as well. But the council feels the need for a personal emissary here—someone they can trust implicitly. And given your well-known dislike of the Kraaken, you're the perfect choice. Plus you even have a reason for making the journey."

"Very well. But I want an absolute guarantee that if this brother is up to no good, the Kraaken will be gotten rid of."

"Then I suggest that you go to see His Majesty and get that guarantee. I'm sure he'll be delighted to see you," he added with a chuckle.

"No doubt he will." She smiled. "Especially when I tell him it's past time that he starts setting up those free schools, now that he's finally doing something about the sewers."

Chapter Two

Two days later, Jillian boarded the handsome ship, accompanied by four Royal Guards. The day was clear and bright, with a stiff breeze that pushed against the furled sails.

She stood on the deck that smelled pleasantly of wood and newly applied varnish. Timor had come to see her off, as had their cousin Helza, the ship's owner. Both men were now departing. She waved one last time at Timor, then scanned the busy harbor for signs of the Kraaken priest, Brother Averyl.

But there was no sign of him, and she allowed herself the faint hope that the Kraaken had changed their minds. Thanks to the priests who acted as their spies in the city, they undoubtedly knew that she had been selected as escort for their recruiter. And she didn't doubt for one minute that they knew how she felt about them. As a niece to the king—and an outspoken one at that—her opinion regarding the brotherhood would certainly be well-known to them.

Then she saw a Kraaken boat gliding into the harbor, headed for the section reserved for smaller craft. Their boats were easily recognizable, since they were painted the same gold color as the long cassocks worn by the brothers themselves.

Jillian glared at it and at the two men in the boat as they tied up at the dock. She'd seen the brothers only a few times in the years since they'd visited Talita. The only ones who ever left the island were the recruiters, invariably older men with sanctimonious expressions and arrogant walks.

As she watched now, trying to stifle her anger, the one brother started toward her ship, moving easily through the crowds that parted for him. It irritated her to see him accorded respect by the men on the waterfront. Many of them actually bowed as they made way for him.

He was quite tall, she noticed, and broad shouldered as well, hefting his bag as though it weighed nothing at all. He also moved with a litheness that suggested a younger man. Perhaps the rigors of this journey had forced the Kraaken to send someone younger. She tried to see his face, but since she was above him and he was wearing the usual hooded cassock, she couldn't get a good look at him.

She turned away from the railing and went down to her cabin. Protocol undoubtedly dictated that she welcome him aboard, but she'd already decided to walk along the very edges of acceptable behavior with this Kraaken. Brother Averyl was about to learn that not everyone stood in awe of the mighty brotherhood.

Jillian was in her small but comfortable cabin, wondering just how long she could avoid meeting the Kraaken, when there was a knock at her door. She opened it to find one of the cabin boys standing there, holding a lovely crystal decanter filled with a golden liquid.

"Compliments of Brother Averyl, milady," the boy said, proffering the decanter.

Jillian looked at it distastefully, but took it. "Please convey my appreciation and tell him that I will meet with him soon."

When the boy had gone, she opened the decanter and sniffed. She knew what it was. The Kraaken were renowned for the quality of their brandy. All the nobility purchased the costly liquid from them, but she refused to taste it and had berated her brothers for having it in their homes. The Kraaken also made the ornately etched decanters and other lovely glassware, then used both to trade for items they needed from the mainland.

The Kraaken had appeared in the lands of the Lesai more than a century ago. Their origins were shrouded in mystery, but the first brothers weren't Lesai. The rulers at that time had granted them the uninhabited island they now occupied, a large island off the coast that measured more than ten miles in length and nearly the same in width.

Since the brotherhood was celibate, they needed to replenish their numbers and had soon begun to recruit members from among the Lesai, a practice approved by the king at the time, whose generosity might have been tempered with some suspicion.

Always the Kraaken took boys at about the age of thirteen or fourteen, generally from among the peasant classes. To be selected by the Kraaken was considered a mark of honor among the peasants, because the brotherhood was known to subject the boys to rigorous testing and then take only the brightest among them.

No one really knew how many Kraaken there were, or even how they lived, since they forbade any visitors to their island, except for Lesai priests and certain tradesmen, who were permitted no farther than the dock area.

The stories of their magic and their immortality began soon after their arrival, but no one had ever seen any evidence of either. Jillian had once remarked wryly that, if it was true that they were immortal, sooner or later they would overpopulate their island. Timor had countered with a smile that perhaps they would then use their magic to enlarge their home.

She set aside the decanter and decided to go up on deck. They had set sail a half hour ago, and this would be her last chance to see land for more than a week. She hoped wickedly that the Kraaken brother would suffer from seasickness—

a common malady that had never affected her. At least if he did, she wouldn't be forced to endure his company for the entire journey.

Unfortunately, the moment she emerged from the passageway onto the deck, she saw him. His arms were braced against the railing as he stared off to the right at his island home. *Well,* she thought unhappily, *I'd better introduce myself.*

She was less than ten feet from him when he turned in her direction. The stiff breeze suddenly blew the hood away from his head. Jillian stumbled to a halt and grasped the railing. He didn't move, but his gray eyes watched her steadily.

"No!" she cried, her voice a mere whisper. It wasn't possible. She had to be wrong.

"Hello, Jillian," he said, now walking toward her with both his hands outstretched in greeting.

"Connor!"

The name hung there between them, both an affirmation and a denial. It was Connor—and it wasn't. For one brief moment, both the boy and the man occupied the same space. He'd always been tall, but at fourteen, he'd been skinny, too. Now he was both tall and powerful. But his dark brown hair was just as thick and still curled slightly, and those gray eyes were the same. The small cleft in his chin was still there as well, but that chin now seemed more squared, more determined. And the softness of his features had undergone a transformation, reshaping a pleasant-looking boy into a very handsome man.

"It's Brother Averyl now," he said with a slight

smile, his wide mouth curving with a familiar twist. "But it's nice to hear my old name."

Jillian simply didn't know what to say. Connor had been dead to her all these years—a wonderful, cherished memory—and a part of her resented being forced to face this man who was and wasn't the soul mate of her childhood.

"I didn't know you were to be my escort until I came on board," he said, dropping his hands to his sides again when she didn't take them. "Your guards told me that you're making this journey to find some birds. Are you still seeking the origins of the keras?"

She nodded mutely. Her throat felt constricted. How could he stand there so calmly and speak in that low, pleasant voice so different and yet so like Connor's voice?

Of all the torments that could have been devised for her, surely none could be worse than seeing him again. She could not rid herself of the thought that the boy she had loved was still there, trapped in the body of a Kraaken, forever beyond her reach.

"I often think of Talita," he said, turning his head to look back at the rapidly disappearing land. "My mother?"

"She's well," Jillian said in a husky voice. *And what about me, Connor? Did you ever think of me? Or was I never as important to you as you were to me?* The pain of that thought forced her to abandon it quickly.

"She's still at Talita, of course. Memma retired some years ago, so she's housekeeper now."

"And your brothers?"

She told him, paying scant attention to what she said, simply reciting the facts. He turned back to her as she spoke.

"And what of you, Jillian? Your husband doesn't object to your traveling alone?"

"I have no husband. My life is with the keras."

Thick, dark lashes covered his eyes as he dropped his gaze and nodded, but not before she saw something in them. Was it pain?

His mouth curved briefly again. "Your father and your brothers were always overindulgent with you."

She bristled. "They couldn't force me to marry, Connor. And I like the life I have." She hesitated, then let a note of sarcasm creep into her voice. "Can you say the same?"

He was silent for a long moment as he stared at her. Into that void poured a tangle of memories: shared memories of golden days and soft nights, of running through fields and swimming in the lake, of games played in the solarium while the spring rains beat upon the glass—of a perfect contentment in each other's company.

But most of all, there was their shared love for the keras. She had first climbed up to the rookeries with him that last spring they had together—only weeks before the Kraaken had come for him. Later, when he'd thought about it, he realized how surprising it was that Jillian's very protective father had permitted her to go with him. But Conner realized her father had trusted him to take care of her.

"I am content with my life," he said finally.

"There's a difference between being happy and being content," she stated.

His gaze met hers and slid away again. "You still haven't forgiven me, have you, Jillie? I'd hoped that . . . you'd found someone."

"No, I haven't forgiven you—and I haven't found anyone because I haven't looked."

She turned and walked away, forcing herself to move unhurriedly and praying that she'd reach her cabin before the tears started to flow.

Connor turned back to the rail, but her image was burned into his mind. The pretty, lively little girl had become a strong and beautiful woman.

He hadn't really expected it to hurt so much to see her now. He'd had some time to prepare for this meeting, but it hadn't helped.

Jillian was a name whispering in his mind through the many hours of enforced meditation and silence. Jillian was a little girl, filled with boundless enthusiasm and curiosity and love for the keras. She'd been the little sister he'd never had, and then, as the years had passed on the island, she had somehow become the daughter he would never have.

What she had not become to him until now was a woman, and he found himself resenting her for forcing that woman upon him.

He felt the tears come to his eyes and lifted his head into the wind to let them dry. The worst and the best of it all was that she'd never married. His choice had condemned her to a life alone as well. It was no wonder that she'd never forgiven him.

And yet, there was a dark, shameful pleasure in him at that knowledge, too—a bittersweet happiness that they had been so special to each other, so inextricably bound.

Connor thought back to that time. He'd told Jillian—or had tried to tell her—that the decision had been his mother's. But that wasn't true. His mother had left it to him to decide—and he had chosen. It was impossible now for him to get back into the mind of that fourteen year old, but he knew that his decision had been made in part because he'd known the day was coming when things would have to change between them. He was a son of peasants and she was a daughter of the royal family, and the indulgence permitted them as children would have come to an end in a few years.

He hauled himself out of the past and forced himself to consider the present and the immediate future. After twenty years, he had seen her again—and he'd lied to her. It was a necessary lie, and probably one for which she would forgive him—if she could forgive him for anything—but it was still a lie.

Connor had known all along that she would be his escort, just as he had known the nature of her mission. That was why he was here.

On the other hand, he could have been sent for a very different reason. It was entirely possible that those who had conspired to send him on this recruitment mission wanted to get rid of him—and what better way to accomplish that than by placing in his path the greatest temptation he could ever face?

Jillian stumbled into the cabin, blinded by the tears she could hold back no longer. She fell onto the bed, her body convulsed by sobs. She cried out of rage and frustration, out of pain and the sharp, clear sweetness of her memories. And then, finally, she stopped crying because she hadn't cried since she was a child.

She got off the bed, wiped away the last of the tears and then smoothed the wrinkles out of her gown. She was going to see the captain now and insist that they return to port immediately. He wouldn't want to do it, but she knew he wouldn't disobey an order from her.

She started toward the door, then stopped. If they returned to port, then she would never see him again. If they continued, she would be spending weeks, perhaps months, in his company.

She returned to the bed and sat there, thinking. Would it be better to end it now—to send him from her life before she had fully accepted his reappearance? Or should she seize this time, accept it as a gift she'd never thought to receive— a chance to know Connor the man?

Then an ugly thought crept gradually into her mind. Could his presence here be something more than a coincidence? Had he been chosen for this mission because of his old friendship with her? If the Kraaken were really hatching some nefarious scheme, who better to send than the one man among them who could presume upon an old friendship to gain his ends?

The thought horrified her. Would Connor allow himself to be used in such a manner? Would he do such a thing to her? Connor wouldn't; of that she was sure. But Brother Averyl? The dark side of love is hate, and in that moment, Jillian came very close to hating Brother Averyl.

Yes, she decided, it was possible—perhaps even likely—that he'd been especially chosen for this mission. While it was true that Kraaken recruiters were always older men, it was also true that none she'd seen had been so frail that they couldn't have withstood this journey.

The anger that wasn't quite hatred gave rise to a thirst for revenge. Withdrawing her love from Marra, Connor's mother, had never satisfied that need. Marra had always insisted that the decision to join the brotherhood had been Connor's, but Jillian hadn't wanted to believe that. She just hadn't been able to accept the fact that Connor might have chosen to leave her.

But she'd been a mere child then, and no child is capable of understanding the tangled web of human emotions. That Connor had loved her, she didn't doubt even now—but she *did* doubt the importance of those feelings to a fourteen-year-old boy who saw a way to gain the power of magic.

No, if there was revenge to be gained, it should be gained from Connor, who had given her unconditional love—and then abandoned her.

She would continue the journey, and she would watch Connor very carefully, waiting for any sign that his mission was other than recruitment. And if it was, then she would know that he'd come here to betray their love—again.

She remained in her cabin, girding herself for the days and weeks to come, reminding herself over and over that this man was Brother Averyl, a despised Kraaken, and not Connor.

The captain sent his aide to invite Jillian to join him for dinner, and she arrived to find Connor already there. Seeing him again, she felt different. With the shock more or less gone, she found herself facing a stranger. She met his gaze defiantly and had the bittersweet pleasure of knowing this time that she saw pain in his gray eyes. But she would not let herself believe that that pain was the same as hers. No longer would she assume that she had ever meant as much to him as he had to her.

The captain was clearly accustomed to having nobility at his table and was able to keep the conversation flowing effortlessly, despite receiving only limited assistance from his guests. He talked of past voyages and distant lands, then asked Jillian about her quest.

She told him what she'd learned and he expressed an interest in seeing the map the other captain had given her. So after dinner had been cleared away, she brought it and they spread it out on the table. As the two men bent over the map, she told them about the other captain's theory that the birds might have been carried across the sea by a storm.

"That's possible," the captain said, frowning.

"But it's a very long distance. It seems more likely to me that they would have been carried out of the hills and then at some point escaped from their captors. I've never heard or seen of such birds among the Masani, but perhaps they managed to acquire a few. From there, they could easily have been carried across to Lesai in a storm."

"But I've traveled there before," Jillian said, "and I paid agents to search the lands of the Masani to find anyone who might have heard of such birds. No one was ever found."

"Well, if it happened only once and that many years ago, your agents simply might not have found anyone who knew about it. Or perhaps someone did know about it, but also knew that the birds had been stolen," the captain suggested.

Connor, who was still examining the map, spoke up. "If the mountains were their home and they did somehow escape, it makes sense that they would have headed for the mountains near Talita where your ancestor found them, Jillian. If you look at the journey they would have made, the mountains of Talita would be the first place they'd come to that felt like home."

The captain thumped a finger against the map. "You have a long, difficult journey ahead of you, milady. I've never been in the desert, but I've heard stories. Burning hot days and bitter cold nights and nomads who can't always be trusted. Have you ever seen a camel?"

Jillian smiled and nodded. "I saw several of them when I was traveling in the Masani lands. They're very strange-looking creatures, but I know

I'll have to use them to cross the desert."

Connor asked what they were and the captain described them, then inquired if Connor planned to accompany Jillian on that part of the journey. Connor nodded, with a quick glance at Jillian.

"I, too, am eager to see the birds." Then he smiled, and to Jillian, his expression was an aching reminder of the boy. "Besides, this will be my only opportunity to see something of the world."

"You forfeited that opportunity twenty years ago, Connor, by your own choice," Jillian stated coldly.

The captain looked from one to the other of them, obviously confused. Jillian remained silent, regretting her outburst—not for Connor's sake, but for the captain's. So it was Connor who answered the captain's unspoken question.

"I grew up on Talita," he told the captain. "My parents were servants there, and Lady Jillian and I were childhood playmates. My name then was Connor."

"Ahh, I see." The captain nodded. "Then you must be very familiar with the keras yourself, Brother Averyl."

"Yes, I've always admired them. As a boy, I used to climb up to their rookeries, and when Jillian was old enough, I took her up there."

His eyes met Jillian's and she looked away quickly, unable to bear the memories his words invoked. Furthermore, she was sure he knew that and might well continue to use those memories against her at every opportunity.

They talked some more about the journey and about the keras, and then Jillian took her leave. Instead of returning to her cabin, she went up on deck for a stroll in the cool, salt-scented air. If she was to sleep this night, she would need all the assistance she could get.

But the peace of the night was shattered very soon, when Connor joined her at the rail.

"It was my understanding that your purpose in coming on this journey is to recruit from among the Masani," she stated with cold formality. "I had planned to arrange for a Masani escort for you when we reach Trantor, and then to proceed on my own."

That didn't happen to be true. She had promised to keep the Kraaken brother with her throughout the journey, but she was of a mind to challenge his supposed mission right now.

"My recruitment efforts are not necessarily limited to the Masani," he replied, ignoring her peremptory tone. "And *I* understood that I would be accompanying you the entire time."

"And if I refuse to have your company?" she challenged.

"Then I will seek out escorts on my own and follow you."

Jillian felt an unwelcome ripple of memory stirring. This conversation had happened long ago, with different words. Always she had challenged Connor's authority, granted to him as the older one, and always he had somehow deflected it and accomplished his ends.

"Things change—yet remain the same, Jillie,"

he said softly, with a smile in his voice.

She felt his eyes on her, but she kept her face averted as she stared out at the vast darkness of the sea.

"Nothing is the same, Connor," she stated angrily. "You're a Kraaken now."

"Yes, but you're still . . . Jillian."

She clenched the railing. In his brief pause, she had heard the unspoken word *my*. Ownership had never played a part in their relationship before; they had truly belonged to each other, without ever questioning that. But now he no longer belonged to her, while she. . . . Jillian left off that thought and began to walk along the deck. He followed, a shadow from the past that loomed very large in the present.

"Why have the Kraaken decided after all these years to begin recruiting from among other people?" she asked.

"High Priest Jenner has decided that it would be wise for us to begin bringing together men from many lands. I think he sees a role for the brotherhood as peacemakers if war should break out again."

"Why did they send *you?* I thought all recruiters were much older."

"Yes, they are. Perhaps they decided they needed a younger man because of the length of this journey."

She whirled on him suddenly, her blue eyes flashing darkly. "You're lying, Connor! You can't lie to me and expect to get away with it. You were chosen specifically—because of me."

She expected a denial, but to her amazement, he began to chuckle. "You're right; I *was* chosen when they learned that you would be the escort. Your feelings about the brotherhood are well-known among us, Jillie—although I think they do not understand the reason for that dislike. Jenner knows we were childhood friends, and he chose me because he thought you would be less likely to toss me overboard."

He chuckled again. "Perhaps even our high priest is capable of making mistakes from time to time."

She refused to be teased out of her anger. "Why should the Kraaken care about me or my feelings? Jenner must know that however I feel about the Kraaken, I'd never go back on my word to provide protection."

"Jenner believes that you are very powerful. Your priests have told him that you hold considerable authority in court."

"That's ridiculous!" she exploded. "I rarely even go to court, and when I do, my uncle can hardly wait to see the last of me."

"I think you underestimate yourself, Jillian. His Majesty always had a soft spot for you. I overheard him once when he was visiting Talita, telling your father that you were the daughter he'd never had."

"That was long ago—before I started making a nuisance of myself by demanding that he pay more attention to the needs of the poor."

"But from what we've heard, your demands are invariably met."

48

"Aren't you worried that you might not want to go back, Connor?" she asked cruelly, deciding to change the subject, since she knew he was right.

"I have very good reason to want to go back."

"Oh? What reason is that?"

"In five months, I will be thirty-five, and it is at that age that we are granted our powers. Then I will become a member of the Inner Circle."

She said nothing as a chill swept through her that owed nothing to the cool night breeze. He wasn't lying now—and that meant that the stories must be true. The Kraaken *did* have magic, after all. She slanted a glance at him and found him staring at her. She looked away quickly and tossed her head defiantly.

"I don't believe that nonsense about magic and immortality."

"Nevertheless, it is true, Jillian."

We had magic once, she thought with a sharp stab of longing for those simpler days. And in that pain, she recognized the dream that lay hidden in her mind: the hope that Connor would undo what he'd done all those years ago and return to Talita with her.

"What is this magic?" she asked scornfully.

"I can't talk about that."

"Why do you not receive these powers until you're thirty-five? That's a very long wait."

"But a necessary one. We must grow into them, become wise enough to accept them."

"Is that why you seclude yourselves on your island: to become wise? It seems to me that wisdom comes from wide experience."

"Wisdom can also come from long years of study and reflection and meditation, Jillie. That is our way. Staying on the island removes worldly temptations."

She recalled some stories she'd heard and eyed him suspiciously. "But that doesn't always work, does it? I have heard that Kraaken have been known to visit the city's brothels."

"That has happened," he acknowledged. "But very rarely."

"And what happens to them?"

"They must leave the brotherhood."

"If they're caught, that is." She snorted with disgust.

"They are caught when they seek admission to the Inner Circle." He reached out suddenly to take her hand and draw her to a stop. The contact between them was electric, breath snatching, and she knew that he must have felt it as well, because he withdrew his hand quickly.

"Jillian, it is wrong for you to continue to believe that I abandoned you. I realize that the little girl couldn't have understood that, but surely the woman can."

His voice was a soft plea, but she stubbornly shook her head. "No, I don't understand."

"We had no future together, Jillian. Your father didn't object to our childhood friendship, but he would never have countenanced me as a suitor for your hand. You must know that."

She *did* know it—and had known it for years. But knowing it and accepting it were two entirely different matters. To someone who had always

50

gotten what she wanted, no obstacle seemed insurmountable.

"That wasn't the only reason I joined the brotherhood," he went on. "But it played a part. I also wanted an education. Your father was good to me, but I know that he saw no reason why I should be educated beyond the basics. With the Kraaken, I received that education. The brotherhood has wonderful teachers."

She could not dispute that. None of the peasant children on the estate knew more than how to read and write and do simple sums, and the peasant children of Talita were better off than most in that regard.

"You could have chosen the military," she pointed out. "Father would have been happy to sponsor you, and you would have received an education there."

"Yes, I thought about that, and your father *did* make the offer. But I didn't want to be a soldier. I never had the desire to kill and I saw no glory in battle." He stopped and heaved a sigh.

"What I wanted—and what I still enjoy most—is the chance to study things and think about them. It's a pleasant life, Jillian. Often, I disappear into the woods on the island for days at a time, taking books with me. I write poetry," he added with a smile.

Jillian was stunned into total silence, unable to reconcile the boy who'd always been so adventurous with the man who had become so quiet and contemplative. Was he telling her the truth? She'd heard no falseness in his tone, even though she tried very hard. It felt as though he were stealing her memories.

"That's what we look for when we recruit," he said. "We seek boys who want that kind of life."

"But you *weren't* that way, Connor," she insisted, clinging to those fading memories.

He smiled, and even in the dim light, she could see the amusement reflected in his pale eyes. "I didn't spend *all* my time with you, Jillie. Remember the times you accused me of ignoring you? I wasn't, though; I was just off somewhere, reading and thinking. Your father told me once that he thought I'd read more of the books in the library than he ever had."

She felt tears welling up in her eyes. She'd never really known him, after all. She felt bereft—lost without the comfort of those memories.

"You couldn't have understood that need then, Jillie," he said gently. "You were too young. Besides, it's not your nature to be quiet. And I think that hasn't changed."

She looked up at him as the tears began to spill down her cheeks. He reached out to brush them away gently, his fingers warmly caressing her skin.

"Did you truly love me, Connor, or did you just . . . tolerate me?"

He smiled. "I truly loved you, Jillian—and I still do. My feelings haven't changed. You've been my muse all these years, when I've sat beneath a tree or along the shore or in my room. It is through you that I've found the words to put onto paper."

"Connor!" His name came out hoarsely from a suddenly constricted throat. But he may not have heard it, because he turned abruptly and disappeared.

Jillian had never known such anguish in all her life. After Connor's departure all those years ago, she'd been sad and angry and badly hurt. But now her feelings were vastly more complicated: a dark, seething mass of contradictions. She cherished her memories, but didn't trust him. She loved him still, and yet she wanted to hurt him.

She knew she'd made a mistake by asking if he loved her. She'd made herself vulnerable. Such a thought would never have occurred to that child, and she greatly resented its appearance now. But she knew that she'd given him reason to believe he could use her in the brotherhood's nefarious schemes.

But worst of all was the realization that he'd kept a part of himself hidden from her even then—that he'd actually had a life apart from her, when she'd built her entire existence around him. With brothers who were too much older to be playmates and only sporadic visits from her cousins, she'd had only Connor and had wanted no one else.

Connor had even been educated alongside her by her tutors. Partly, it had been because she had demanded he be taught with her, but partly it was because only when he was there, bent to his studies, did she pay any attention to her own.

For the next few days, she succeeded in avoiding him except for the meals they took with the captain, during which both of them engaged in polite conversation for the captain's sake while carefully avoiding each other's glances.

She wished that he'd stay in his cabin, but he apparently liked being up on deck as much as she herself did. Every time she went there, she saw him either standing motionless at the rail for long periods of time or sitting somewhere with a book in his hand, as though he were determined to prove to her that what he had said about himself was true.

And she also came, albeit belatedly, to see that aura of calm that surrounded him. Even the captain remarked upon it to her, saying that Brother Averyl seemed to be a man who was content to live within himself. The captain found that quality admirable and said that he'd tried to cultivate it himself during his long periods at sea. Jillian, restless and eager to get on with her quest, found it annoying. She had far too much time on her hands, time she found herself spending in unwise thinking about Connor and the Kraaken.

One evening, the captain asked Connor about his writing. Connor replied that he was keeping a journal—mostly for himself, but for the others as well.

"I've always kept journals," he went on. "Even as a child. I have stacks and stacks of them. It's interesting to reread my own thoughts from time to time."

"*I* never saw any journals," Jillian stated sharply.

Connor smiled at her—that indulgent smile she supposed she must have loved as a child, but certainly didn't now.

"I kept them hidden. I had to. You were a terrible snoop."

I still am, she thought, wondering if she could get a look at his journal somehow.

"I keep it locked in the trunk," he said, his eyes dancing with laughter. The cabins came equipped with locked trunks.

The captain roared with laughter, by now quite accustomed to their verbal sparring. Jillian flushed with embarrassment. She sometimes forgot just how easily Connor could read her mind—just as he always had. Unfortunately, the reverse was no longer always true.

Jillian excused herself from the captain's table shortly thereafter, as the two men began a discussion about philosophy. The captain had been educated in the military schools, as all ships' captains were. In peacetime, the Lesai maintained only a small navy, but having merchant ships commanded by military men allowed for rapid conversion if more vessels were ever needed.

Jillian went up on deck, strolled around a bit, then climbed up to the bridge, where several men stood watch. She remarked to them on the roughness of the sea.

"Aye, milady, we were just talking about that. It's unusual for this time of year."

"Do you think there could be a storm?" she

asked. "The stars are still out."

"Let's hope not," the watch commander replied. "This is a new ship, and while she's well built, we all need to settle into her a bit before we hit rough weather."

Chapter Three

Jillian awoke in the darkness, jolted out of her sleep by the rolling and tilting of her bed and the distant shouting on the deck. A storm! Awake now, she could feel the trembling and heaving of the ship as it struggled to make its way through angry seas.

She wasn't truly afraid, because she'd been through a storm at sea before, but she thought uneasily about what the watch commander had said. The ship was new and untested and the crew were as yet unfamiliar with its idiosyncracies.

Then there was a loud knock at her door, and she stumbled from the bed and grabbed her cloak before picking her way carefully across the heaving floor to open the door. One of the young cabin boys stood there, and from the look on his pale, drawn face, she guessed that this must be his first encounter with a storm at sea.

"Cap'n says to tell you that it's going to get real bad, milady. He wants you to stay in your cabin and suggests you use the ropes to tie yourself to your bunk so you don't get hurt."

Jillian nodded as she clung to the doorframe for support. "I've been through a storm before. I'll be fine." Then she thought about Connor. "Have you spoken to Brother Averyl? Is he all right?"

"I'm going there now, milady," the boy said, his face becoming paler and paler in the dim light of the lantern he held. She was sure he was going to become sick at any moment.

"Why don't you go about your other business?" she suggested gently. "I'll go speak with him."

The boy hesitated, then nodded and thanked her before taking off down the corridor as quickly as possible. His lantern swung wildly as he stumbled from side to side, hurrying to the stairs that led to the deck.

Jillian lit a lantern in her cabin and then started toward Connor's cabin, just down the corridor. She was caught somewhere between genuine concern for him and a wicked wish that he'd lose some of his accursed composure.

The ship was now pitching so wildly that walking was nearly impossible, especially with a lantern in one hand. Jillian kept her knees loose as she'd been taught and let herself sway with the motion of the ship. But she'd gotten only halfway to Connor's cabin when his door opened and he staggered out and turned in her direction. With her thick, curly hair disheveled from sleep, she could well imagine the sight she must present in the light of the swinging lantern.

They made their way carefully toward each other, not trying to speak above the groans and shrieks of straining timbers and the shouts of men on the deck above. When they were within a few feet of each other, he reached out to take her arm, whether to steady her or himself she couldn't guess. But she *did* note that, while his expression was grim, he didn't appear to be sick.

"We're to stay in our cabins and tie ourselves to our bunks," she told him, doing her best to ignore the heat generated by his touch, even through her heavy cloak.

He nodded. "We're closer to my cabin. Let's go there."

Without waiting for her response, he began to propel them both to his doorway. Together, they stumbled into his cabin and onto the narrow bunk.

"I've been through a storm before," she told him, annoyed that not even this could penetrate that insufferable calm around him. "It's not as dangerous as it may seem."

"So the captain told me earlier. The sea was running heavy before I left him for the night, and he was worried because the ship's so new."

She was clinging to a sturdy bedpost at one end of the bunk, while he had grabbed hold of the post at the other end. "This is one of Helza's ships. You remember my obnoxious cousin. About the only good thing I can say about him is that he demands the best, both in his crews and his ships."

Then they were both silent, listening to the roar of the sea and the myriad other sounds of ship and men doing battle. The ship was lifted and then dropped, almost as though a giant hand were toying with it, and she remembered suddenly the little boats Connor's father had made for them to sail on the lake at Talita. She recalled how they'd sailed them in the shallow water, then sent them out into the deeper part of the lake, creating man-made waves with their splashing.

Connor reached out to take her hand, covering it warmly with his. "An adventure, Jillie." He smiled. "Somehow, that seems appropriate, now that you've come back into my life again."

In spite of her determination not to let him draw her back to those times, she laughed. "Don't hold me responsible for this, Connor. Doesn't it—"

Her words were abruptly cut off as they heard the unearthly shrieking of splitting wood above them, followed seconds later by a horrendous crash and more shouting.

"A mast?" he asked, gripping her hand more tightly.

"I think so."

Despite her earlier lack of fear, Jillian now began to grow uneasy. No damage had been done to the ship during the storm she'd encountered on that other voyage. And the rolling and pitching of the ship was far worse than she could remember from that previous time.

The lantern she'd brought with her began to swing crazily from the wall bracket where Connor had hung it, casting strange patterns of light and shadow over them as they sat there, their faces raised to the unseen destruction above them. He released her hand and got up.

"I'd better put out the light before it breaks loose and starts a fire."

She watched him as he staggered across to the lamp and turned it off, leaving the cabin in total blackness. Even in his gold robe, he was invisible to her until she felt his hand reach for hers once more. And then the ship lurched wildly again, and he was sent tumbling against her. They both fell backward onto the bed in a tangle of arms and legs as she was forced to let go of the post.

He propped himself over her, reaching out with a hand to grasp the post again. "Are you all right? Did I hurt you?"

"I'm fine," she said huskily, but she wasn't. The sudden contact with his hard body had sent a strange heat through her, a frightening awareness of sensitive, vulnerable flesh beneath the layers of clothing.

She pulled herself away from him and sat up, clinging to the other post. His silence was unnerving. Could he have felt what she'd felt?

How dangerously foolish she'd been to let herself think of them still as children, living in blissful ignorance of the forces that controlled men and women. She could forgive herself for that, though, because until this moment she'd never felt that aching hunger. And she knew she could not afford to feel it now. Nor could he, for that matter.

How she longed to be back in that innocent time, when they ran through fields of flowers or swam and played in the lake, tickling each other, hugging, touching—blissfully unaware of the powerful forces gathering within their bodies.

After a few moments of relative calm, the ship began once more to struggle through waves and troughs, rising and falling with the whims of the roiling seas.

"I think I'd better go up on deck and see how bad it is," Connor said, breaking the long silence between them. Jillian heard—or thought she heard—a huskiness in his voice and wondered if he, too, had been momentarily lost in their shared past.

"No!" she said quickly, reaching out blindly to find his hand. "We'll go together."

Their arms wrapped around each other, they made their way slowly down the corridor, stumbling and nearly falling several times before they reached the stairs. Jillian felt his great strength. Even as a skinny boy, Connor had been amazingly strong, or so it had seemed to her then. Now she felt the well-developed muscles of a man and thought with some obscure satisfaction that he must not spend *all* his time reading and writing poetry.

He went up the steps first and pushed open the hatch. Water poured through, cold and salty. It drenched them both as she climbed up behind him, then stood in the open hatchway, peering out at a terrifying scene.

In the darkness, lit only by the few of the ship's

lights that had survived the storm, they could see that the main mast had been snapped off, its jagged ends wrapped in sodden sails. A few men were on deck, moving about by means of ropes that were secured to the rails at one end and iron rings at the other. Jillian had expected to see more men up here and hoped that meant the others were safe below deck.

A lamp was still burning in the bridge and she could see several figures there, including the captain. The Royal Guards were nowhere to be seen and she hoped they were below, tied to their bunks. Only one of them had ever been to sea before, and they were, in general, a rather effete lot, given to fancy uniforms and parades and little else.

One sailor made his way carefully to them, moving from one taut line to the next. "Cap'n says he thinks we're through the worst of it," he said as he floundered past them. "Stay below. You'll be safe. She isn't going to capsize."

As soon as he had passed by, a huge wave broke over the railing and rolled toward them. Connor dragged them both back and closed the hatch, but not before some of the water had reached them. Thoroughly soaked, they stumbled back down the stairs. Connor wrapped an arm around her as they started along the corridor.

"You'd better change into something dry. I'll wait for you out here."

She fumbled through the darkness of her cabin and found dry clothing, then rejoined him, and they made their way back to his cabin, where he dug out some dry clothes as well.

"I'll go outside and change," he said, then closed the door behind himself. When he returned a few minutes later, the gold cassock was gone. He wore instead a pair of rough seaman's trousers and a heavy sweater. She stared at him, realizing only now how much she hated his Kraaken garb.

"Do I seem more like Connor now?" he asked as he sat down on the other end of the bunk.

"Yes," she admitted. But then, before she could quite stop herself, she added, "But I'm not sure that's wise."

"Neither am I," he admitted, but he still reached out to take her hand again.

Connor told himself that nothing that was happening now was wise. Even though the only contact between them was through their clasped hands, he could still feel the lush, womanly curves that had been pressed against him.

Removed completely from the company of women at an age when he'd just begun to think about the enticing differences, Connor was astonished to discover the power of that difference. He knew about it, of course, but knowing about it and actually *feeling* it were two different matters altogether.

And added to that was a volatile mixture of emotions that resulted from its being *this* woman—his Jillian, whom he'd kept in his heart as a little girl.

Gradually, the storm subsided, although the ship continued to move through rough seas. At some point in the darkness of the night, Jillian let go of the post and clung to Connor instead, then fell asleep curled against him, her dark head resting on his shoulder.

Connor remained awake for a time, thinking about a spring day twenty years ago, when they'd made their first—and last—climb together up to the rookeries, then sat together like this on a ledge, perfectly content in their wholeness.

It was the completeness of innocence—an innocence long gone now. He prayed that he would be able to resist this temptation, this power that had its origins in that long-lost innocence. He *had* to resist it—for both their sakes.

The calm the next morning was as unsettling in its own way as the ferocity of the night had been. Dawn had brought clear skies and gentle winds that would have made the events of the night seem like no more than a nightmare, if it hadn't been for the devastation around them.

Jillian and Connor stood on the deck, where the water had dried to leave a crusty layer of salt on the polished planking, and they listened to the captain's account of the damage and loss of life. Four men, including two of Jillian's Royal Guards, had been swept overboard, and although a search was underway, it seemed unlikely that they would be found alive. Three more men had suffered fatal injuries.

The main mast was gone and two other masts were damaged. So, too, were most of the sails, although they at least could be repaired. Sailors were already busy at work on them.

The captain took them to the bridge, where he showed them the map. "As near as I can tell, we're about here," he said, pointing. "But we won't have a proper fix on our position until nightfall. The nearest land is here, and we're going to make for that."

"What's there?" Connor asked, bending over the map.

"Nothing, as far as I know. I don't even know what the coastline's like there, since I've never sailed south of Trantor. But it's land, and the currents will help to carry us in that direction."

He looked up from the map and frowned at the blue sky, then lowered his weary gaze to the litter-strewn deck. "She's a good ship, for all that. I've been sailing these seas for nearly twenty-five years, and I've never seen the like of that storm in these seas—and especially not at this time of year."

"How far will we be from Trantor when we reach land?" Jillian asked.

"About three or four days' ride, if we had horses," the captain replied, smiling grimly. "At least double that if we have to walk. But we might come upon some help before that."

"What about the boats?" she asked. "Couldn't we use them when we get closer to shore to row to Trantor?"

The captain shook his gray head. "We lost two boats, and the third one is damaged. We can patch it up enough to get us to shore if we have to anchor out, but that's about it. Besides, if the map is accurate, we'd be rowing against the current all the way."

Jillian glanced up at Connor, who had remained silent for some time. But he had turned away from them and was staring out at sea, seemingly lost in thought.

She thanked the captain, then left so he could get back to his work. Connor followed her silently back down to the deck, where they picked their way carefully past debris and tired sailors who were attempting to clear it away.

"What's wrong, Connor?" she asked as they continued to walk toward the stern, where there was less damage.

"Nothing," he replied in a distant tone.

"Well, I hope you're not still blaming me for this adventure, because I'm certainly not looking forward to walking for a week."

Connor dropped an arm across her shoulders and hugged her, laughing, then abruptly withdrew again, as though he'd only belatedly realized what he'd done.

"I'm not blaming you, and at least we're alive."

She thought that both his laughter and his words sounded forced, but said nothing. They were both tired. She had fallen asleep at some point, cradled in his arms. Then they'd both been awakened at dawn by voices in the corridor that turned out to be the guards who had come to inform her of the deaths of their mates, only to discover her missing from her cabin.

After they had gone, it occurred to Jillian that her behavior must have seemed scandalous, appearing as she did, all disheveled and obviously just awakened in the cabin of a Kraaken brother.

She slanted a glance at the silent Connor, wondering if he might be concerned about gossip the guards would carry back to Lesai. She decided she would find a way to let the commander of the Royal Guards know that Connor was an old childhood friend.

But that explanation, while certainly true, rang hollowly in her own mind. Their childhood was far behind, and what *she*, at least, had felt last night was disturbingly adult. In fact, as they had come awake this morning, sprawled on the narrow bunk, wrapped in each other's arms, Jillian had awakened to a new and wondrous reality.

The feeling hadn't lasted, of course. After only a few seconds, they had disengaged themselves, silently acknowledging that reality, while at the same time denying it.

Jillian stifled a yawn, then told Connor that she was going back down to her cabin to take a nap. He merely nodded, still lost in his unknown thoughts.

After she had gone, Connor stood at the rail, watching two sailors scurry up a mast to take down a damaged sail. The ugly thought that had been circling him last night was now staring him full in the face.

Could that storm have been the result of Kraaken sorcery? Did their influence reach this far? Was it possible that Jenner and some of the others might fear him so much that they wanted to kill him?

Neither Connor nor anyone else outside the Inner Circle knew just what magic they possessed, but of course Connor and others had speculated about it endlessly. Some of the brothers believed that the rains that seemed always to come at exactly the right time for their crops were brought by Kraaken magic. If they were right, then wasn't it possible that the Inner Circle had also sent the storm?

Quite apart from the threat to himself and the others, Connor was haunted by the possibility that Kraaken sorcery could be used for such a purpose. Indeed, one of the things he and the others outside the Inner Circle often talked about was the use of their as-yet-unknown powers for the benefit of all.

Could he really represent that much of a threat to the Inner Circle? Raised to respect them, Connor had never openly challenged them, even though he sometimes chafed privately against the rules. But it had simply never before occurred to him that they might view him as a threat— especially now that he was mere months away from joining the Inner Circle himself.

That he had attained a position of power within the ranks of his brothers he didn't question. He'd never sought such a role, but it was clear that the others looked upon him as their leader. The members of the Inner Circle were immortal, but by tradition, the position of high priest was passed on at some point, and Connor knew that many of his brothers saw him as a successor to Jenner.

Connor frowned. If he *did* threaten the Inner Circle, was it only because of that, or could it possibly be because of his mission? The whole thing was shrouded in the annoying secrecy with which the Inner Circle accomplished their ends. Brother Seka, his mentor and the one who'd first spoken to him of this mission, had been very secretive indeed, demanding his promise that he would speak to no one—not even others of the Inner Circle—of his true purpose.

Unable to resolve those troubling questions for the moment, Connor turned to another equally disturbing problem: Jillian. He still could not quite shake the thought that she had been brought together with him again as a test—a test that some might be hoping he'd fail.

He stood there reliving those moments before they'd fallen asleep in each other's arms, and then that blissful instant when they'd awakened together—before reality had intruded. And before he could quite banish the thought, he wondered if Kraaken magic and the promise of immortality could possibly mean more to him than the magic of making love to her.

"Land ho!"

Jillian and Connor, along with everyone else within hearing of that welcome cry, immediately began scanning the misty horizon as the sailor far up in the crow's nest of one of the remaining masts shouted and gestured again. But from their vantage point on deck, they could see nothing as the wounded ship moved at its agonizingly slow pace through calm seas.

"Whatever else we find," Connor said, "we'd better find some game. The captain said that our food stores are low. Some were damaged by water and others that had been stored on deck went overboard in the storm."

He turned to Jillian with a smile. "The captain was quite concerned about you, considering the ordeal that we face. But I told him that while you might be a noblewoman, you are scarcely fragile."

She laughed. "Perhaps he'll begin to believe that when he sees me in trousers."

A short time later, they could all see the vague, gray hump of land in the distance growing larger and more well-defined by the moment. A shout of joy arose from the sailors at the imminent end to their ill-starred journey.

Jillian went down to her cabin and began to sort through the two trunks she had brought with her. She certainly had no intention of burdening any of the crew with a wardrobe she could leave behind.

Having already borrowed a seaman's bag, she began to fill it with the bare necessities, including the two bags of gold coins she planned to use to purchase the services of guides and to buy some birds if she were lucky enough to find them. Her fine gowns, intended to be worn during her stay in Trantor, were left behind. Her friends there would just have to accept her as she was.

Then she changed into trousers and shirt and

laced up the high boots she used for her climbs to the rookeries. She returned to the deck, and to say that she diverted the men's attention from the approaching land would be an understatement. Mouths dropped open and the men stared at her unabashedly. The Royal Guards, having apparently heard of her eccentricities, were somewhat less shocked.

Connor's wide mouth twitched with amusement that glittered as well in his gray eyes. He himself had continued to wear rough seamen's clothing, although she suspected that the gold cassock would reappear before they reached Trantor.

Together, they watched as the land ahead took on sharper definition, and now they could see as well the dark shapes of huge boulders strewn along the coastline.

"It looks as though you might get an opportunity to demonstrate your climbing skills," Connor remarked as they stared at the steep cliffs that rose from the narrow, rocky beach.

"I'll manage it better than *you* will," she challenged.

"There's a rock cliff at one end of the island and a few of us climb it regularly. I think I'll manage."

The clusters of boulders reached out nearly a half mile from shore, forcing the captain to anchor the ship beyond their reach. Jillian paced the deck impatiently while the sailors furled the remaining sails and secured the ship as best they could. They had managed to find a small cove that would afford some protection for the vessel until the captain could arrange for some help in Trantor.

When he saw her seaman's bag, the captain's eyes went quickly from shock to admiration. He gave her a slight bow.

"Milady, it's clear that I underestimated you. Does that cliff look more difficult than your rookeries?"

"No. It's not even as high and there appear to be a number of good footholds along the way."

He chuckled. "Then perhaps I'll stop worrying about you and start worrying about myself instead."

The remaining boat had to make several trips before they were all on the rocky shore, together with their belongings and remaining supplies. Eager to be away, Jillian went on the first boatload, together with Connor and the guards.

Because of the rocks, they would have to leave the boat and wade through the shallows to the narrow strip of beach. Jillian pulled off her boots and laced them together, then rolled up the legs of her trousers. Connor did the same, and they splashed through the water, racing for the shore.

His longer strides brought him to dry land first, and as she joined him a moment later, they both laughed, sharing the sheer pleasure of the moment and remembering other times like this along the shores of the lake at Talita.

Dressed as he was now, Connor seemed more like the boy she had loved. Her heart ached for what they'd had—and could never really have again.

How can you be one of them? she demanded silently. *How can you be content to spend your life with them—and not with me?*

When they were all finally gathered on the shore, Connor suggested that he and Jillian go up the cliff first to secure the ropes for the others. There was much consternation among the sailors, but the captain agreed, and another man offered to join them, saying that he had done some climbing as a youth.

So they all secured ropes around their waists and set off. Jillian had been certain that she could climb faster than Connor, but she soon fell slightly behind. Her only consolation was that the third member of their party was some distance behind her.

About halfway up, they reached a ledge wide enough to accommodate the two of them. The sailor stopped on a smaller ledge off to their right, out of sight around a rocky outcropping. Shouts of encouragement drifted up to them from the beach below.

"They're probably making bets as to when I'll fall," Jillian observed dryly.

"Or when *I'll* fall." Connor laughed. "A Kraaken brother and a noble lady are rather unlikely climbers."

She smiled. "Just imagine the stories they'll carry back to Lesai. High Priest Jenner could be very displeased," she added wickedly.

"He is frequently displeased with me." Connor

shrugged. "But I've done nothing to trouble my conscience."

Not yet, she thought, then drew in a breath sharply. Would she really try to seduce him? The thought hovered there, bringing a powerful awareness of him as they sat side by side on the ledge. If she did, and if she succeeded, she could win him away from the accursed Kraaken. She knew Connor well enough even now to know that his sense of honor was too strong for him to break his vows and then try to remain in the brotherhood.

I can't do that to him, she told herself, but she only half believed it.

The remainder of their journey proved to be even less arduous than the first half, and they were soon standing on the top of the cliff, staring down at the others who had begun making their way up the ropes.

Jillian wandered off to have a look at their surroundings, her mind still filled with guilty thoughts of seducing Connor. Unfortunately, she really had no idea how to actually go about such a thing. Unlike other women, she didn't simper or flirt outrageously, and she couldn't see herself doing that now. Still, the idea of it lingered, sending small shivers through her even as she considered it.

She saw that they were on a wide plateau thickly covered by fir trees. There was no sign of human habitation, however. The area appeared to be as uninhabited as the captain had suspected.

What she did find were wild strawberries, now

at their ripest, and she gathered a handful and ate them, then gathered a second handful to take back to Connor.

He was busy helping to maneuver the ropes as they hauled the last of the crew up the face of the cliff. She showed him the berries and he opened his mouth expectantly. So she popped them in a few at a time, and when he had eaten them all, he bent to kiss her cheek.

"Thank you. I haven't tasted them in years."

"You would have if you'd stayed where you belong," she replied acerbically, then turned away. Moments like this had become a torture for her, and she knew that much more of that torment lay ahead.

Finally, all the men and all the supplies had been hauled up the cliff. They rested and ate from their stores of food, then began the long trek north to Trantor. Before long, they came upon a well-beaten path that was probably the route of migratory animals—a lucky find that made their journey considerably easier.

At day's end, they set up camp in a small ravine, where a clear, cool stream rushed over mossy rocks. Along the way, the Royal Guards had managed to bag some game, so they enjoyed their first fresh meat in days.

After dinner, the captain, clearly exhausted after his struggle up the cliff, and no doubt concerned about his beloved ship, retired to a far corner of their campground and went to sleep. The sailors drew out their pipes and began to play or sing old sea chanteys. The guards sat together, talking quietly. Jillian looked around for Connor and saw that he'd disappeared.

The moon was bright and nearly full, and she soon found him, sitting cross-legged along the mossy bank of the little stream. She started forward to join him, then stopped. His utter stillness was unnerving. It felt to her as though only the shell of the man was there, the mind having gone somewhere she couldn't follow. So she turned away and instead found a spot for herself farther down the stream's bank.

Connor had been quiet and distracted most of the day, trying her already limited patience. Jillian sat there thinking about him and suddenly recalled times when he'd been that way as a child. How could she have forgotten that? She could see herself so clearly now, trying to force him to play some game or go off somewhere, while he'd sat there, seemingly content to do nothing.

So he was right when he'd told her that he hadn't changed. Her memories of their shared childhood had apparently become very selective over the years. She'd simply chosen to forget everything about him that had irritated her.

Some twigs snapped behind her, and before she could turn, a hand touched her head lightly in a caress, and then Connor was sitting down beside her.

"Can this be Jillian, sitting here so quietly?" he asked wryly.

"Well, what else is there to do?" she snapped, annoyed at how much she'd managed to forget about their childhood and irritated at the rush of warmth his presence brought.

He laughed. "Now I *know* it's Jillian."

"At least I haven't spent the entire day moping," she replied irritably.

"I haven't been moping. And I heard everything you said."

She narrowed her eyes at him. "That's the difference between us, Connor. I talk, and you think. I don't hold secrets."

"And you think I do?"

"I *know* you are. You've been acting this way ever since the storm."

He said nothing. She let the silence drag on. She was remembering now that her rare silences had generally produced results in the past.

Finally, he sighed. "Something *has* been on my mind, and it has to do with that storm."

"What do you mean?"

"I hope I'm wrong, but I'm worried that the storm could have been the result of Kraaken sorcery."

"*What?*" Jillian stared at him, aghast. "Have you lost your mind, Connor? How could they do that?"

"The real question isn't how, but why," he observed.

"All right, why, then?"

"It's possible that High Priest Jenner might be trying to get rid of me. He wouldn't dare try anything on the island, where my death could easily be traced to their magic."

"Why would he want to get rid of you?" Jillian

was astounded, though not so shocked that she couldn't take a small measure of satisfaction—and even hope—from his words.

"Because he may see me as a threat. I told you before that in a few months, I will become a member of the Inner Circle, with powers of my own. Many of the younger brothers see me as their leader, and we all would like to change some things. It's possible that Jenner views me as a rival."

"How is the high priest chosen?" she asked, her shock by now having given way to curiosity about the inner workings of the hated Kraaken.

Connor shrugged. "No one outside the Inner Circle really knows. Supposedly, the choice is made by the powers they invoke in their conclaves and not by the members themselves."

"Do you really believe they could have magic so powerful that they could send a storm to attack us at sea?"

"I don't know. Their powers are a closely guarded secret."

"And you've never actually seen them perform any magic?"

He shook his head.

"It doesn't exist, Connor," she stated flatly.

He reached over and took her hand, holding it gently between both of his. "I know you want to believe that, Jillie, but—"

She pulled her hand free. "It doesn't. They've been lying to you. They use the lure of sorcery to get recruits. How else would they get them?"

"Jillian, you must accept the fact that I have

committed myself to them. I made that choice long ago, but it doesn't mean that I don't love you."

"Hmmpphh!" She snorted disdainfully. "Some love *that* is, Connor, when you haven't seen me for twenty years, and you would *never* have seen me if you hadn't been sent on this journey."

"Nevertheless, I love you," he stated quietly.

Since she didn't doubt that he loved her in his own way, she ignored that declaration. "You love *me*, but you choose to stay with *them*, even if they're trying to kill you."

"The Kraaken are no different from any other group of people. Some are good and some are not so good. Murder schemes are not unheard of among your nobility."

"I certainly wouldn't try to use them as an example of humankind at its best," she scoffed. "And the Kraaken are supposed to be saintly and above such faults."

He chuckled. "Only to those on the outside."

She decided to abandon this line of conversation. "Is it possible that they chose you for this mission because they know how you feel about me?"

His gray eyes met hers and he nodded slowly. "Yes, it's possible. There were two times after I joined the brotherhood when I considered leaving, and they know it was because of you and the keras."

"You shouldn't have let them talk you out of it," she said in a voice that trembled slightly.

"No, Jillian, I made the right choice—for both

of us. And they didn't try to talk me out of it; the decision was mine."

In the silence that followed, Jillian tried not to think what might have happened if he'd chosen differently. Instead, she focused on this supposed threat to his life that she didn't really believe, since she didn't believe in Kraaken magic.

"Will they know that they've failed?"

"To kill me, you mean? I don't know."

"But they could try again."

He nodded grimly. "We have no choice but to remain together until we reach Trantor, but then I think we'd better separate. I don't want you at risk if they're trying to get me."

"No!" she stated emphatically. "I have the guards. They'll protect us both."

"Jillian, love, if I'm right, the guards cannot protect us. But you'd be safe if you stay away from me."

"I'm *not* going to stay away from you, Connor!"

The next day, Jillian was uncharacteristically silent as she mulled over what Connor had told her. She was still disinclined to believe in Kraaken magic, but her disbelief was tempered somewhat by his words. After all, even the captain, a man with years of experience at sea, had never seen the likes of that storm.

What if it was true and Jenner and his henchmen *did* want to kill Connor? Would they try again, or would they simply assume they'd gotten him the first time? In any event, once Connor and the others reached Trantor, word would quickly get back to Lesai—and then to the Kraaken—that Connor had survived the storm.

Jillian was determined to protect Connor—and just as determined to make him see that he had to leave the brotherhood. Surely, despite what he'd said, he must be having some doubts about the Kraaken now. All she had to do was to keep him safe and let those doubts grow—and then he would be hers again.

That, she thought with some satisfaction, was a much better plan than trying to seduce him, which she couldn't bring herself to do in any event.

Unfortunately, by day's end, there were some dark thoughts beginning to whisper through her mind. She began to be tormented by the possibility that Connor had made up the whole story as a way of persuading her to let them go their separate ways—so that he could carry out some evil Kraaken plan.

She wanted—desperately wanted—not to believe that. The boy she remembered would never have been capable of such a thing. But the Kraaken had had twenty years to change him, and if there were times when she and Connor still seemed as close as ever, there were also times when she felt as though she scarcely knew him.

They camped the second night within sight and smell of the sea again, since the track they'd been following skirted the edges of the cliffs once more. In the morning, they had all let themselves believe that surely they would come upon a village, but by evening, they had seen no evidence of one.

As the captain had pointed out, there might well be settlements close by, but the travelers couldn't afford to wander all over looking for them. Instead, they must keep heading north, staying close to the sea, since that route would take them to Trantor.

There was no singing and little talking around the campfire this night. Everyone—Jillian included—was tired after two days of walking and the unwelcome prospect of at least another three or four days ahead.

The Royal Guards were taking turns guarding the encampment through the night, even though they'd seen no sign of people. As the captain had pointed out, while it appeared that they had no cause to fear an attack by two-legged creatures, the same could not be said about the four-legged variety. There was some evidence that mountain lions inhabited this wild land.

Tired from the long trek and exhausted as well from the effort required to keep her doubts about Connor away, Jillian fell asleep quickly, wrapped in her blanket and lying between the captain and Connor.

At first, Jillian thought that she'd been awakened by a nightmare, but then she quickly realized that instead, she'd awakened *to* one.

Darkness surrounded her, pressing in threateningly. The moon was gone. The campfire had gone out. Instinctively, she turned to Connor. He wasn't there. His blanket lay in a heap, as though quickly tossed aside.

A chill shot through her. The Kraaken! She jumped at the sound of a low voice near her ear.

"Run, milady! Get into the woods quickly. Something's amiss!"

It was the captain, struggling to his feet as he spoke. She could barely see him, even though he was only a few feet away.

Confused and terrified for Connor, Jillian stood up and tried to see into the all-encompassing blackness. Why were there no stars? What had happened to the campfire? For the first time, she began to believe in Kraaken sorcery and the thought paralyzed her.

Then shots were fired, the sounds strangely muffled. Shouts and screams followed quickly, but they too seemed distant, oddly muted.

Connor! Where was he? She wanted to shout his name, but when she opened her mouth, no sound came out. Then suddenly, she was engulfed in something and struggling to free herself even as she was being lifted from the ground. Once more, she opened her mouth to scream, but this time a hand was clamped over her mouth.

Her assailant carried her only a short distance before unceremoniously dumping her onto the ground. Immediately, she began to fight her way out of the blanket that had covered her. Her flailing hands connected with a muscled thigh, but she had only a moment to understand that whatever had attacked her was real, and not a Kraaken trick, before strong fingers touched the base of her neck—and her world went black.

Chapter Four

Jillian was once again being transported, wrapped tightly in a blanket. Her entire body felt strange, weak and tingling. She cried out in protest, irrationally happy to be able to make a sound. A face bent close to hers in the darkness.

"It's over, Jillie. You're safe."

"Connor," she said, flooded with relief just as her anxiety about him had come back.

He carried her back to the campfire that was being rebuilt by one of the sailors. Connor set her down near the fire and knelt before her. "How do you feel?"

She dismissed the question. "What happened? Where are the others?" She could see only two other men besides Connor, both of them sailors.

"The camp was attacked. Besides us, there are only the two sailors and one of your guards."

"The captain?" she asked, looking wildly around in the flickering light of the fire. She'd grown quite fond of the man.

"He's dead, Jillie. They're all dead."

She stared at him, as yet unable to believe his words. "B-but. . . ."

Connor stood up and ran a hand distractedly through his hair. He was bare chested and silhouetted against the flames and he seemed so huge and powerful and remote.

"I don't know what happened," he said harshly, then glanced behind her. "Here comes your guard. Maybe he can explain."

"I don't know what happened," the man said as they both began to hurl questions at him. His tone was defensive. "I took the first watch. Donner had relieved me and I was just falling asleep when we were attacked. But I never saw them, and all the bodies are ours."

"But how were they killed?" Jillian asked. "I heard only a few shots."

"There were no wounds on any of them, except for one of the sailors, and I think he might have been shot by Donner. He probably thought he was one of the attackers."

"If there are no wounds, how are you sure they're dead?" Jillian asked, clutching the blanket more tightly against her as the thought of Kraaken magic began to torment her again. But why would they kill everyone? It was Connor they wanted.

"They're dead," Connor assured her. "I checked them all myself."

"But why didn't they kill me, too?" she cried. "One of them carried me off into the woods." She reached up to rub the back of her neck, recalling those fingers that had touched her there.

"That was me," Connor said after a pause.

"You? What did you do to me?" She continued to rub her neck.

"I put you to sleep for a time, that's all. It was the only thing I could do to get you out of harm's way and keep you quiet."

Jillian trembled as she thought again about Kraaken sorcery. But Connor said he knew nothing of it. "H-how did you—"

"A touch," he replied, indicating the back of his own neck. "Lightly applied, it merely puts one to sleep for a time. But when more pressure is used, it can kill."

Jillian stared at him in disbelief, but Connor turned to the guard. "Do you know of such methods?"

The man shook his head quickly, and Connor went on. "It's something we were taught, along with other means to defend ourselves. I was told that such things are known only to the Kraaken."

Then, without waiting for Jillian to respond to that, he turned to the sailors, who had by now joined their group. "Since I doubt that anyone will be getting any more sleep tonight, I suggest that we bury the dead. There are enough stones about to build cairns and we'll send someone back for their bodies when we reach Trantor. As soon as daylight comes, we'll start out again."

Jillian sat there silently as the men began their grim task. She wasn't cold, but she still shivered uncontrollably beneath the blanket, reaching up every few seconds to touch the back of her neck. Who was this man who could kill with a touch? Echoes of his firm, commanding tone as he spoke to the other men kept tormenting her as she stared into the fire.

"Do you think it was the Kraaken who attacked the camp?" Jillian asked quietly as their diminished group trudged north through a misty gray morning.

"I don't know what to think," Connor replied distractedly.

She took a deep breath and spoke with uncharacteristic carefulness. "When I woke up, you were gone, Connor. Where were you?"

"I must have heard something. I'm just not sure. All I know is that I woke up and saw that the campfire was out and sensed danger. So I went to find the guard. He was already dead. Then I came back and got you. There was a heavy fog, and I couldn't see anything. After I left you in the woods, I came back and discovered that everyone else was dead, except for the five of us."

"I don't understand any of this, Connor. If it was the Kraakens, how did they do it? And why didn't they kill *you?*"

"I don't have the answers, Jillian—and please don't blame all of the brotherhood for what could only have been the actions of a few."

"You'll have to forgive me if I don't feel charitable toward the Kraaken right now," she stated angrily.

"We don't know for certain that it *was* them," he pointed out.

"Who else could it have been?" she scoffed. "You said yourself that the Kraaken have methods that no one else has: silent ways of killing."

Connor had no answer to that and nothing more to say to her as they walked on through the damp, dreary day.

With the captain dead, the role of leader of their small group might have been expected to fall to the remaining Royal Guard or to the first mate, who was among the surviving sailors. But instead, they turned to Connor, upon whom that responsibility seemed to sit lightly.

For her part, Jillian kept her distance from him, wrapped in her sadness at the loss of the captain and the other men, and her suspicions regarding Connor.

Ever since he'd told her about his lethal skills, she'd been fighting herself. He'd been gone when she awakened to that living nightmare—and he alone seemed capable of such stealthy killing.

But when she forced herself to consider the possibility that he could have murdered the others in their sleep, she was thankfully stopped by the question of *why* he would have done it. It simply made no sense, even though the alternative— Kraaken sorcery—made no sense to her, either.

She stared at his tall, erect figure as he walked

some distance ahead with the first mate. Surely not even the accursed Kraaken could have turned Connor into a killer. Even as a child, when boys seemed naturally determined to fight, Connor had been unwilling to do so. She recalled boys on the estate taunting him from time to time, but he'd always walked away.

"Milady, begging your pardon, but just how well do you know Brother Averyl?"

Jerked from her reverie, Jillian turned sharply to the guard who walked beside her. "What do you mean, Sergeant?"

Taken aback by the sharpness of her question, the guard stammered. "I-it's just that he's admitted he knows how to kill quickly and silently, milady, and no one saw strangers in camp." He paused, then hurried on. "We haven't seen anyone since we came ashore, and no one could know we're here."

"Brother Averyl is not a killer," Jillian stated and hoped that the guard couldn't hear that small doubt in her voice.

Late in the afternoon, they reached the crest of a hill and saw in a narrow valley before them a small mining town. Everyone but Connor was elated at the prospect of their long trek coming to an end. Instead he issued a caution.

"We can't assume that they'll be as happy to see us as we are to see them. We must stay together and be wary."

Then he called a temporary halt and disappeared into the woods. When he returned, he was once more wearing the gold cassock of the

Kraaken, together with a gold chain that held the intricate gold-and-emerald symbol of his order.

"This might buy us some fear—or at least some respect," he explained as they started down toward the town.

And as they reached the bustling community, it appeared that Connor was right. Jillian was rather surprised to hear the name Kraaken in a few whispered conversations. She hadn't realized that the brotherhood was well-known beyond the borders of Lesai.

Not that she didn't attract considerable attention herself, once people noticed that there was a woman in the midst of this bedraggled group of strangers. She even saw several people staring at the ornate ring she wore because she was a member of the royal family of Lesai, but she doubted that even someone who recognized it would believe she wore it legitimately.

She was the only one among them who spoke the Masani tongue fluently, so she acted as interpreter when Connor strode up to a group of men gathered before one of the mining company buildings. At Connor's request, a man went off to find the manager. He returned a few minutes later with a short, stocky, gray-haired man, who, as it turned out, spoke quite passable Lesai.

Connor introduced himself and then Jillian. The manager bowed politely to her, even though she could see that he had his doubts about her identity. She didn't want to think about what she must look like at this point. Never one to dwell upon her appearance, Jillian nonetheless suspected that she must look no better than some of the ragged women who stood staring at them in the town square.

There were few horses to spare in the town, but Connor managed to procure enough for their party, thanks to a liberal supply of gold coins. More gold assured that reliable men would be found to return to the temporary graves and bring the bodies of the others to Trantor.

The town boasted only one small inn, but they were able to secure enough rooms for them all, with the sailors and the remaining guard sharing accommodations.

In short order, Jillian was luxuriating in her first real bath since setting out on this journey. Aboard ship, she'd been forced to sponge bathe, and since that time, she'd done little more than rinse her face and hands in the stream along the way.

A maid took away her filthy clothing to be laundered and she put on the only other things she'd brought with her: another pair of trousers and a clean shirt. It amused her to see the minimal deference accorded to her by the girl, who clearly thought Jillian to be anything but a lady.

She ate dinner in her room, devouring every bit of the dull fare as though it had been prepared by the palace cooks. Connor had invited her to join him for dinner, but she had declined, saying that she intended to remain in her room. Then, with her stomach well filled for the first time in days, she fell asleep before dark.

When she awoke sometime later, Jillian was at

first convinced that she was reliving the attack on the camp. Angry shouts jolted her from her bed, and at the same time, she heard running footsteps in the hallway beyond her securely bolted door.

She went over to the single window and looked down into the courtyard. In the light spilling out from the tavern next door, she could see a group of men, two of whom she thought she recognized as being the sailors from her party.

Angry words were soon followed by punches and a brawl quickly erupted. Then suddenly Connor was there, wading into the melee in an attempt to stop it. Upon seeing his Kraaken garb, most of the men backed off, but a few persisted— and then one of them swung at Connor.

What happened next happened so quickly that Jillian had no time to fear for Connor's life. He easily deflected the man's blow, then spun about so fast that she could only guess that he'd kicked the man. Another man jumped him from behind and Connor twisted about yet again, flung the man away and rendered him motionless with a sharp, chopping blow to his neck.

This was apparently too much for the rest of them, because they melted away quickly into the darkness, leaving only Connor and the two sailors, whose voices carried up to her.

"My thanks, Brother Averyl. They followed us from the tavern, spoiling for a fight." There was a pause, and then the sailor said, "If you don't mind my saying so, sir, I've never seen anyone fight like that. Is that what the Kraaken taught you?"

"We don't all have these skills," Connor told

the sailor. "There's been no need for us to defend ourselves on the island. But some of us have chosen to study such methods."

The man thanked him again and they all disappeared from view as they entered the inn.

Jillian returned to her bed in a daze. Gone forever was that earlier image of a boy who refused to fight. And she was haunted by his statement that he'd *chosen* to learn such deadly skills.

"Cousin Jillian! Even for *you*, this is a surprise!"

"Then you'd have been even more surprised if you'd seen me yesterday." Jillian smiled.

She wasn't sure just what had gotten them past the guards at the ambassador's residence: her ring, her guard's tattered uniform or Connor's cassock. But it was clear that the men had had doubts about them all.

Jillian introduced Connor and her cousin stared at him. "Connor? Not the Connor who—"

Connor smiled and bowed slightly. "Yes, milady, the very same Connor. But it's actually Brother Averyl now."

Kathe shot Jillian a quick look that said they certainly had much to talk about. But for now, she led them into the family dining room and ordered food from one of the hovering staff.

Jillian explained their situation. Kathe was upset at the loss of life—particularly the captain, who had been a guest at her table in the past. But by the time Jillian had finished, Kathe was unable to hold back a grin.

"This couldn't have happened to anyone but the two of you. It's just like the adventures you had as children. I envied you so."

"This one was a bit more deadly," Jillian reminded her. "Kathe, have you heard of any outlaws in that region?"

Kathe shook her curly head. "No, although I'm not all that familiar with it. But the Masani seem to have gotten rid of the bands of outlaws that used to roam the rural regions. You'll have to ask Trevor about it when he returns. He's at court at the moment."

Jillian wasn't looking forward to asking Trevor anything. She detested the pompous ass and wondered for the millionth time why Kathe had married him. He was a dozen years her senior and certainly had nothing to recommend him as far as Jillian could see, while Kathe herself was bright and pretty and had always been one of Jillian's favorite cousins.

A man in the uniform of major in the Lesai army was shown into the room, and Jillian repeated her story to him. After expressing his sadness at the loss of life, he inquired about the ship, saying that he would commission a Masani vessel to bring it to Trantor under tow.

Connor said that he had the map the captain had carried with him, on which he had marked the location of the crippled ship. The two men left the room, and Kathe turned eagerly to Jillian.

"Connor! I can't believe it! How handsome he is, Jillian. Those eyes of his. That's how I recognized him."

"Might I remind you that he's Brother Averyl now—a Kraaken?" Jillian stated dryly, speaking the last word with obvious distaste.

"But I saw the way he looks at you. He loves you, Jillie."

"I know that. He's even said so. But he loves the Kraaken more," she said bitterly. "And I don't even know if I can trust him at this point."

She told Kathe of her suspicions and saw her own doubts reflected in her cousin's face. But when she had finished, Kathe shook her head. "He couldn't betray *you*, Jillie. No one could change that much."

"He betrayed me once before," Jillian pointed out in that same bitter tone.

"No, he didn't," Kathe insisted. "You could never have married him. You know that. You even admitted it to me once."

Probably just to shut you up on the subject, Jillian said silently. She'd heard those words all too frequently in the years after Connor's departure, but she'd never accepted them.

"I'm sure that Trevor could arrange to get him another escort who could be trusted to keep an eye on him," Kathe said, turning to more practical matters.

But Jillian shook her head. "No. I've accepted the responsibility of watching him myself, and that's what I'm going to do. Besides," she went on in a bleak tone, "if he really can't be trusted, I need to know that myself."

"Oh, Jillian," Kathe said, reaching out to touch

her arm sympathetically, "you really still love him, don't you?"

Jillian was saved from having to reply by the return of Connor and the major, who told Jillian that the ship should be in port at Trantor within a few days.

"I wish, milady, that your wonderful birds were capable of crossing the sea with their messages. As it stands now, it will be a week or more before Lord Helza can be informed."

"That is my hope as well, Major," Jillian replied, then explained her purpose in coming here.

The major looked at her thoughtfully. "I've never heard those stories. I must tell you, milady, that you would be undertaking a long, difficult journey. The desert is treacherous in itself, and not even the Masani venture very often into those mountains."

"Nevertheless, I am going there. I will require several guards, since I have only one left, and I will also need someone who speaks the language of the desert tribes. Once I make contact with them, I hope to find a guide into the mountains."

The major glanced at Connor. "Brother Averyl has already informed me of your requirements and I will see to them as soon as I deal with the ship."

"The major says that we should take only a small party into the desert, Jillian, since a larger force could seem threatening to the nomads."

"Then you still intend to accompany me?" she asked.

He nodded. "I can be armed as well, if someone will teach me how to fire a rifle."

"It seems to me, Connor, that you did quite well without one last night."

Connor was clearly surprised. She hadn't told him that she'd seen the fight. The major looked from one to the other of them questioningly, but it was Jillian who explained about Connor's skills.

The major frowned thoughtfully for a moment, then shook his head. "I seem to have heard tales of such fighting skills somewhere, though not in connection with the Kraaken."

"If you can recall where you heard it, it might be of help in finding the men who attacked our camp," Connor said. "And I would also like to know."

Listening to this exchange, Jillian couldn't help thinking that Connor was trying too hard to sound casual about his own interest, and she reminded herself yet again that he might be here for more than mere recruiting.

They remained in Trantor for a week, resting and preparing for the next part of their journey. The bodies of the captain and the others were brought to Trantor, then sent home to Lesai aboard another of Helza's ships. Both Jillian and Connor were part of the formal party that saw them off on their final journey, and Jillian sent along a note of condolences to the captain's widow, together with a promise to visit upon her return to Lesai.

They were presented at court by Trevor, and

Connor obtained permission to recruit from among the Masani. Trevor had passed along to the Masani king Jillian and Connor's suspicions regarding this mission, and it became apparent that he took the warning to heart. He sent his men out to find suitable boys and had them brought to court, where Connor was permitted to talk to them through court-provided interpreters.

Connor selected three boys, whose parents were then brought to court in order to gain their approval. All promised to give the matter serious consideration and render their decisions upon Connor's return from the mountains.

"Don't you worry about bringing boys into what may be a den of treachery?" Jillian asked him.

"No, because we will need good men if we are to change things. And I've never said I was sure that any of the brothers were responsible for the storm or the attack."

"But if they weren't, then who was?" she demanded.

"The storm may simply have happened, and as for the attack on us, it could have been a roving band of outlaws."

"I don't believe that," she scoffed.

"That's because you *want* to believe it was the Kraakens."

"You're the one who first raised that possibility," she pointed out angrily. "Why have you changed your mind? And why have you also changed your mind about accompanying me? Before, you said it would be better if we split up."

"If the Kraaken *weren't* responsible, then I have no reason to separate myself from you."

"But you don't know that they *weren't* responsible."

Connor chuckled. "We are talking in circles, Jillian—something we once did often. Nothing is certain at this point, but I've made my decision."

"You've made your decision based on your blind allegiance to that pack of schemers, Connor."

She stalked away and Connor watched her with a smile that drained slowly from his face when she had disappeared. He'd told her the truth: he wasn't certain of anything at this point. But during their final days on the road, he'd thought long and hard about the possibility that the attack had been the result of Kraaken sorcery. For all his faults, High Priest Jenner seemed unlikely to go to such extremes, and if he had, Connor suspected that he would have been more successful.

But it was the other possible explanation for the attack that had forced him to change his mind about going his separate way. He could have been mistaken about the target of the attack. It could be Jillian, and not himself. He knew little about the Lesai court now, but what he recalled from his childhood was that there had always been intrigues—and even the occasional suspicious death. And he knew that Jillian, however much she denied it, held great sway over her uncle, the king.

He'd heard of her championing the cause of the poor, and knowing her, she'd undoubtedly run roughshod over any opposition. There were always people who saw any bettering of the condition of the poor as a threat.

Or there was even the possibility that some unknown enemies wanted to make certain her mission didn't succeed so that they could pursue it themselves. She'd told him that there were a few others now attempting to breed keras, and he knew it was a lucrative business.

Connor was painfully aware of the dangers of the situation. If he was wrong and Jenner *was* trying to have him killed, he could be putting Jillian in grave danger by staying with her. But if someone was trying to kill *her*, and he went his own way, she would be in even greater danger.

In the end, though, he knew that his decision had been made because he wanted to be with her for as long as possible, to build up a store of memories that would have to last him a lifetime.

They left Trantor behind and rode through the rolling farmlands to the west of the city, where newly planted crops stretched from horizon to horizon. In addition to Henka, the remaining guard, they had acquired two Masani Royal Guards as escorts. More men had been sent ahead to the garrison at the desert's edge to make contact with the nomads and to hire camels and a guide for the journey across the desert.

Jillian, as always, was impatient, eager to reach the mountain tribe said to possess the birds, and it was with ill grace that she waited while Connor spoke with several recruit prospects rounded up in the various farming villages.

Upon learning of her suspicions regarding Connor's mission, Trevor had seen to it that the Kraaken brother was followed whenever he left the ambassadorial residence. They discovered that Connor had hired himself a young interpreter, then gone about the city inquiring after tales of men with unique fighting skills.

The youth Connor had hired had been persuaded by means of still more gold to keep Trevor and his men informed, but according to Trevor, Connor's quest had been in vain.

Trevor was of the opinion that Connor was probably only seeking to aid in the as-yet-unsuccessful attempt to find their attackers, but Jillian wasn't so sure. However, in the absence of any other explanation, she was forced to set aside her doubts.

In his rich golden robe, Connor drew considerable attention in the villages, and she noticed that the boys, both here and at court, seemed instinctively to like and trust him. One of the Masani guards had been appointed to act as his official interpreter, but Connor asked her to be present as well, saying that he wanted to be sure his words were being translated properly.

"His Majesty obviously doesn't trust me," Connor told her. "So I can't afford to trust him, either."

"What makes you believe you can trust *me*, Connor?" she challenged. "You know how I feel about the Kraaken."

He laughed. "I trust you, Jillian. Lies are impossible between us."

She wasn't so sure about that, because she continued to believe that he was concealing something from her. She didn't for one minute believe his rather casual dismissal of the storm and the attack on them. And she was still unsettled by that fight she'd witnessed and the indisputable truth that the seemingly gentle Connor was also a deadly fighter.

Still, there was one thing she *did* believe without question, and that was that he would never harm her, nor allow harm to come to her. She had only to meet his gaze to see the strong, clear light of his love for her.

How will I give him up again? she asked herself over and over as they rode toward the desert. And yet she knew it would happen.

The fertile fields gave way to flat, sere plains, a foreshadowing of the desert that lay ahead. Thriving towns were replaced by tiny, poor villages whose inhabitants eked out a minimal existence farming the hard-baked earth. The faces that watched them were gaunt and suspicious, and Jillian was glad for the presence of the Masani guards, who had already told Connor that he would find no recruits among these illiterate people. But it was from them that Jillian received her first report of the birds she sought.

The villagers spoke such heavily accented Masani that she had trouble understanding them as one of the guards spoke to the village elders on her behalf.

"They *have* seen such birds, milady, but only rarely and only soaring high overhead," the guard reported.

"What do you know of their origins?" she asked in the Masani tongue.

The men turned to the guard as though seeking his approval before answering in their guttural accents. The guard translated. "They call them ven-yawas, birds of the high mountains. They believe that the birds come from the mountains beyond the desert, from an enchanted place."

"An enchanted place?" Jillian frowned. "Why do they say it's enchanted?"

The men spoke with many pauses and shrugs and the guard turned back to her. "There are old stories, told to them by their fathers and grandfathers, of men who live forever in those mountains, in a place of great beauty and riches."

When they had left the village behind, Jillian turned to Connor and asked what he thought about their stories. She'd seen his keen interest.

He shrugged. "They are poor people living a harsh existence. It is understandable that they might invent such tales. But it may also contain at least a grain of truth."

The Masani guard joined in their discussion. "None of these people can read and write, milady, and therefore they must pass their history down by word of mouth. It is customary among such people to treasure storytelling and to place great value on the talents of the teller as well."

"Which means," Connor said, "that with each generation the stories are embellished still more."

"Exactly." The guard nodded. "But I agree with Brother Averyl that they cannot be dismissed completely. Besides, I once heard similar tales from the nomads when I was stationed in Shereva. They, too, are great storytellers."

The travelers arrived at the garrison town of Shereva early that evening. Jillian was surprised to find that it was a fairly sizable town, and a thriving one as well. The guard explained that, in its way, Shereva was as busy a trading center as the port of Trantor, serving as the focal point of trade between the desert tribes and the Masani. Connor asked what the trade consisted of.

"The nomads have certain spices and oils made from desert plants that are highly prized among my people, and they trade them for gems and gold. Because they have no permanent homes, they carry their wealth with them as jewelry." He smiled. "Be prepared to see even the men wearing much gold, including gold earrings. Some decorate their camels with it as well."

The Mesani guards were put up at the garrison, while Jillian, Connor and Henka were taken to an inn not far from the great stone fortress that overlooked the town. They decided to rest for a few days before setting off across the desert, and Jillian was eager to explore the markets the guard had told them about—not so much for herself, but rather to find gifts for her family and friends.

Early the next morning, after her first comfortable night's sleep in days, Jillian started out of the inn to visit the markets. But before she had gone far, Connor suddenly appeared at her side.

"I'll come with you," he said when she told him of her destination.

"What could you possibly find of interest there?" she asked, not wanting to show how pleased she was to have his company. Always now, she felt that terrible pain of wanting to be with him and knowing it could not last.

"Perhaps some spices," he replied as they walked along the busy street. "Our cooks might enjoy something new, and if we are to have Masani boys among us, it would be good to provide them with something familiar."

The market, which sprawled over many blocks in the center of town, consisted of numerous permanent shops and even more numerous temporary stalls. And as Jillian and Connor entered the crowded area, they saw their first nomads.

Darker skinned than either the Lesai or the Masani, both men and women wore loose, flowing white garments and gold jewelry that glittered in the sun. Jillian was enchanted by their language, which had a strange, musical quality.

Connor watched them for a time, then turned to her. "Perhaps we should outfit ourselves like them. After all, they live in the desert, and however strange their clothing may look to us, I'm sure it must be comfortable."

"I'd feel as though I were wearing my nightclothes," Jillian said as she, too, stared at the strange garments. "But I think you're right."

They found a shop that had bolts of the gauzy cloth on display, and when Jillian told the shopkeeper what they wanted, the man nodded.

"Milady will find that such garments are perfect for the desert," he assured her. Then, after being promised nearly double the asking price, he told her they could be ready the following day. He also recommended sandals and gave them directions to a shop that sold them.

After purchasing sandals as well, Jillian and Connor made their way slowly through the market, buying spices and oils and sweet cakes that they washed down with a strong, sweet tea. Jillian also found some of the special cream that she'd been told would protect her skin from the dry desert air.

At one point, Connor stopped to examine a lovely and unusual shawl. Jillian was surprised when he handed over some gold to the stallkeeper.

"For Mother," he said, answering her unspoken question. "You can give it to her when we return home."

She felt a chill as she envisioned herself presenting the shawl to Marra, with Connor only a memory once again. "Why don't you visit Talita and give it to her yourself?"

"I cannot, Jillian. I must return to the island."

"Why?" she demanded. "Are you afraid that, if you come to Talita, you'll never go back to the Kraaken?"

"Yes," he said simply, then turned away.

* * *

They dined that evening at the garrison, as guests of the commander, who was very curious about the Kraaken priest and the noblewoman who had come so far to seek birds. He, too, had heard the tales of great birds seen occasionally high above the desert, and he'd also been told by a chief of the nomadic tribes that they came from an enchanted place in the distant mountains. But being a highly practical man, he had discounted such stories.

He talked at great length about the desert, however, and it was clear that he found it fascinating.

"In the spring, when the rains come, there are flowers there far more beautiful than anything in the palace gardens," he told them. "And there are what the nomads call *fazaras*—places around springs where trees and grass grow in the middle of barren land."

He spoke of great sandstorms more blinding than the worst snowstorms in the mountains back home, storms that left the land totally transformed—until the next storm came along and changed it yet again.

"Do these storms happen often?" Connor asked with some concern.

"Not often—and *too* often," the commander replied with a grim smile. "But your guide will know the signs. Sometimes, it's possible to outrun them, and other times you must simply make camp and remain inside your tents until they pass."

"Outrun them on a camel?" Connor asked incredulously. He'd seen several of the strange beasts earlier.

The commander laughed. "Don't let their ugliness fool you, Brother Averyl. They're capable of great speed. In fact, in the desert, they can outrun the swiftest horses."

After dinner, the commander took them up on the garrison wall that sat on a slight rise at the edge of town. Twilight was just settling over the land. To one side of the wall lay the town, where lamps were just being lit in the houses. On the other side lay a ridge just slightly higher than the top of the garrison. There were no lights in the valley between, and the ridge itself was just barely visible as a smoky, purplish-hued line.

"The desert is just beyond that ridge," the commander told them. "I hope you've been warned about how cold it gets out there at night."

"Yes, we have," Jillian replied, "although it's hard to believe that any place so hot during the day could become that cold at night."

"It does, believe me; and the change is very sudden. Sometimes, I think that the sorcerers we spoke of earlier come down out of their mountains each night and cast a spell on the place."

He cast a quick glance Connor's way, but only Jillian saw the speculative look in his eyes. Connor was staring at the ridge, his thoughts apparently far away.

Surely it must be a nightmare!

Jillian couldn't breathe! Something huge and

soft was pressing against her face. She began to struggle against it automatically even as she fought her way out of sleep.

And then, abruptly, she knew it *wasn't* a nightmare! As she thrashed about in the bed, her legs and arms encountered muscled flesh. She twisted and kicked out and connected solidly with something that produced a startled grunt of pain.

Her attacker's grip on the pillow covering her face loosened, and Jillian quickly wriggled out from under it and away. The room was too dark for her to see her assailant, but she had a vague impression of a pale, meaty face and a thick neck on a short, heavy body. He had rolled off the bed to get away from her blows. She slipped off on the other side, then began to raise herself from a crouch just as he lunged across the bed toward her.

She sidestepped his outstretched arms and he fell across the bed heavily. The high headboard struck the wall with a resounding *thunk* and the bed itself groaned in protest.

Jillian ran for the door, only to discover that it was still bolted. She began to fumble in the darkness with the bolt as she heard him getting up to launch another attack.

Then there was a loud pounding from the other side of the door, and Connor's voice was calling out to her. She turned, certain that she was about to be attacked again, but her assailant was leaping out the window.

She finally managed to open the door, then ran

to the window in time to see a dark shape drop down from the low roof beneath her window and disappear into the darkness.

"Jillian! What happened?"

Clad only in his trousers, Connor came across the room toward her. She turned away from the window as the full horror of the attack overcame her. Shaking badly, she reached for the bedpost, then sank onto the bed.

"Someone attacked me! He was trying to smother me with a pillow. Then he jumped out the window."

Connor went to the window and looked out, then came back to her. "Are you certain that it wasn't just a nightmare?" he asked as he sat down beside her.

"Yes, I'm certain," she said angrily, then caught her breath with a sob. "Connor, he was trying to *kill* me."

Connor drew her into his arms and stroked her sleep-tangled curls. "Nightmares can sometimes seem very real," he said soothingly. "And after what you've been through—"

She pushed away from him. "It *wasn't* a nightmare, Connor. I'd left the window open and he must have come in that way."

"Were you able to see him at all?"

She shook her head. "Not very well. He was fairly short and heavy, and I think he had dark hair—unless he was wearing a dark cap. His breath stank of beer," she added, wrinkling her nose in distaste.

"Why didn't you scream?" he asked. "I only

woke up because I heard a sound, like something hitting the wall."

"That was the bed. It bumped against the wall when he threw himself across it to grab me. I guess I didn't scream because it all happened so fast. I was too busy trying to save myself." She took a shaky breath. "Connor, why would someone want to kill me?"

"I don't know," he replied, drawing her back into his arms again. "But you're safe now."

And she *did* feel safe—safe enough to begin thinking about the fact that she was wearing only a light shift, while he was half naked. As they sat there, wrapped in each other's arms, she could feel the tension begin to gather, threading its way from her to him, whispering of darkness and of flesh pressed to flesh, separated by the flimsiest of barriers. She raised her face and stared at him, wondering if he felt what she felt—seeking the answer in his eyes.

"Jillian," he murmured, his hand gliding slowly over her hair and curving about her neck. "My dearest Jillian."

The darkness became a palpable, throbbing presence, heavy with a desire previously unknown to them. Their heads moved slowly toward each other, their breath intermingling as they stared into each other's eyes and recaptured in an instant all the closeness they'd known so long ago. Then they began to edge beyond that.

Connor made a sound low in his throat, and a soft sigh escaped from her parted lips. It was a silent acknowledgment that they stood at the edge of childhood friendship, testing its outer limits.

And then their lips met slowly, so very tentatively, clinging to the moment, trembling on the brink of the next.

It felt so very right—and so wrong. This was Connor, her dearest friend. And this was Jillian, his little sister. And they were both surrounded by very adult bodies that were urging them on to a path that was exciting—and terrifying.

They both withdrew, retreating into a tangle of emotions that left them speechless for a long moment. Finally, he released her and got up from the bed to close and lock the window.

"Would you like me to sleep in here—on the floor?"

In that brief space between his question and the qualification, Jillian felt her body saying yes. But aloud, she said, "No, I'll be fine. He won't come back now."

Connor came back to her, kissed the top of her head lightly, then said good night and slipped out the door. She got up to bolt it behind him, the sound far greater in her mind than in reality as she heard the echoes of her lie. She wasn't fine, and she knew that she'd never be fine again.

As she lay back down in bed and tried to reclaim the sleep that had been stolen from her, the attack was almost forgotten. For one brief moment, Jillian had glimpsed a magic that was far beyond anything she and Connor had known in childhood. And she wanted that magic.

Chapter Five

"Henka says that he might have seen the man who attacked you."

"Oh?" Jillian looked up from her breakfast. She certainly hadn't forgotten the attack, but the horror of it was buried beneath the wonder of its aftermath.

"He says he was just coming back from the garrison and he saw a man running away from the inn. He didn't get a good look at him, either, but he fits your description."

"So now you believe me," she said, belatedly recalling that he'd tried to talk her out of it.

"I believed you last night, too."

"You did not!" she exploded, overreacting out of the tangle of her emotions. "You said it was a nightmare. I have bruises, Connor, and they're real!"

He smiled and shook his head. "Why does every conversation we have sound like we've had it before?"

"Probably because we have," she groused, wondering how he could be acting as though nothing else had happened last night. Then she lifted her chin defiantly as she thought about the attack. "I think I surprised him by fighting."

Connor smiled. "No doubt you did, but that just proves that he couldn't have known you."

"Why, Connor?" she asked, her mind now fully occupied with the attacker. "Why would someone try to kill me?"

"His motive could have been robbery," Connor stated. "Henka seems to think that's the most likely explanation. The man could have seen us in the marketplace yesterday, and if he did, he would have known you have money. The innkeeper admitted that there've been some problems in the past, although he didn't recognize the man from the description."

Something in his tone caught her attention. "But you don't believe that. Why not?"

He hesitated for only a moment, then gazed at her steadily. "Even before last night, I'd started to wonder if the attack on our camp might have been directed at *you,* and not at me."

"So *that's* why you're now insisting upon accompanying me. I knew you weren't telling me the truth about that. But why would anyone want to kill *me*?"

"Is it possible that you've angered someone at court?"

"I'm sure I anger a lot of people at court, even though I'm rarely there. But none of them would do something like this. The days of such court intrigues are over. It isn't like it was when we were little."

And that was true. She knew there were those at court who regarded her as a nuisance or even a threat to their fortunes. But the worst they would do was to try to turn her uncle against her or to discredit her in some way.

"Then what about your rivals—the other breeders?"

She started to shake her head, then stopped, thinking about that possibility for the first time.

"You told me that the demand for keras has never been greater, so obviously, there's money to be made from breeding them."

She sighed. "Yes, that's true."

"Who are the other breeders?"

"You wouldn't know them. They're small landholders in the northern mountains. I don't really know them well, either. They're not succeeding because they're trying to breed the keras in captivity.

"A few years ago, they tried to establish rookeries in their own mountains, but the birds kept returning to Talita to breed. They had banded them, and I saw to it that they were returned, but I refused to return the chicks, and that didn't please them. But the royal decree that gives Talita ownership of all chicks regardless of the ownership of the parents remains in effect."

116

"I assume that word must have gotten around about your search."

"I'm sure it did. I didn't attempt to keep it secret." She sat there, thinking about the possibility he'd raised. "For centuries, the northern mountains have been the most lawless part of Lesai. The people there have a long tradition of blood feuds and of taking the law into their own hands. They'd never try to kill me at Talita or anywhere in Lesai, for that matter, but here. . . ." She trailed off uncertainly.

Connor laid his hand over hers. "We'll have to be very careful, Jillian. If we're right, they'll be getting even more desperate after two failed attempts."

They left the inn and went to the garrison, where they met their guide for the journey across the desert. He was a tall, handsome youth, whose dark eyes shone with a frank curiosity about the golden-robed priest and the noblewoman who dressed like a man. The garrison commander told them that he was the son of the most powerful of the desert chieftains and, in an aside, said that this chieftain was also the most trustworthy.

Connor told the commander about the attack on Jillian and their suspicions about her rivals. The commander frowned.

"Most likely, they hired a local man, but without a better description, there's probably not much hope of finding him. And it could indeed have been a robbery attempt. A foreign noblewoman would make a good target for thieves.

"But whichever it was, I don't think you need

to fear an attack once you get into the desert. More likely, they'll wait here for your return. It would perhaps be better if you stay here at the garrison then."

Jillian thanked him and said that they would indeed accept his offer upon their return. The commander gestured to the rifle tied to Connor's horse.

"I see that you're armed, Brother Averyl. Do you carry a knife as well?"

When Connor said that he didn't, the commander turned to his aide and told him to find a knife for their guest.

"I'd like to have one, too," Jillian said.

The commander stared at her, clearly shocked. "But, milady—"

"I've carried a knife before," she stated. "And considering that it's *my* life that's at risk, I want to be armed."

He glanced at Connor, who nodded; then he told his aide to bring two knives. "Rifles are fine, but they're not much help if your enemy mounts a sneak attack up close. I've heard that you have some, ah, unusual fighting skills, Brother Averyl, but a knife could still save your life."

It was clear to Jillian that the commander was uncomfortable with the idea of a knife-wielding woman—and a noblewoman at that—but she was grateful for his acquiescence to her request, even if it *had* come courtesy of Connor's sufferance.

The aide returned with a pair of short-bladed, wicked-looking knives, then offered to instruct Jillian and Connor how to use the weapons. The two were taken to the section of the garrison set aside for arms practice. There they saw a line of posts with heavy padding that showed the results of much use.

"The best way to attack with a knife," the soldier told them, "is with an upward thrust like this."

He lunged forward and brought his arm up in an arc, slashing at the padding. Jillian winced. Connor slanted her a glance.

"*Have* you carried a knife before?"

"Well, no, except to cut ropes and such," she admitted. "Have you?"

He shook his head, then began to practice under the watchful eye of the soldier. "Good," the man said. "You've got good moves."

Jillian watched as the soldier demonstrated the best places to strike and how to parry a knife thrust as well. Connor became very good very fast, and Jillian recalled that he'd always been good at sports and games. As the soldier said, Connor used his body well.

Connor's graceful moves and the soldier's comment had a strange effect on her. Before long, she was paying less attention to the instruction—and far too much to Connor as she replayed yet again that kiss last night. Not even his Kraaken cassock could keep her mind from drifting off into some delightful fantasies.

When the soldier was satisfied that he'd taught Connor all that was necessary, he turned with obvious reluctance to Jillian. Connor, seeing his hesitation, intervened.

"The Lady Jillian and I are old friends, Sergeant. I'll teach her what she needs to know."

The man left with obvious relief. Connor smiled grimly at Jillian. "Well, I taught you how to swim and how to climb up cliffs, but I never expected to be teaching you how to kill."

He was patient, as he had always been with her, countering her tendency to try too much too soon and her irritation at being told how to do anything. She practiced with the padding until he was satisfied that the upward thrusting motion had become second nature to her. Then they picked up the blunted wooden knives used for hand-to-hand combat practice.

Jillian knew this was deadly serious, but it nevertheless quickly became a game to her, not unlike the many games they'd played as children. Both of them were soon so caught up in their parries and thrusts and feinting that they failed to notice the audience they were attracting. Connor was quick, but Jillian was smaller and nearly as fast.

At one point, she managed to catch him off guard and struck at him with a cry of triumph. In a lightning-quick series of moves, he parried her thrust and then hooked a long leg around hers and sent her tumbling to the ground.

"That wasn't *fair*, Connor," she sputtered angrily. "You're using those Kraaken tricks."

Laughing, he reached down to help her to her feet. "If you ever have to use that knife, I wouldn't count on having an opponent who believes in fairness."

Then laughter drew their attention to a group of soldiers gathered nearby. Jillian pulled herself up haughtily and gave them a withering look that sent them away quickly. Connor chuckled.

"Well, milady, I think we've provided enough entertainment for one day."

"It wouldn't be the first time," she grinned as she dusted herself off, then began the mock battle once again.

"I think I'd prefer to walk across the desert," Connor said, eyeing the camels doubtfully.

"It can't be as uncomfortable as it looks," Jillian replied hopefully.

And it wasn't. The two beasts knelt at an order from their guide, and Connor and Jillian both mounted, then clung to the big saddles as the camels got ungracefully to their feet, emitting sounds that clearly showed their reluctance. Jillian turned to look longingly after their horses as they were led away. She also did not fail to note that the ground was much farther away than from the top of a horse. The camels were half again as tall as the horses had been.

After bumping along uncomfortably for a short distance, they both adjusted quickly to the unusual rolling gait of the creatures. And then their first sight of the desert captured all their attention.

As they paused at the top of the ridge, the world before them changed far more abruptly than they could have imagined. What lay before them was an ocean of white sand that stretched in undulating waves toward the distant horizon.

"I feel as though we've stepped off the world," Connor said in a voice filled with awe.

Jillian felt disoriented, even a bit frightened. "How can he possibly know where he's going?" she asked of their young guide, who was riding somewhat ahead of them. "There are no landmarks and the land itself must change all the time."

One of the Masani guards turned to her. "That's why we need him, milady. None of us would venture far out here without a guide. But he knows his way somehow. His people use the sun and stars and the winds, much like sailors do."

The analogy was very apt. They were soon surrounded by the sea of sand. Behind them, the ridge, their only landmark, was rapidly becoming no more than a dark smudge on the horizon. Jillian would have felt much better if she could have seen the mountains that were their destination, but the youth told them that three days at least would pass before they could see the end of their journey.

The heat that had descended upon them even before they ventured into the desert soon became so oppressive that it seemed to be sucking the very life out of her. Jillian thought that, by the time this journey was over, she might be a dry, withered old woman, despite the creams and oils she so diligently applied.

She glanced over at Connor, who was dressed like her in the loose, white robes they'd ordered. He'd even acquired a headdress similar to the one their young guide wore: a length of gauze twisted about his head with the ends making a curtain that fell to his shoulders. She herself wore a loose hood of gauze that covered her hair and provided at least some protection from the burning sun.

At first, she kept scanning the heavens, hoping to catch a glimpse of the great birds, but before long, the sun had become such a searing white ball that she couldn't look up anymore.

Their guide had earlier told her that he'd seen such birds only once, but his father had seen them many times. Their name for the birds translated into birds of the roof of heaven, though it sounded far lovelier in their own language.

Hammat said that there were tales among his people too of sorcerers who lived in the mountains and had tamed the great birds. None of his people had ever seen the sorcerers, but he'd heard that the hill tribes saw them regularly.

He spoke passable Masani, but when Jillian asked him if he and his people believed these tales, he switched to his musical tongue, then paused to think before he returned to Masani.

"My father says that there are many things in this world that we are not permitted to understand."

Jillian smiled, thinking that both father and son would make good diplomats, since their first rule seemed to be never give offense. Obviously, he didn't know whether or not *she* believed in sorcery, and therefore chose words calculated to prevent giving offense.

It was impossible for her to guess how much

progress they were making. The camels seemed to be moving at a very slow pace, but the travelers had long since lost sight of the ridge behind them.

Hot as it was, though, Jillian didn't sweat, and that at least made the heat bearable. Such breeze as existed flowed through the layers of gauze, touching her skin and making her glad she'd worn only the most minimal undergarments.

Finally, when the sun began to slip down from its height, Hammat deviated for the first time from the straight line he'd been following. And a short time later, they were in the shade of a tall dune Jillian hadn't even noticed. From a distance, it had appeared to be no more than another of the small ripples of sand that made up the desert.

"We will rest here for a time," Hammat told the others, sliding easily off his camel.

Jillian slid somewhat less gracefully off her own beast and watched as Hammat scrambled up the side of the dune in a blur of sand. When he reached the top, he turned slowly in all directions before sliding down again to rejoin them as they sat in the welcome shade.

One of the guards asked what he was looking for, and the youth shrugged. "Signs of a tsaweh—a sandstorm. I feel one, but I do not see it."

"How do you feel it?" Jillian asked, recalling unhappily what the commander had said about the storms.

Hammat seemed to consider her question for a long time, then shrugged again. "I cannot explain it. We all feel them coming, but sometimes they go elsewhere."

"That certainly covers all possibilities," Connor said with a low chuckle.

Their party grew quiet, and soon Jillian saw that all of them, even Hammat, had fallen asleep. She turned to Connor, who sat beside her, his head thrown back as he rested against the hill of sand. His eyes were closed as well, but they opened quickly when she started to get up.

"Where are you going?" he asked lazily.

"Well, I'm *not* going to sleep," she retorted. "Someone should stay awake. What if we're attacked?"

"The camels will warn us," he replied, stifling a yawn.

"How do you know that?"

"I asked. Don't wander off, Jillie. It would be easy to get lost."

"I won't go far," she replied over her shoulder as she set out.

Walking in the sand proved to be easier than she'd anticipated, perhaps because of the sandals. She thought about climbing up the dune as their guide had, but decided against it. She had no desire to spend the rest of the day covered with sand.

Or many days, she thought unhappily, wondering when they would come to one of those garden places the commander had spoken of. If there were springs there, surely she could bathe or, at least, wash herself.

She decided to walk around the tall dune.

Keeping it in sight meant that she couldn't possibly get lost. So she walked the length of it, then emerged once again into the blinding glare of the sun.

Her thoughts turned once more to Connor's belief that she could be threatened by the other kera breeders. At first, she'd given some credence to the idea, but the more she thought about it, the more doubtful she became.

While there was a certain lawlessness to the people of that region, she just couldn't see one of them attempting to kill a daughter of the royal family. They cherished the independence granted to them by her uncle too much to risk it in such an endeavor.

Besides, she thought, what point would there be to killing her? The keras would still belong to Talita, and nothing would change for the other breeders. And if they intended to bring back some of the birds she sought, how could they explain that? No matter how they tried to hide them, someone would find out and guess what they'd done.

Still, someone was obviously trying to cause harm to her or to Connor—or perhaps to them both. Why? What was it about them that made them such a threat to someone?

She harkened back to the earlier fear of the court that the Kraaken had a reason other than recruitment for sending Connor with her. So often, it seemed to her, her original thoughts on a subject proved to be the correct ones. But if the Kraaken *did* have some evil scheme in mind, Connor hadn't carried it out. He'd been followed too closely in Trantor, and he'd had no opportunity since then.

Then it occurred to her that Connor might well have been sent to stir up trouble, but had decided to disobey his orders. From what he'd told her, he didn't always agree with his superiors.

Still, that fact would certainly have been known to High Priest Jenner and the others. So why had they chosen to send him, especially since they'd also known that *she* would be his escort?

She stopped walking and stared at the complex patterns of lines in the sand, thinking about the complexities of her own situation. Then, when thoughts of Connor began to veer from his purpose to his kiss, she started walking again, turning to head back to the others.

She raised her head to see where she was in relation to the tall dune—and stopped. It had vanished! She drew in a sharp breath as she recalled that she hadn't seen it before, either, until their guide had led them into its shadow.

Panic nibbled at the corners of her mind. Her feet wanted to move, but she had no instructions to issue them. All around her were the rounded waves of sand—any one of which could be the dune where they'd sought shelter.

She looked for her footprints in the sand, only to realize that they were vanishing rapidly, lost in swirls created by the quickening breeze.

Terrified now—too terrified to be angry with herself at the moment—she cupped her hands around her mouth and shouted for Connor. But the breeze seemed to snatch away his name and scatter it over the empty sand.

I can't have gone far, she told herself. *And it would be better if I simply wait here until they find me.*

Having thus assured herself, she sat down at the base of a dune, then began to berate herself for her foolishness.

Time passed. She drifted into a reverie, thinking about a time when she was perhaps six or seven and had gone off into the woods alone, seeking the lovely wildflowers she knew grew there. She'd been warned not to wander off alone—which, of course, was why she'd done it.

It was nearly dark when Connor and her father had found her, crying and hungry. Connor had been off somewhere, but when he'd come home to find that she was missing, he'd guessed immediately where she was.

As she sat in the desert, Jillian closed her eyes, slipping still deeper into her memories, then opened them quickly when a shadow fell across her face.

"Are you ready to admit that you're lost?"

Shading her eyes, she stared up at the tall figure in white standing before her.

"I was resting," she said, rising quickly and brushing the sand off her robe.

Connor lowered his face to within inches of hers. "You were lost. I've been following you."

She shrugged. "Then I suppose that we're both lost."

He roared with laughter. "That's just what you

said when your father and I found you in the woods that time—remember?"

She *didn't* remember that; all she could recall was how happy she had been to be found and how grateful she'd been that Connor had thought to bring along her favorite sweet cakes.

"When we found you, the first thing you asked was if we were lost, too."

"Well, I'm not lost now."

"Fine. Then you can lead us back to the others."

Jillian had begun to see the trap she'd set for herself before his words were even out of his mouth, and she started to look around, hoping to spot his footprints. But there were none to be found.

"All right," she said huffily, "I'm lost. But I knew you'd find me."

Connor laughed and took her hand. "I've never known anyone to show less grace about being wrong. Come along, Jillie. The others are waiting. It's time to be off again."

Overhead, the sun had been a blinding white light. Now, as it sank slowly toward the barely discernible horizon, it glowed with a glorious red-gold light, hanging before them in a sky as bleached of color as the land beneath it.

"We've changed direction," Connor said, breaking a long silence as the camels moved tirelessly across the sand.

Jillian looked up to see that he was right. She'd pulled the gauze hood across her face and had very nearly dozed off in the saddle, thanks to the steady rhythm of the camel's movements. The sun had been slightly to their right; now it was off to the left.

Since Connor spoke no Masani, Jillian asked their young guide about the change of course.

"There is a fazara ahead, lady. We go there," he replied.

Jillian brightened at that news, recalling that that was the name of the garden places. She relayed the information to Connor and they both stared doubtfully at the endless desert before them.

"I'm not sure I'll believe it even if I see it," Connor remarked, squinting into the glaring sun.

Jillian laughed. One of the stories the garrison commander had told them was about hallucinations that sometimes came upon people lost in the desert. The word for them in the nomad's language translated as things that are not there.

"I don't even care if it's real or not," she replied. "All that matters is that I *believe* it's there."

Connor smiled. "This is sounding like the beginning of a long philosophical discussion of the sort the other brothers and I often have on the island."

Jillian lapsed into silence. He often made references to his life there; whether for his own benefit or hers she didn't know. But they never failed to send a chill through her, reminding her that he had a life apart from her, a life to which he would be returning.

She had dozed off again when exclamations from her fellow travelers jolted her awake. She opened her eyes to see them all staring intently at some point ahead of them. Shading her eyes with her hand, she, too, peered off into the seamless world of white—and saw a small, dark spot far ahead. To judge from the change in the sun's position, she must have slept for some time.

"If you had napped when the others did, you'd be able to stay awake now," Connor said teasingly. "That's the fazara, or so Hammat tells us. It will take another two hours to reach it."

During those two endless hours, the dark spot grew ever larger, even though it still lacked definition. The sun sank lower and became redder, losing the last of its golden light and coloring the sand a lovely rose pink. For the first time, Jillian began to understand how this strange place could be called beautiful. The desert was an artist's palette, and the sun was the artist.

She glanced over at Connor and saw the smile on his face as he stared off ahead of them. It seemed so very right that she should be sharing this with him. He turned her way suddenly, catching her staring at him.

"I'm happy to be here, Jillian, and happy to be seeing it with you. I never dreamed that we'd be sharing an adventure like this one day."

There could have been many other adventures, she said, but only to herself. She had stopped saying such things to him. They sounded like petulant whining to her own ears. Somewhere along this journey, she'd given up her anger with him, allowing it to fade instead to regret.

But how will I ever be able to give him up again? she asked herself. *Can I accept that this is all there will ever be for us?*

Gradually, the dark place ahead of them became a small copse of strange trees and tall grasses full of people and animals. It was much larger than she'd originally thought, and there appeared to be quite a few people there as well. Hammat brought them to a halt when they were still some distance away, and Jillian could see some men gathering at the edge of the fazara, staring in their direction.

"These are not my people," he explained. "It would be better if I go alone and speak to them first."

Then he left before they could ask any questions, and they all sat there uneasily as he dismounted and was immediately surrounded by rifle-toting men. The guards fingered their own rifles, although they didn't raise them.

"Will there be trouble, do you think?" Jillian asked one of the Masani guards.

"No, I don't think so, milady. Few in the desert would dare to offend Amari's son. He's the most powerful of the chieftains, and he's known to exact a heavy revenge from anyone who crosses him. Since we're traveling under the protection of his son, we should be safe."

After what seemed like hours, but was in reality only moments, Hammat remounted his camel and rode back to them. The other men returned to the encampment.

"We are welcome," their young guide announced with a satisfied smile.

They rode into the fazara, feeling a wonderful coolness the moment they left the white sands behind. The change was startling. Not only was it much cooler, but Jillian could smell and feel the moisture in the air, and ahead of her, through the dense trees, she could see water. By the time they dismounted, she could hear the shouts and laughter of children and the sounds of splashing.

Hammat led them to a spot some distance away from the group of nomads, who had all stopped to stare at them. Jillian didn't detect any hostility in the looks they received, but she nonetheless stayed close to her own group. For the first time, she began to think about how far she was from everything familiar—and how much farther she had to go to reach her destination.

"In here, it's easy to believe that the desert is nothing more than a dream," Connor said, coming up behind her.

"Yes, but it's going to become a recurring dream," she reminded him. "We have much farther to go."

He turned toward the sounds of the children playing in the water. "Hammat says that they'll be called to dinner soon. Then we can use the pool. But don't wander off alone, Jillie."

"Is that Hammat's warning—or yours?"

"Mine. I think we're safe here, but we need to be cautious."

A short time later, they heard adult shouts, and

then the sounds of the children died away. Connor suggested that they go to the pool. Smoke drifted their way from the other encampment, bringing with it the aromas of exotic foods.

"I told the others that you would want to bathe," Connor said as they made their way through the dense undergrowth to the pool's edge. "They will wait until later."

The large, sparkling pool, apparently fed by underground springs, lay at the very center of the fazara, surrounded on all sides by the strange, lush plants that grew in this improbable place. Jillian bent to dip her hand into the water, then pulled it back quickly.

"It's cold!"

"Too cold for bathing?" Connor teased. "I seem to remember a little girl who was always the first one into the lake at Talita in the spring."

"I wait a bit longer now," she told him as she stared at the inviting water. Cold or not, she wanted very much to strip off her clothing and jump in. She cast a glance at Connor and tried not to think what she was thinking. He smiled and took a few steps away, then turned his back to her.

"I'll wait here until you're in the water."

After a quick look around, she hurried out of her robes—an easy task, given the minimal amount of clothing she wore. Then she waded into the water, shivering at the cold.

The bottom of the pool dropped away sharply after a few yards, and Jillian began to swim, then turned to look over her shoulder at Connor. He had sat down on a rock to remove his sandals, and when he stood up again, she quickly turned her head and continued to swim toward the center. But in her mind, she saw him remove his robes to reveal that lean, muscular body that made him a very different man from the boy she remembered—a man capable of arousing feelings in her that heated her body even in the cool water.

A short time later, Connor's dark head appeared as he swam with long, powerful strokes toward her.

Jillian's breath caught sharply, and she became achingly aware of her own naked body, separated from his only by the clear water. She felt heavy and awkward in her movements, yet at the same time almost insubstantial, as though her very familiar body were no longer really hers.

At no time did Connor come that close to her as they both swam around the pool. But she could still feel him, as though a current ran from one to the other of them, humming with desire, taunting her with the unknown.

Finally, she started back to shore, then stopped as the water became shallow. Connor was still swimming in the middle of the pond, and as she looked his way, he turned and struck out for the opposite side, keeping his back to her.

She scrambled through the shallow portion of the pool, feeling both vulnerable and yet powerful in a strange sort of way. How little attention she'd paid to her body all these years, and yet now, it seemed she could think of nothing else. Except, of course, for *his* body.

As she hurried into her clothing, she felt a certain anger at being forced to think of such things. A part of her still wanted the lost innocence of their childhood, even as another part whispered ever more urgently of pleasure to be found in losing that innocence. Did he feel the same? Perhaps not, since he had the power of his vows to keep his thoughts from straying.

Connor reached the far shore, then turned back. She was standing on the opposite side of the pool, watching him. As he came closer, he could see how the wet fabric clung to her, becoming translucent in its dampness.

She was so beautiful, her body a wonder of womanly curves. Even though he lacked any experience of women, Connor knew that none could be as lovely as she was.

He wondered if she would turn her back when he reached the shallows and what he would do if she didn't. It felt like all their childhood games—and yet it wasn't. There could be no winner in this game—only losers. He could lose everything, and she would lose him. Breaking his vow would destroy him as a man, and there would be nothing left for her.

And yet, as he swam steadily toward her, Connor could hear that soft whisper, telling him that it might be worth it. He could burn his very soul—but what a glorious flame!

At the very last second, as though she too were weighing the consequences, she turned her back to him and moved away from his clothing. In the fading light, he could see the outline of her body: the long, slim legs, the gentle swell of her hips, the hollow of her waist. Aching with a hunger that could never be satisfied, Connor waded out of the pool and put on his clothes.

When she judged that she'd given him enough time, Jillian turned around to find Connor sitting on the large rock near the pool's edge, staring at her. His gaze didn't waver as she walked back to him. She knew that her damp clothes still clung to her because she felt their coolness against her suddenly heated skin.

She sat down next to him and he took her hand in his.

"We could hurt each other, Jillian. That's something we could never have done as children."

She nodded, knowing what he meant and, at the same time, secretly thrilled to realize that, vows or not, he was thinking the same thing she was.

"In all these years and in all my thoughts of you, I kept you as a little girl, even though I knew the image wasn't true. It was easier that way."

"Do you regret seeing me again, Connor?" she asked. It was a question she'd asked of herself about him and one she hadn't been able to answer.

He shook his head as he continued to hold her hand. "No. I knew I'd be seeing you."

"You did? But I thought you said—"

"That wasn't exactly the truth," he admitted. "They told me that you would be my escort. I could have refused to come, but I think Jenner knew I wouldn't. Maybe he's even hoping that I won't survive the temptation."

Jillian said nothing. What she wanted to say was that she hoped he wouldn't survive the temptation, either. But she'd come to understand that she would lose him either way. If he broke his vow, he wouldn't be able to live with himself—and he'd be lost to her just as surely as if he'd kept it and returned to the Kraaken.

"Was there never a time when you wanted to marry?" he asked. "Surely there were many suitors for your hand."

"There were, but I didn't want any of them. I knew I could never have what I'd had with you with any of them." She paused, then stared hard at him. "I'm sure it would make you feel better to have found me married, but surely you knew that I hadn't."

"No, I didn't know that. I deliberately didn't ask about you because I couldn't face either answer I would have received. But I *did* hope that, when I met you, you would tell me that you were happily married. I truly wanted that for you, even though it would have hurt."

"If you wanted happiness for me, Connor, you—" She stopped abruptly as a figure appeared out of the woods, hovering in the lengthening shadows.

Seeing her look in that direction, Connor turned, too. Then they both stared as the figure moved toward them hesitantly. It was a woman— one of the nomads. She stopped about ten feet from them and stared at Connor, then suddenly began to speak rapidly in her own incomprehensible tongue.

Connor stood up and approached her slowly, asking if she were lost, even though his words were meaningless to her. Then, all of a sudden, she rushed forward and threw herself at his feet. Jillian stared in shock as the woman picked up the hem of his robe and pressed it to her lips.

Clearly as shocked as Jillian was, Connor reached out to try to raise the woman to her feet, but she got up swiftly and backed away from him, once more chattering away. And then she was gone, melting back into the shadows.

Jillian hugged herself, shivering. The woman's behavior had thoroughly unnerved her. Connor just stood there, frowning and staring off to the spot where she'd disappeared. Finally, he turned to Jillian.

"Do you think it's because we're foreigners?"

"I'm a foreigner, too," she pointed out. "But she didn't pay any attention at all to me."

Still somewhat shaken by the woman's strange behavior, they walked back to their camp. Jillian suggested they ask Hammat for an explanation.

"Do you remember any of the words she used?" she asked. The woman had spoken in such a low voice that Jillian hadn't been able to make out the words.

Connor hesitated before answering. "I'm not sure. She was speaking so fast. But I heard one word several times. It sounded like Kraaken."

"Oh," Jillian said, relieved. "Then she must have known who you are. Perhaps Hammat told them."

"He might have." Connor nodded. "But it's still strange that she would have behaved that way."

But Hammat said that he hadn't told the other tribe who any of them were. He had merely stated that they were foreigners traveling under his father's protection. Seeing how shocked they were at the encounter and obviously curious himself, he told them he would make inquiries.

Hammat was gone for some time, during which Connor and Jillian ate the meal prepared by the Masani guards. When Hammat returned, he seemed distracted. It took several minutes of questioning for him to tell them what he'd learned.

The woman was a peshtara, a word in the nomadic tongue that translated roughly as far-seer. "She knows things," Hammat said. "Things that are unknowable to the rest of us. We have one such woman in our tribe as well—my aunt."

"So she knew that Connor was a Kraaken," Jillian said. She'd always heard that such seers existed, though she'd never met one herself. There was even such a woman who was regularly consulted by her aunt, the queen.

Hammat nodded, but clearly there was more to the situation. Still, it took some time to get the rest of the story out of him.

"She says you are a very great man, Brother Averyl—one favored by the gods, although you choose not to join them."

"What?" Jillian asked, exchanging a confused look with Connor.

"What did she mean?" Connor asked.

But Hammat shook his head. "She didn't say. Peshtaras never explain. They only report what they see."

Both Jillian and Connor were still thinking about the strange woman and her even stranger words when they fell asleep in their bedrolls. Jillian wondered if she could have meant that Connor would choose to leave the brotherhood, but Connor was thinking very different thoughts: thoughts about his true mission that he'd kept secret from Jillian.

Chapter Six

"You choose not to join them." The old woman's words kept running through Jillian's mind as the travelers set out again soon after dawn the next morning.

Already, the desert sun was a warm presence against her back—a welcome presence now, because she'd discovered that the garrison commander hadn't exaggerated about the cold nights out here. Even in her bedroll, she'd barely managed to keep warm.

She kept seeing the woman as she'd knelt before Connor and kissed the hem of his robe. The woman's behavior was as unnerving as her words, harking back to a primitive time when kings had been worshiped devoutly, a time when men—or a few men—had enjoyed limitless power.

Jillian shivered, partly from the lingering chill of the night, but more from her thoughts. No matter how she tried to see it differently, the far-seer's behavior and words suggested that what Connor had said about Kraaken magic and immortality was true.

She looked over at him as he rode beside her, his face turned away as he watched the fazara disappear behind them. Already, it was no more than the faint dark spot they'd first seen yesterday.

If the woman's words had had any effect upon him, he hadn't let it show. Her attempts at forcing him to talk about the woman had resulted in nothing more than teasing words about her past failure to believe in such things. "They're primitive people, Jillie, with primitive beliefs."

She knew that was true, but even so, she could not get it out of her mind. And neither could she let go of the other thought that flowed from it. If Connor would choose not to become one of them—one of the Inner Circle—then that must surely mean that he would choose *her* instead.

Was that the reason for the smile the old woman had given her this morning, as they were taking their leave of the tribe? Jillian had already mounted her camel and was waiting for the others when she saw the woman standing alone at the edge of the group.

When Jillian first saw her, the far-seer was staring intently at Connor, but then suddenly she had turned to look directly at Jillian. They had stared at each other for a long moment, and then, just before the woman turned away, Jillian had seen a smile flicker across her weathered face. She thought the woman might even have nodded, but she wasn't so sure of that.

I'm being a fool, she told herself disgustedly. *The desert sun has affected my brain, and I've let my hopes run wild.*

She thought instead about the new information their guide had obtained regarding the hill tribe believed to have the birds she sought. At her request, Hammat had spoken with the chief storyteller among the nomads. The man said that those who possessed the great birds lived very high in the mountains and were not part of the hill tribes. They were great sorcerers who dwelt in the highest places, living in solitude with their birds.

"You're very silent this morning, Milady Jillian," Connor said teasingly.

She pulled herself from her thoughts and told him what Hammat had learned from the story-teller. "Our journey could be even longer, if the story is true."

"Well, we should know the truth when we reach the hill tribes. The closer we get to the source, the more accurate the tales should be."

Jillian raised her head to scan the heavens. Already, the pinks and blues of the morning sky were fading into that bleached-out color she'd come to associate with the desert. Soon it would be nearly impossible to discern the horizon.

"I keep hoping to see one of the birds," she said wistfully.

"Everyone has told us that the sightings are rare," Connor reminded her.

As before, Hammat brought their party to a halt shortly after midday, and they all sought the shelter of a tall dune. This time, Jillian napped with the others. The desert heat was slowly sapping her strength, and the novelty had worn off as well. Hammat had already informed them that there would be no fazara tonight; they would have to make camp in the desert.

Late in the afternoon, as the sun began its fiery descent, they set out once more. Hammat said that they could continue their journey into the night, with the moon and the brilliant canopy of stars to guide them. So they rode steadily westward as the sinking sun grew ever larger and redder, bathing the desert in its ruddy glow.

Jillian waited eagerly to see the wondrous sight she'd seen the day before. In the final moment, before the sun vanished below the horizon, there was a sudden burst of colors far more breathtaking than the loveliest of rainbows.

She drew in her breath, then exhaled in a soft sigh as both desert and sky were lit by those eerie colors for one brief instant, before beginning a rapid fade toward deeper blues and purples and grays.

Then she turned to Connor and their eyes met in mutual acknowledgment of the beauty—and of the pleasure each took in sharing it with the other.

Soon, they were riding beneath a cold blackness, pricked by the light of a million stars and a half-moon that was ascending slowly into the vault of the heavens. Jillian sat in the saddle, huddled within her bedroll for warmth as the temperature dropped sharply. The body heat from the tireless camel helped warm her as well, and she thought perhaps she should just sleep in the saddle tonight, although it was doubtful that the camel would approve.

They made camp shortly before midnight in the shelter of a dune. Hammat offered to set up one of the small tents for her, but since she doubted that it would be of much value, she thanked him and said she would sleep in a bedroll, as the others were.

The last thing she saw before sleep claimed her was Connor sitting alone at the small campfire, his body totally still as he stared into the flames.

"Something is troubling our guide," Connor said the next afternoon, breaking a long silence between them.

Jillian looked questioningly at Hammat, who rode some distance ahead between the Masani guards. Henka, her own guard, rode slightly behind them. He'd been brooding and silent since they set out, and Jillian assumed he was regretting this assignment. The highly pampered Royal Guards weren't accustomed to such hardships, living as they did among royalty.

"Why do you think so?" she asked after watching Hammat for a few moments.

"Twice already, he's left us and ridden to the top of a dune to stare off to the south. And he's also been uncharacteristically quiet."

Jillian shrugged. "I assume he rode up there to get his bearings. Surely you don't think he's lost?" The thought horrified her.

"No, I'm sure he's not. I was thinking that he might sense a sandstorm."

That possibility pleased her no more than the prospect of being lost. She scanned the southern horizon herself, but saw nothing but endless patterns in the sand beneath a milky sky. The horizon was completely invisible. This time, even when she stared hard at it, she was unable to find the line between desert and sky.

"I know," Connor said when she mentioned it to him. "That's what made me think of a sandstorm—that plus the fact that he's changed our course somewhat. We're now traveling more north than west, and we're also past the time when he usually stops to rest."

Jillian kicked her camel in a fruitless attempt to get it to overtake Hammat. She'd already discovered that, while the beasts would stop and start easily enough—albeit begrudgingly—they refused to increase their speed once they got going.

"Henka," she called to the guard. "Please tell Hammat that I wish to speak to him."

He shouted to their guide, who promptly brought the party to a halt, then turned to her.

"Is something wrong, Hammat? Is there a sandstorm coming?"

He hesitated, then nodded. "But I believe we can outrun it, Lady Jillian—that is, if we don't stop to rest."

"Fine, let's try. I have no great desire to see a sandstorm up close."

But the storm gained on them. It was a frightening thing to watch. Each time Jillian turned toward the south, there was less desert to see. Many times, she had watched thunderstorms approaching, but this was nothing like that. Land and sky simple blurred together into a single dun color. There was no distant rumble of thunder or flash of lightning—just the usual vast silence of the rapidly vanishing desert.

And then, finally, there was the wind that picked up suddenly and began to whip around them, making the camels nervous and clawing at her loose robe. It was a strange sort of wind, almost mischievous in nature, as it changed directions quickly, blew itself out and then rose again from yet another direction. It felt to Jillian like a living thing.

Ahead of them, Hammat urged his camel to a greater speed and the others followed. He passed the word back that they could not hope to out-run the sandstorm now, but must seek shelter instead.

By the time they came to a halt, the winds were howling, whistling and rasping—a cacophony that made it nearly impossible to be heard, except when one shouted as loud as possible. And even then, the wind snatched away the sound.

Even Hammat seemed to be frightened now—perhaps, Jillian thought, because he knew he'd waited too long. With the eternal optimism of youth, he'd undoubtedly believed he could outrun the storm.

Pitching the tiny tents would have been a wonderful comedy if their situation hadn't been so very desperate. Ropes flew like snakes off into the wind. Canvas flapped loudly, adding to the nearly unbearable level of noise.

Helping as best as she could, Jillian wondered why Hammat hadn't chosen a spot that would keep them out of the wind. But however misplaced his earlier optimism might have been, she trusted him to know what he was doing now.

The camels needed no urging to kneel down in the sand with their rumps all facing the rising wind. When Jillian saw Hammat go over to them, carrying pieces of cloth, she struggled through the storm to him.

The cloths proved to be large, gauzy bags with string threaded through one end. After watching him drop a bag over the first camel's head, then tie the string securely around the beast's thick neck, she helped with the others. The cloth was fine enough for the animals to breathe through, while at the same time keeping the sand out of their eyes and nostrils. The camels made no objection; it was obvious that they'd been through this many times before.

As Jillian and Hammat worked, she asked him why he'd chosen this spot, rather than one that would have taken them out of the full force of the wind. In fact, they weren't anywhere near the tall dunes. The spot he'd chosen was nearly level.

"It is impossible to get out of the wind," he shouted. "At least here, we will not be buried in the sand too deeply."

Jillian stared at him, aghast. She simply hadn't thought about how fragile the miniature mountains of sand were, even though she'd seen how the winds had sculpted this strange land.

By the time Jillian and Hammat had covered the camels' heads and checked to be certain their burdens were as securely tied down as possible, the others had succeeded in pitching three of the small tents. The tents were each intended to hold one person only, but since there was no time left to put up the others, they would have to share. The full force of the storm was bearing down on them too quickly for them to do any more work, except for dividing up the water and some food to carry into the tents.

Connor, his face completely covered by the ends of his turban, held open a flap and motioned with his hand. Jillian needed no further encouragement to crawl inside. She had covered her face as best she could, but her skin and her eyes and throat were already rubbed raw by the blowing sand.

Inside the small tent, the wind whistled through openings and the sand made a strange hissing sound as it struck the walls. It seemed a very fragile source of protection indeed, but it was still welcome.

The tent was high enough for Jillian to stand upright, but Connor had to stand in a slight crouch as they busied themselves brushing sand from their faces and hands and clothing. When she had finished cleaning herself as best she could, Jillian reached for the water they carried in oiled skins.

"Be careful with the water," Connor warned her in a raspy voice. "We don't know how long it will have to last."

She nodded unhappily and took a small sip, barely resisting the temptation to pour it all down her parched throat. Then she handed the water to Connor, who also swallowed only a small amount.

They sat down in the middle of the tent and listened for a time to the violence around them. She reached for his hand. "I'm glad you couldn't set all the tents up."

He squeezed her hand. "Frightened?"

She arched a dark brow. "And I suppose you're not?"

He chuckled. "Maybe a little. After all, even Hammat seemed nervous, and he's undoubtedly been through many of these storms."

They soon fell into reminiscences about thunderstorms at Talita, which tended to get many violent spring storms. And that led to yet another excursion into their shared childhood. Jillian was touched by the abundance and clarity of Connor's memories, which rivaled her own and sometimes exceeded them.

Accustomed to the swift passage of thunderstorms, they both kept expecting the sandstorm to move on. Several times, the wind *did* seem to die down a bit, but each time they were about to get up and venture outside, the storm seemed to renew its fury.

"How long can this go on?" Jillian asked impatiently after it had tricked them for the third time. "Surely the storm can't last for days."

"Hammat says it could, and there's no way to predict how bad it'll be. Why don't we both try to get some sleep? If it ends during the night and the sky clears, we could make up for the time being lost now."

He spread their bedrolls out in the small space, then drew her down beside him. Jillian had been so preoccupied with the storm that only now did she think about their forced intimacy. And then she wished she hadn't.

At first, they simply lay there, side by side, without touching. But then Connor's hand found hers and covered it. Jillian's body sang with the current that passed between them, sending tiny tremors along all her nerve endings.

Does he feel what I feel? she wondered. *Or have the accursed Kraaken taught him to control such feelings?* She wanted to ask him, but couldn't bring herself to form the words, and this hesitancy—so new to their relationship—irritated her.

She drifted into a light doze, her thoughts becoming muddled and scattered, but filled always with Connor. And at some point during her drifting, she moved closer to him and he fitted her against him. The last thing she remembered before she fell away into sleep was the soft brush of his lips against her brow and a barely audible whisper: "Jillian, my love."

*   *   *

Jillian awoke slowly, reluctant to leave a dreamworld where Connor made love to her, his lips and hands roaming over her, drawing from her wondrous sensations. It all seemed so real—right up to the moment when she opened her eyes.

At first, she was disoriented and frightened. It was so dark, and the air around her felt so dense and still. The first thing that registered on her awakening brain was Connor's absence. Surely he'd been here; she hadn't dreamed that, too, had she? No, she knew she hadn't; she remembered his arm around her, the hard pillow of his chest and his soft words as she'd fallen asleep.

And then she realized that it was quiet again: the enormous silence of the desert had returned. The storm was over. Connor must have gone outside to see how the others had fared.

She had just sat up when the tent flap was abruptly pulled back and a figure appeared. Connor's name was on her lips, but she stiffled it as she realized that it wasn't Connor: it was Henka, her guard.

"Where's Connor?" she asked, her voice shrill with fear.

"We need your help, milady," Henka said urgently. "One of the tents collapsed. There are men buried beneath it in the sand."

Jillian crawled quickly from the tent. "Where's Connor—Brother Averyl? Is he all right?"

"He was trying to help them," Henka said, his voice taut with tension. "He . . . had an accident."

"What?" Jillian turned sharply to the guard, then froze. He was carrying one of the hammers they'd used to secure the tent pegs, and as she turned toward him, he swung it in an arc toward her head.

Already unbalanced because she'd turned toward him, Jillian flung herself sideways and fell to the sand. The hammer struck a painful, glancing blow to her shoulder and she cried out. Then she quickly scrambled to her feet and started to run.

She ran blindly into the darkness, screaming, unable to see any of the others and certain of only one thing: Henka was trying to kill her. Even as she ran, she knew it must have been him all along. But there was no time to think about his treachery now. She could hear him behind her, breathing heavily as he struggled through the sand, his much greater weight making it more difficult for him to run because he sank farther into the sand.

Suddenly, something loomed ahead of her in the darkness. She couldn't see what it was, but she veered away from it at the last moment. Behind her, she heard Henka swear and then fall heavily.

Jillian turned to see him struggling to free himself from something, and she realized that it was one of the ropes that had secured a tent. He still had the hammer in his hand, but in the other hand, he now held a knife.

"Connor! Help!" Her shout seemed tiny in the desert stillness, and there was no answer.

"He won't help you," Henka hissed, baring his teeth as he threw away the hammer and came at her with the knife.

The emotions that swept through her in that instant should have paralyzed her. Connor was dead, killed by this man who was determined to kill her as well. But instead of rendering her helpless, that knowledge enraged her. She could taste the bitterness of her anger as she reached into the folds of her robe and withdrew the knife she'd hidden there, strapped to her bare waist.

And now, as Henka lunged at her, Connor's lessons came back to her. She raised the knife, surprising Henka momentarily—just enough time for her to sidestep his thrust and strike a blow of her own!

Henka cried out in surprise and stumbled backward, then slowly crumpled to the sand as a stain spread over the front of his white shirt.

The paralysis she'd managed to avoid earlier struck her now as she watched him fall to the sand. For a moment, he struggled to get to his feet again, making horrible sounds, and then he fell back and lay still.

Jillian raised her hand to her mouth to stifle her cry, then jerked it away again as she realized she still held the bloody knife. She flung it down with a strangled sound, staring at the guard's lifeless body. The stain covered the entire front of his shirt.

"Connor!" she cried, looking around her wildly. "Connor!"

Her blood was pounding so loudly in her ears

that she almost missed a low groan from some-where nearby. Or had it only been the wind that was still swirling around her, though with much less force now.

"Connor! Where are you?" She started to run through the sand in the direction where she thought she'd heard the sound. And then she heard it again, more clearly now.

"Here, Jillie."

His voice was weak, but there was no doubt that it *was* his voice. Where was he? He sounded so close, but she could see nothing, even though her eyes had by now become accustomed to the faint starlight.

"In the tent," he said in that same weak, muf-fled voice.

Then she realized that his voice was coming from beneath a small dune. Protruding from one end was the piece of rope that had tripped Henka—and probably saved her life.

"Jillie? Are you still there?"

"I'm here," she told him. "Are you hurt?"

His response was slow in coming, but he told her he was fine. "I just can't move very much. The tent collapsed. Where's Henka?"

"He's dead," she said flatly, trying not to think about that blood-soaked body and the way the knife had felt when she'd plunged it into him. She was busy following the rope to the tent itself, digging through the sand. Her shoulder ached, and that was enough to drive away any guilt she felt over the guard's death.

"Dead?" Connor croaked. "What—"

He stopped in midsentence. Jillian, who was still digging, saw the hill of sand shift and heard a dull thump from somewhere inside it.

"Connor?" she cried out in terror.

It seemed forever until she heard his muffled response. "Can't move. Something on top of me. The tent pole, I think. And something else."

Jillian never knew how long it took for her to dig her way through the sand. Connor had lapsed into silence, after saying that he was having trouble breathing. Then at last her hands touched a tautly stretched piece of canvas.

She needed a knife. Telling Connor that she would be right back, she staggered through the sand to Henka's body and began to search for her knife. But it was his knife she found first—the knife he would have used on her, she reminded herself grimly as she picked it up.

She slit the fabric carefully, since she had no idea where Connor was. When she had opened it wide enough, she pulled the edges apart and peered in. It was pitch-black inside, but then she heard a deep sigh.

"Air," he said, his voice weak. "Better now."

"All these people dead—and we still don't know why."

Jillian reached out for Connor's hand, needing to reassure herself again that he was alive. He laced his fingers through hers and squeezed gently.

Above them, the stars were fading as dawn approached. A cool wind had sprung up, but it was still much warmer than on previous nights, the result, she supposed, of the storm.

They sat atop the highest dune, staring off to the east, facing the dawn rather than the devastation behind them, where tent poles stuck up out of the sand and scraps of torn canvas littered the landscape.

After she had freed Connor, they'd discovered that part of what had been pinning him down was the body of their young guide. Then they'd dug through the sand until they found the collapsed tent containing the bodies of the two Masani soldiers.

Connor had explained to her that Henka had awakened him after the storm had passed, saying that the tent he'd shared with Hammat had partially collapsed and he needed Connor's help in getting the guide out. When they reached the partially buried tent, Henka had struck him from behind—undoubtedly with the same hammer he'd swung at Jillian. But when Connor had awakened, buried in the sand, he'd assumed that the tent pole had struck him as it collapsed.

The Masani soldiers were dead when Connor and Jillian reached them, and although they might have died in their collapsed tent, it seemed more likely that Henka had killed them as well. It was clear to them both that his plan had been to make it look as though all had died as a result of the storm—which was why he'd used the hammer rather than his knife, until desperation drove him to attempt to use it on Jillian.

She shivered, still unable to think of the

murderous Henka without reliving that moment when she'd stabbed him. Connor drew her closer, settling her against his chest.

"You had no choice, Jillie," he said softly. "I'm just sorry that I wasn't there to protect you. I should have suspected him earlier."

"Why? You had no reason. He's—he *was* a Royal Guard."

"Yes, but something happened aboard ship that should have made me suspect him—if not at the time, then certainly after that attack on our camp."

He told her that he'd been up on deck late one night, when he had suddenly sensed someone behind him and had turned to discover that Henka had come up behind him.

"What should have made me suspicious was that I didn't hear him. Before, he'd worn his boots and it's impossible to walk on a deck in them without making noise. But that night, he was wearing soft shoes, and there was something in his movement when I turned that should have warned me. He apologized for startling me, then left a few minutes later."

"But why?" Jillian asked again. "He certainly wouldn't have been acting on his own."

"No, he wouldn't have," Connor replied grimly. "Someone must have paid him well."

Well indeed, she thought. The Royal Guards were handsomely paid already—and very carefully chosen. Still, it was clear that he'd been corrupted, but by whom and for what reason?

The most likely candidate, she knew, was

someone at court. But despite Connor's earlier suspicions, Jillian still could not believe that anyone at court would want to get rid of her. She was, at best, an annoyance to some of them, and she just couldn't see even the worst of them taking such a risk.

"It *has* to be because of the birds," she said aloud. "That is, if *I'm* the intended victim."

Connor remained silent—*too* silent, she thought. She knew him so well that she could distinguish even the quality of his silences, and this one felt ominous. She was reminded again of the long years they'd spent apart—more than enough time for his loyalties to shift, if not enough time to destroy his love for her.

The sky grew lighter still, and the distant horizon became more distinct, rimmed now with a faint pinkish light that edged perceptibly toward red.

"We should do our best to mark this spot, and then move on," Connor said, his voice loud in the preternatural stillness.

Still lost in her thoughts, Jillian was slow to understand what he was saying. Finally, though, his words penetrated the fog in her brain, and she drew in a sharp breath. They were alone now: utterly alone in the middle of the desert.

"Move on," she echoed. "Connor, what will we do?"

"Except for the detour to reach the fazara and then to outrun the storm, we've been heading due west," He replied matter-of-factly. "So we'll continue in that direction."

"We could go back," she ventured.

He shook his head. "I think we're about half-way now. Hammat said that we would come to another fazara, and that he expected to find his people there."

"But it might not lie directly in our path. How will we find it?"

"The one behind us would not be directly in our path if we went back, and we'd be just as likely to miss it. With only the two of us now, we have more water and food." He paused to wrap an arm around her shoulders. "We'll make it, Jillian. I know we will."

An hour later, they set out, riding their camels and leading the others. All of the animals had survived the storm quite well, although they registered the usual protests at being forced to resume their journey.

Behind them, they left the scene of carnage largely undisturbed. Connor buried Henka in the sand while Jillian kept her distance. She knew that however much the guard had deserved to die, his face and his bloodied chest would haunt her dreams for a long time.

She grieved for young Hammat, whose ready smile and exuberance were gone forever, and for the Masani soldiers who'd proved to be good company, even if they hadn't been able to fulfill their roles as protectors.

Just before they left, they climbed together up the side of the tallest dune in the area, carrying an undamaged tent pole and a scrap of the red tent fabric. Hammat had told them that each of

161

the nomadic tribes had a particular color that identified their tents.

Connor planted the pole as deeply as possible in the top of the dune, and they fastened the fabric scrap to the top. Now, as they rode away, she turned back one last time and saw the scrap of red fluttering in the morning breeze. It looked almost festive, even though it marked a scene of death.

Hour after hour, they rode across the blazing sands, with the sun overtaking them to hang directly above them, and then finally beginning its long descent to the western horizon. They weren't as adept as Hammat had been at finding a suitable resting place, but finally, they came upon a sheltered spot and dismounted wearily.

Propped against a hill of sand, they had nearly fallen asleep when Connor startled her by suddenly leaping up. She opened her eyes and saw the problem at once: they'd forgotten to tether the camels.

She leaped to her feet as well and followed Connor as he ran after the camels. Fortunately, the beasts didn't move any faster now than they did when they were under human control. They also instinctively stayed together, so that capturing two of them brought the others to a halt as well.

After leading them back and hobbling them as Hammat had always done, Jillian and Connor returned to their nap, laughing at their foolishness, their arms around each other's waists.

"We shouldn't be laughing," Jillian said in the midst of a giggle. "This isn't a game."

"No," he agreed as his own laughter died down to a chuckle. "But it feels like one. It feels as though you've given me back my childhood, Jillie."

She stared at him, thinking that he looked as though he'd lost those years. True, he didn't exactly look like a boy again, but something in him had changed these past few weeks—something she could see in those clear, gray eyes that regarded her now with amusement gleaming in their depths.

She wished that the little girl in her would surface again as well. In some ways, she had: the long journey and the wonders of the desert brought out a childlike sense of awe, and Connor brought back memories to add to that. But she could not look at him through the eyes of a child. When she stared at him, she felt altogether too adult for comfort.

And she wondered again how he managed to avoid that—or to control it. He continued to be physically affectionate toward her, but try as she might, she could see no difference between the behavior of Connor the man and Connor the boy.

Except, of course, for that kiss: the one time his control had slipped and allowed the needs of the man to come through.

She wanted it to happen again—and didn't want it to happen. She wanted to triumph over the Kraaken who'd stolen him from her, but she didn't want to see him lose his soul. And if the truth be told, she feared losing her own as well. She'd spent too many years controlling her own destiny, dependent upon no one but herself for her happiness. What she'd surrendered unknowingly to Connor as a child, she was not quite so willing to give up now.

But still, she could not look at him as he rode easily in the big saddle without thinking about the pleasure of having that lean, hard body pressed against hers. And as she drifted off to sleep next to him, she fell into a dreamworld where no doubts existed, where Connor and she surrendered to each other without regrets.

"Wake up, Jillie. It's time to go."

She felt fingers brushing the hair from her face, then caressing her cheek. She made a low sound in her throat and nestled still closer to him.

Her head bobbed up and down as he sighed, and she could feel the strong, steady beating of his heart. He shifted his position slightly and she realized that her hand rested on his thigh. She opened her eyes, but didn't move. She hadn't fallen asleep in his arms, but at some point, they'd moved together—drawn by the need for contact, the hunger of flesh for flesh.

"Jillie," he said, more firmly this time. "Wake up."

And so she did, staring down at her hand where it lay against his soft robe. Beneath it, she felt the rock hardness of his thigh. For one breathless moment, she could envision her hand creeping up, moving to touch that part of him she didn't yet know and wouldn't even be able to imagine if it weren't for all the naked statuary that adorned the palace grounds. What she felt as she thought about it now was both a childlike curiosity and a very adult hunger: a powerful, almost enervating mixture.

He removed the temptation, which was growing by the second, through the simple act of picking up her hand and pressing it to his lips.

"Jillie, Jillie," he murmured, almost as though speaking only to himself. "How much I want you."

She stiffened suddenly, startled at his admission and knowing now how wrong she'd been. But he misinterpreted her movement and quickly got to his feet. She waited for him to say something, but when he finally did, it was merely to discuss their journey.

They rode west into the lowering sun, detouring every now and then to climb the side of a dune in the hopes that they'd see a dark spot on the horizon that marked a fazara. But there was nothing to be seen except for the endless, windswept desert, now tinged with a ruddy glow as the sun neared the horizon.

Then they paused once more to watch as the sun disappeared in a blaze of colors even more spectacular than they'd seen before, but just as fleeting.

This time, with her mind still on those moments when she'd awakened in his arms, Jillian caught the thought that had been hovering in her mind from the first time she'd witnessed this spectacle. When the tears stung her eyes again, she

165

understood. What they could have was like that brilliant flash of beauty. And what they'd both be left with would be the darkness and the chill that followed.

They continued their journey well into the night, hoping as they climbed each rise that the darkness ahead would be sprinkled with the lights of campfires at a fazara. But always, what lay ahead was an impenetrable blackness, and finally they found a spot to shelter in for the remainder of the night.

After they had eaten their unappetizing food and drunk the small amount of water they allowed themselves, Jillian went off to feed the camels while Connor got out their bedrolls. They'd spoken very little since they'd awakened earlier in each other's arms, and when she came back to the campfire, she saw that he'd put down their bedrolls on opposite sides of the fire.

Tired, dirty and sore where her shoulder ached beneath a huge purple bruise, Jillian said nothing as she settled in for the night. Connor remained sitting at the campfire, facing her but staring into the flames.

And strangely, this night, her dreams were not about Connor, but about a golden bird much larger than her keras that swooped down from the dun-colored desert sky.

Chapter Seven

For the first time in her life, Jillian was truly frightened and aware of the fragility of her own existence. Her fascination with the unique world of the desert had given way to an understanding of its dominion over them.

Another day had passed with no sign of a fazara—or of any other living thing. They still had adequate water and food, but were rationing both carefully, since they had no idea how long it would be until they reached either a fazara or the end of the desert.

They spoke little, except for the communications necessary to two people traveling together. Connor seemed to have retreated into himself, to some inner place known only to him—while Jillian often found herself edging toward a sort of stupor that left her only half aware of her surroundings.

Suddenly, in the midst of one of these dazes, the sound of her own shrill cry jerked her back to reality—just as she slipped off the camel's back and tumbled to the sand. Then she cried out again as her injured shoulder was jolted by the impact. The camel moved on a few paces, then stopped and lowered its head, staring at her impassively.

Connor dismounted quickly without waiting for his animal to kneel. Jillian was whimpering with pain and massaging her shoulder when he reached her.

"I must have fallen asleep," she admitted sheepishly before he could say anything. "I've fallen asleep before. I don't know what happened this time."

He knelt before her. "You weren't fully asleep before—only in a sort of trance."

He helped her to her feet after ascertaining that she'd suffered no real injury. She started back toward her camel, by now angry with herself for her weakness. Her irritation held a bit of the child—the little girl who'd always resented the fact that the older and stronger Connor could outrun her or outlast her at their games.

Connor took her arm. "Ride with me, Jillian. The saddle is big enough for us both."

She pulled herself free. "No, it won't happen again."

But an hour later, despite her best efforts, it *did* happen again. This time, however, her fall was broken by Connor, who had seen her listing to one side and maneuvered his camel close to her, then reached out to encircle her waist as she started to slide.

He ignored her protest and hauled her in front of him on his saddle. "You remind me of the little girl who always protested that she didn't need her nap—just before she fell asleep." He chuckled, his breath fanning against her ear as he urged the camel forward.

"And you remind me of the smug little boy who always made so much of being three years older," she grumbled.

He laughed again, but then his laughter was cut short. "Jillie, look!"

"Where?" She peered into the desert, trying to see despite the glaring sun. The excitement in his voice could only mean a fazara, but she saw nothing.

He reached out to cup her chin and lift her face to the nearly colorless sky. "Up there!"

And then she saw it! High above them, a great bird drifted in wide circles. She gasped, forgetting all about fazaras and everything else. She was accustomed to seeing the keras flying at great heights and was therefore able to judge that this bird was at least half again as large as a kera.

They both sat there in silent wonder, watching the bird as it circled and circled, staying directly above them. Then, without any conscious intent, Jillian raised her arm and began making the circular motion she always made to summon the keras. Connor's one arm was wrapped securely around her waist, but he raised the other one in the same gesture at the exact moment she did.

Both of them drew in sharp breaths as the bird began a slow, spiraling descent toward them. Jillian thought of the treats she'd packed among her belongings. But they were out of her reach on one of the other camels.

In the end, it didn't matter. The bird stopped its lazy spiral when it was still more than a hundred feet above them. In the glare of the late-day sun, she could not see it clearly, but she *could* tell that its feathers were a pale golden color—much lighter than those of her keras—and the tips of its great wings were rimmed with white.

Then, abruptly, the bird split the silence with a piercing shriek and flew away, staying lower than before as it moved off in a southwesterly direction.

Connor pointed the camel's nose in the same direction and kicked it into motion.

"Do you think it wants us to follow it?" Jillian asked, even though the question sounded absurd. There'd been some cases where keras had led their masters to safety, but they had been bonded with those masters over long years.

Connor didn't answer her, not even when she turned in the saddle to stare at him. His face was still lifted to the sky, although the bird was no longer visible. Leaning against him as she was, she could feel the tension in his body, almost as though he were straining to leave the saddle and join the wondrous bird.

"Connor!" she said more sharply, unaccountably frightened by his behavior.

Finally, he lowered his gaze to her and she felt him relax. But for that first second, the gray eyes that now stared at her were seeing something different.

"We'll follow him," he said after another moment. "If they're in the desert only rarely, then it's likely that he'll lead us out."

He lapsed into silence again as they rode on, this time with the setting sun off to their right. Jillian, even given the great respect she had for the intelligence of keras, wondered at Connor's certainty that they should go in this direction. But she remained silent. She could feel him behind her, his body pressing against hers as they both moved with the rhythms of the camel's gait—but she could also feel his absence, as though body and soul had separated.

What has happened? she asked herself. *Something happened to him that didn't happen to me.*

Jillian was thrilled at this firsthand evidence that such birds existed, but her pleasure was tempered by her bewilderment over Connor's behavior.

Then she realized that he hadn't seen keras for a long time, and his reaction probably stemmed from that. He'd loved them as much as she had. She had no idea when the last of the keras on the island had died, but it must have been at least four or five years ago.

The Kraaken had always owned keras, but after Jillian took over the breeding, she'd refused to replace them as they died off. She'd even taken considerable satisfaction from the knowledge that she would be depriving Connor of something he loved. It was the only way she could punish him.

What a magnificent bird, she thought excitedly. Surely she could persuade those who had them to part with a few. It might take many years, but eventually, even a few of them would improve the breed.

Lost in thought, Jillian no longer paid any attention to Connor's continued silence. She had no idea how long it was before he broke it, but the last of the day's light had drained from the sky.

"Do you see them?" he asked excitedly.

She immediately looked up into the heavens, assuming that the bird had returned and wondering how Connor could see it in the growing darkness.

"Ahead of us," he said. "Lights!"

Then she saw them: many small lights clustered in the darkness. "A fazara," she whispered, wondering even in her relief if the bird *had* led them there.

"Let's hope that the nomads welcome us," Connor said as they rode steadily toward the lights.

"It's probably Hammat's tribe," she replied, then realized what he meant. "Do you think they'll blame *us* for his death?"

"They might," he acknowledged. "And if it isn't them, they might be hostile simply because we're strangers."

They were apparently spotted when they were still some distance away, because a small group

172

of men on camels approached them. Connor brought the camels to a halt and they waited in a tense silence until the men reached them, then spread out in a circle around them.

Their leader was a lean, dark, hawklike man. Jillian noted that he wore a bright red turban just like Hammat's and wondered if this was his father. She recalled what the garrison commander had said about the man's thirst for vengeance.

He began to talk rapidly and excitedly in his own tongue, then finally stopped his camel directly in front of them. "My son. Where is he?"

Jillian swallowed hard. The man spoke Masani with a very heavy accent, and she knew she had to make herself understood, even though it wasn't her native tongue, either. His question was addressed to Connor, but since Connor didn't speak Masani, it was she who answered.

"We are very sorry, but your son is dead. Our guards are dead, too. We are the only ones left."

His dark eyes bored into her, but he said nothing. Instead, he turned the camel around faster than she'd ever seen one move, spoke a few sharp words to the others, then rode back to the fazara.

The other men took up positions behind them and on either side and indicated that they were to ride to the camp. Connor's arm tightened around her waist and he urged the camel forward. Then he bent close to her ear.

"Don't worry, Jillie. We'll be all right. They won't harm us."

173

She bit off a sharp reply. This was no time to harangue him for what was obviously an attempt to soothe her. But she knew they were in trouble. Not even the fact that she was a member of a royal family and that he was a Kraaken brother would help them now. If she could not convince Hammat's father of their innocence, they would surely be killed.

They were led to the area where all the tribe's camels were grazing, and after they'd dismounted, the men ushered them into the camp itself. People surrounded them on all sides, staring at them in silence—a silence that was broken suddenly by a woman's cry. Then Jillian heard a series of keening and wailing sounds not unlike the cries she'd heard among peasants at Talita when a family member died. It was an agonizing sound, one that had never failed to make Jillian wonder if such people cared more deeply for their loved ones than her own kind did.

Nothing happened for what seemed to be a very long time. They stood in the center of a circle of silent, staring people. Cooking smells surrounded them and the smoke from the nearest campfire drifted over them. Then Hammat's father reappeared.

"Tell me," he ordered, his expression giving nothing away.

Jillian chose her words with great care, explaining about the storm first, and then going on to tell the chieftain how his son had died and how she and Connor had marked the graves. She kept expecting him to interrupt and ask questions, but he remained silent until she had finished. Then he spoke one word: "Why?"

Jillian had known that he would ask this, and she wished she had an answer. But lacking that, she did the next best thing: she made one up, choosing the one he might be most likely to believe.

"I have come here seeking the great birds that live in the mountains. I believe that the man who killed your son was hired by people who want those birds for themselves. That man tried to kill us as well, but I . . . killed him instead."

For the first time, she saw a recognizable emotion on the chieftain's face. Unfortunately, that emotion was disbelief.

"*You* killed my son's murderer?" he asked incredulously.

Too late, she realized that she should have said Connor had killed him. It was clear that the man didn't believe a woman to be capable of killing the man who had taken his son's life. To his way of thinking, that might make his son seem weak.

"Yes," she said, meeting his stare with her own.

"And him?" He gestured to Connor. "Why did he not avenge my son's death?"

"Because the killer had hit him, and—" She struggled with the words and finally came up with something that she thought made the point.

"This man was in your employ?" Hammat's father asked, ignoring Connor again.

Jillian realized he meant Henka and nodded. "He is—was a member of the Royal Guard, who

175

protect the family of the king. I am a member of that family. The king is my uncle."

His dark eyes swept over Connor with obvious contempt. "And this man, too, is one of your guards?"

"No. He is a priest—a member of the Kraaken brotherhood."

For the first time, there were murmurs from the silent crowd that watched them. Jillian glanced at Connor, puzzled. He shrugged, his eyes returning quickly to the chieftain, who raised a hand to silence the group.

"Why is a Kraaken here?" he asked, his gaze resting on Connor now with a certain wariness. "Kraaken have not come to the desert before."

Jillian was trying to think of a way to explain Connor's mission when there was a sudden flapping of wings, followed by a piercing shriek. Her head—and the heads of everyone in the camp—turned in that direction.

The bird sat on a low branch perhaps thirty feet away, just beyond the gathered crowd. It was too dark to see the bird clearly, but the firelight reflected off pale golden feathers as the bird sat there motionless, watching them watch it.

Jillian was so fascinated that she failed to notice when the people nearest the bird began to back away. When that fact belatedly registered, she tore her gaze away from the bird and turned back to the chieftain.

But he wasn't staring at the bird; instead, his gaze was fixed on Connor, and even in the dim light, she could see the fear in his eyes.

* * *

The campfires of the nomads were no longer visible, but Jillian still worried that she and Connor might be attacked at any moment. Connor, however, seemed unconcerned as he dropped some more wood onto their small fire.

They were camped in a tiny clearing at the far end of the fazara. The moon had risen to bathe them in its color-deadening light. She'd noticed before that the nights weren't quite so cold here in the midst of the thick foliage, but it scarcely mattered this night, because a chill had seeped into her that owed nothing to outside temperatures.

The sudden reappearance of the bird had shaken her badly. In a strange way, it had affected her even more strongly than Henka's attempt on her life and his death at her hands. She had the unmistakable sense of things slipping beyond her control—a very unnerving situation for a woman who'd always been in complete control of her life.

And worst of all, the bird itself frightened her— an absurd situation for one who had spent her life among such creatures. But she could feel the difference, even if she didn't understand it.

"Is it still here, do you think?" she asked as she peered nervously into the darkness around them.

"Perhaps," Connor said as he sat down beside her, then turned to stare at her. "It frightened you, didn't it?"

Not even to Connor would she admit such a

thing. "I just don't understand why it suddenly reappeared like that—and why it came so close. Everyone told us that they'd seen them only from a distance, flying high overhead."

Connor wrapped his arm around her, drawing her close. "Just be grateful that it did. It might well have saved our lives."

Jillian rested her head against his shoulder and thought again about that look of fear on the chieftain's face. He'd been looking at Connor, but his fear must have been directed at the bird.

"I'm surprised that the chieftain had heard of the Kraaken," she said, thinking about the conversation that had preceded the bird's appearance.

"The garrison commander probably told him about me," Connor said with a shrug. "The important thing is that I'm sure they'll leave us alone now."

"You were sure of that before," she said skeptically.

"Yes, I was," he admitted, then hugged her. "In another day, we should be out of the desert—and now you know that the birds exist."

It was clear that his words were intended to cheer her up, but Jillian continued to sit there in a worried silence. It felt to her as though answers were just beyond her grasp—even though, at this point, she didn't even know what the questions were.

They ate their unappetizing food mostly in silence, and when they had finished, Connor told her that he'd discovered a small spring-fed pool not far away.

"We can safely bathe there," he said. "The others will use the large pool at their camp."

Jillian roused herself from her stupor at the thought of this luxury. She decided she would also wash her clothing. Even here in the lush fazara, where the desert seemed only a distant memory, the air was very dry and the gauzy fabric would dry overnight.

Connor led her through the woods to the pool that shimmered invitingly in the moonlight, and she let go of her bleak thoughts and thought instead of the pleasure of feeling clean again. She was so focused on that thought that she began to remove her robe without giving any thought to Connor. When she suddenly remembered his presence, she shot a glance at him to see that he'd moved away from her and turned his back as he unbelted his robe.

The long, uncomfortable days and nights and the deaths that had surrounded them had kept away the hunger she felt for him. But now, here in this isolated and beautiful place, the feelings all came flooding back, leaving her filled with a languorous heat.

She flung away her clothes and stood there for a moment at the edge of the pool feeling a strangely pleasing vulnerability in her nakedness and wondering if Connor were watching her. Then she stepped into the water and cried out in surprise!

"A hot spring," Connor said, coming up behind her. "There's one on the island as well, but it has an ugly smell to it."

She hadn't really intended to turn to him, but she did. For one long moment that seemed to stretch beyond forever, they stared at each other in the moonlight.

He's beautiful, she thought, surprised that she would use such a word. Connor had always had a slight bronze cast to his skin, as had his father, who had come from a people who had originally inhabited the lands that were now Talita. In the moonlight, he looked even darker, but not so dark that she couldn't see the light sprinkling of darker hairs on his muscled chest and the thin line that trailed down across his flat belly to. . . .

Jillian turned away and moved deeper into the pool. The slick bottom dropped off sharply and she plunged in, enveloping herself in the warm water. But the water felt almost cool now as it slipped over her heated body. She'd had no experience of men, but she'd seen enough animals to know that one of her questions had indeed been answered. There was no doubt that he wanted her. If the Kraaken had taught him self-control, that control had failed.

The knowledge sang through her, making her feel powerful and weak at the same time. The far-seer's words came back to her again. He would choose *her*—not the accursed Kraaken. He would return with her to Talita. Only her uncle, the king, could prevent her from marrying him—and that was an ancient right that hadn't been exercised in many years. Besides, if he were faced with the choice of letting her marry Connor or having his niece live with a man without benefit of marriage, he would certainly give in.

Jillian swam about in the pool, conscious of Connor's presence close by, but lost in the future she was now certain they had—a future at Talita, where they would once again share their love for the place and for the keras. Together, they would see her dream of improving the keras become reality.

She came out of her reverie only when she turned—and nearly collided with him as he swam behind her. They were in a more shallow part of the pool and she scrambled to get her legs under her as Connor did the same. The water just barely covered her breasts, but left him bared to the waist. Connor reached out to brush away the strands of wet hair that had fallen across her face.

"You are so beautiful, Jillian," he said softly. "One day, perhaps I'll be able to find the right words to describe the way I see you."

Instead of feeling pleased, Jillian felt as though she'd been slapped. Something in his tone—a sad, wistful note—told her that she wouldn't be there when he found those words. Anger surfaced quickly from the melange of emotions colliding in her brain.

"You want me, Connor! You want me more than you want Kraaken sorcery. Admit it!"

But he didn't. Instead, he simply stared at her, and in the darkness, she couldn't read his emotions. She turned abruptly and waded out of the pool, then gathered up her clothing and began to rinse it out.

Most women would probably have felt the shame of rejection, but Jillian felt only anger: an anger directed both at Connor and at the Kraaken who had seduced him with promises of magic and immortality.

False promises, she fumed. *He believes them because they got him at an early age, when he was still impressionable.*

Connor walked out of the pool toward her, but she kept her eyes averted as she did her best to scrub the garments clean. She even continued to ignore him as he came over and squatted down beside her.

"I *do* want you, Jillian, but I cannot break my vows."

She snorted in disgust. "How can Kraaken magic be worth more than we could have?" She turned to glare at him. "Is it the power, Connor? That must be it—not the magic itself, but the power you think it gives you. The Kraaken have no power, or they won't when I get finished with them. I'm going to destroy your precious brotherhood, Connor. My uncle and his advisers distrust them already. We'll see how well your magic works against the Lesai Army."

"Jillian," he said softly. "You don't understand."

"I understand, all right. The Kraaken took a boy who'd already been filled up with his father's tales of the ancient glories of his people, and they let you think you could regain that."

"That's not true. The magic has a purpose,

Jillian. It's not sorcery—not what you're thinking."

"Then what is it?" she demanded.

"It's about finding a oneness with the old gods and rising above human greed and lust and impure thoughts of all kinds."

"That's nonsense, and besides, it hasn't worked, has it?"

Driven to extremes by her anger, she leaned closer to him, until their faces were scant inches apart and their naked bodies were nearly touching.

"It hasn't worked because you want me. And your thoughts will never be free from that, Connor. We belong together."

He said nothing, but he didn't move away from her, either. And then the anger drained from her, leaving only pain in its wake. She turned away abruptly and rose to her feet.

She was reaching for the blanket she'd brought along to cover her after her bath in the pool, when he came up silently behind her and took it from her, then wrapped her in it.

His hands slid over her as he drew the light cover around her, and she heard his sharp intake of breath as he touched her breasts. Then, with a groan, he buried his face in the curve of her neck, his lips moving softly over her warm, damp skin.

"Jillian," he murmured, making her name itself a caress as his hands cupped the fullness of her breasts and he drew her back against him.

They were both trembling as the blanket fell

away and they followed it to the ground. His mouth covered hers hungrily, demanding a response she was more than willing to give. She arched to him, drawing yet another groan from him as their bodies collided in a fire storm of sensations.

Connor hadn't intended for this to happen. He'd wanted only to make her understand. But he'd wanted to touch her, too, to feel for just a moment her softness and her body's wondrous curves.

But now the desire roared through him, out of control—far more powerful than even the sandstorm. And it was fed by the knowledge of her own hunger as he felt her tremble beneath his touch.

He still believed he could control it, could end it when he wanted to—or that maybe she would end it when she knew she could have him.

He was telling himself this lie even as he trailed his lips and tongue down across her throat to the soft swell of her breasts. He was still making himself believe it as his mouth closed gently over the rosy crest and his tongue teased the hard nub that it quickly became.

And he fought to hold on to that belief as his hand glided down over her, coming to rest on that secret part of her, his fingers twining themselves through the wiry curls that hid the very core of her womanhood.

Then it no longer mattered. Nothing mattered except her. She filled his world to overflowing—strong in her own need, yet still trembling from the force of it as he was, too.

The sharp cry pierced the night, freezing them both on the very edge of the precipice. He raised his head and saw the brief glint of pale gold in the moonlight. Then he heard the flutter of the great wings as it ascended into the heavens, where it was outlined for a moment against the stars.

Connor looked down at her and saw the tears glistening in her eyes. Even as he watched, they spilled over onto her cheeks. He bent to kiss them away, bracing himself for her wrath and knowing he deserved it. There was much he didn't understand, but he was sure she must be suffering the agony he now felt—and unlike him, she didn't deserve such pain.

"I didn't mean to seduce you, Connor," she said in a choked voice. "I thought about doing that once, but I knew it was wrong."

He sat up and took her hand in his, bending to kiss it softly. "You seduce me by existing, Jillian. You are my weakness. That can never change."

Jillian heard the anguish in his voice, felt it pierce her very soul. Gone was that feeling of triumph, and in its place was a desolation so profound that it paralyzed her. The far-seer had been wrong—or Jillian had misunderstood. Connor would not choose her because the choice wasn't his to make. Perhaps it never had been.

Instead, he would carry her in his soul forever as the one thing that kept him from achieving his goal. He would never truly rise above his very human need for her, although she was certain that he would spend a lifetime trying.

She withdrew her hand from his and he scarcely

seemed to notice. He was still sitting there beside the pool as she wrapped herself in the blanket and made her way back through the woods to their campsite.

And only when she was falling asleep did she think about the bird and the uncanny timing of its appearances.

Chapter Eight

Jillian awoke slowly, for a time sliding back and forth from her sensuous dreams to the world of reality just beyond her closed eyelids. She clung to the dreams as long as she could, but they gradually retreated, leaving her to face the morning.

Connor was still asleep, his body turned away from her. She stared at him until she felt tears threatening, and then she flung off her blanket and got up.

To keep her thoughts away from him, she concentrated instead on the day ahead. Did they dare approach the nomads again to ask for a new guide—or at least to ask for directions? She couldn't see that they had any choice, even though she feared seeing the chieftain again. He'd had plenty of time to rethink his decision to let them go—a decision she suspected he'd made only because he'd been shaken by the appearance of the bird.

The fire had burned down to embers, so she built it up again. Then she put on a pot to boil water for the strong tea they carried with them. Her clothing had dried, and she dressed quickly, then went to get their food stores.

Their belongings were piled in an untidy heap at the edge of the clearing, and as she searched for their food, she wondered why Connor had left them in such a mess. Then she stopped abruptly and frowned.

The camels! They were gone! Had he forgotten to hobble them? They'd led them here when the nomads had let them go. Well, even if Connor *had* forgotten to hobble them, they wouldn't have gone far. Even camels must surely prefer the fazaras to the desert.

She searched their campsite in ever-widening circles, but saw no sign of the camels. Finally, she decided that they must have returned to the nomads' herd where they'd originally been tethered. They were, after all, herd animals.

She returned to the campsite and saw that Connor was still asleep. Had he sat up most of the night with his thoughts, no doubt berating himself for his brief loss of control? Deciding that she'd rather put off facing him as long as possible, she set off alone for the nomads' camp. Connor's presence wasn't needed in any event; she was the only one who could speak with the chieftain.

As she made her way through the thick woods,

she wondered if she should just go to the herd and take back their camels or try to speak to the chieftain. Then it occurred to her that she'd *have* to speak to him. The camels belonged to him; furthermore, without their packs, she wouldn't know which camels she should take.

I should have brought along some gold, she thought. That might have helped to persuade the chieftain to let them keep the camels. Well, she could always offer it and return with it later.

It had been dark when they left the nomads' camp, but Jillian was sure she was walking in the right direction. Still, it seemed to be taking her much longer to get there than it had the night before.

Finally, she stopped and stared around her. Even though her gaze took it all in, she didn't believe it. They were gone!

There was no doubt that this had been their campsite. The charred remains of fires were there, scattered about the trampled ground. Where she remembered the camels being kept, there were piles of droppings. The large pool she'd glimpsed was just where it had been.

Gone! The tribe had gone, probably with the dawn, and had taken all the camels with them. She was astounded, then enraged at the cruelty of their desertion. And slowly, she saw the reason behind it as she thought about the chieftain's thirst for revenge. He had decided to kill them slowly, by leaving them stranded in the desert. Perhaps he'd even justified his actions on the basis that they'd left his son's body in the desert, too.

She walked slowly back to their campsite, in no hurry to reach it now. Already, she hadn't wanted to face Connor; now, she had even less reason to wake him.

But he wasn't there! Such was her state of mind at the moment that she was sure he'd been kidnapped by the nomads. Then she realized they were long gone, and Connor must have awakened and become worried about *her*.

"Connor!" she shrieked, not yet trusting the rational side of her mind, which told her he had to be around somewhere.

There was a flash of white amidst the trees and he came running toward her, not slowing even when he could see her and must have known that she was unharmed. She ran, too, and they collided in a tangle of arms and legs that very nearly toppled them both.

"Where were you?" he demanded. "I thought—"

"They're gone."

"The nomads? Where are our camels?"

"They took them," she said, her words ending in a sob.

"Are you sure?" he asked in disbelief.

She nodded, struggling to control herself as she wrapped her arms around him more tightly. "It was revenge—for Hammat. They left us to *die*."

Connor was silent as he ran his hand soothingly along her spine, then kissed the top of her head. Jillian remained pressed against him, feeling his rocklike strength, listening to the steady beating of his heart.

If she had to die, at least she'd be with him.

She felt an odd sort of peace knowing that, but a far stronger part of her wanted to live and to find a way to stay with him then, too.

"We won't die," he said with quiet assurance.

"What will we do?" she asked, raising her head to look up at him. There was hope in her voice, even though she was sure he was merely trying to soothe her.

"We'll start walking," he said in that same assured tone. "We'll have enough food if we're careful, and enough water as well."

"*Walk?* Across the desert?" Her hope faded.

"We've walked before. We can rest during the hottest part of the day and walk at night. We'll have bright moonlight for a few nights. It's nearly full."

Her protest died in her throat. She understood what he was saying. They had to try. Neither of them was the kind who could simply sit and wait for death. But despite his seeming confidence, she knew they'd never survive.

They stood there in each other's arms until the horror of their situation gave way to memories of last night. It seemed to happen at the same time for them both, because they disengaged with an awkwardness that was uncharacteristic of either of them. And they both kept their eyes averted as they walked back to the campfire.

After a breakfast of strong tea and the hard biscuits that had become a staple of their diet here in the desert, they began to sort through their supplies.

All their clothing would have to be left behind,

save for what they wore on their backs. Both of them had bags of gold coins, though Jillian's was the heavier. They argued about the gold. Connor wanted to leave most of it behind, taking only what they might need to purchase food and new clothing when they reached the hills. But Jillian insisted that she had to take it all.

"I will need it to buy some birds, and cages for them as well."

Connor finally gave in, and they took two blankets and fashioned them into backpacks, securing them with strips of cloth they tore from a pair of his trousers. Then they began to walk through the woods to the brightness beyond the trees.

Already, the desert seemed unbearably hot to Jillian after the coolness of the fazara, and the sun was as yet far from reaching its zenith. But they set out into the face of a strong breeze she knew would die down as the day progressed.

Connor kept scanning the milky skies, and after Jillian saw him look up for the fifth or sixth time, she couldn't resist saying, "Are you expecting the bird to return and help us again?"

The moment the words left her mouth, she regretted them. They were all too potent a reminder of the bird's appearance last night.

Connor turned to her, and she saw her thoughts mirrored in his eyes. His wide mouth curved briefly into a smile. "I'm not sure that I believe it helped us last night."

The awkwardness returned again as they stared at each other. Jillian hated the tension between them and suddenly hated their bodies as well, for destroying that old easiness between them.

"Do you think it was mere coincidence that it appeared each of those times?" he asked. There seemed to be nothing more than curiosity in his tone.

"What else could it be?" she asked, uneasy with this discussion as she began to think about the tales they'd heard.

"The stories could be true, Jillie. The bird might not have appeared on its own."

Of course he'd believe that, she thought. *If he believes in the magic of the Kraakens, he'd easily accept that sorcerers lived in the mountains.*

"Why would it have been sent?" she asked, testing his thinking.

"Because those who train them want to help us," he said calmly.

"Do you really believe that?" she asked, knowing that he did. "But how could they have known we *needed* help?"

"They're said to possess magic."

She hesitated, then took the plunge. She was sure she would regret her words—but they came out anyway. "Why did it come last night, Connor?"

He was silent for a long time, once again lifting his head to scan the heavens. Then he suddenly smiled and lifted his arm. "There, Jillian! Do you see it?"

She followed his finger and saw nothing. But when she was about to tell him that, she thought she could glimpse something moving toward them across the bleached sky.

Within moments, the bird was high overhead, circling as it had done the first time. This time, it was Connor who raised his arm and began making the circling motion that had always been used to call the keras.

The great bird spiraled down slowly, its huge wings flapping to control its glide. But this time, it came all the way down, settling gracefully to the sand about thirty feet in front of them.

Jillian gasped when she saw its eyes for the first time. Instead of being dark like those of her beloved keras, they were a brilliant emerald green—a shade so startling that she felt unnerved as she met the bird's calm gaze.

Its feathers glistened like spun gold in the desert sun, and its great, hooked beak was pure white, like the tips of its wings. Even its legs were white, ending in vicious talons that would certainly make it a formidable foe.

The bird cocked its head to one side as it watched them, and Jillian found the movement oddly soothing. The keras and many other birds did that, and seeing this bird exhibit such behavior made it more real, and less like a beautiful apparition.

Several moments passed before Jillian realized that, while the bird had looked directly at her several times, its attention was really focused on Connor. She slanted a glance at him to see if he was doing something to attract its attention, but he remained motionless, staring at the bird.

Then she started nervously as it began chuckling. Even though she was accustomed to hearing her keras make that sound, she thought at first it might be coming from Connor. This bird was much bigger than the keras and its chuckle had a deeper, more resonant sound—even closer to that of a man.

If she had had any doubts about this bird being from the species that was the true origin of the keras, they were laid to rest with that sound. She'd never heard another bird make it.

Then Connor repeated the sound, startling her again until she remembered that he'd always been better than anyone else at imitating it. The keras usually responded to her when she attempted to make the sound, but they had been almost entranced when he did it. And this bird was as well. It took a few steps closer, walking instead of hopping; then it stopped once more, its brilliant eyes fastened on Connor.

Jillian felt something—a kind of shudder that passed through her, leaving in its wake a strange sort of uneasiness. She took a few steps away from Connor before she realized what she was doing. Neither he nor the bird seemed to notice.

Later, when she tried to fathom what had happened in those moments, Jillian would be forced to conclude that she didn't even know how long they all stood there like that beneath the burning sun. All she knew was that something was happening that she didn't understand.

Then the moment was shattered as the bird unfolded its huge wings and took off, issuing its high-pitched shriek as it ascended quickly into the heavens, then vanished with astonishing speed in a northwesterly direction. She was still standing there, staring after it, as Connor started to walk in that direction. Then she hurried to catch up, calling out to him.

He stopped and turned to her slowly, and as she came up to him, she thought his gaze seemed unfocused for a few seconds. Then he smiled at her.

"We must go this way. We can walk for a while longer, and then we'll stop to rest."

Now that the bird was gone, taking its mesmerizing presence from them, Jillian felt a surge of jealousy. *She* was the one the bird should have paid attention to—not him. This quest was *hers*.

Before she could put down that rising tide of anger, she asked him sharply, "Did it happen to tell you how much farther we have to go?"

"No," he said, treating her question as though it were normal.

"Connor!" she said, reaching out to take his arm and bring him to a halt. "What happened back there?"

He stared at her for a moment, as though trying to see beyond the question. "Nothing. What do you mean?"

"I—" She stopped, unable to explain what she'd felt, and unable to believe the sudden fear she felt now. She shook her head.

"It was those eyes. I'm . . . not sure how I feel about these birds."

"You want them to be exactly like your keras," he suggested. "And perhaps they're not."

"What do you mean?" she asked as they started to walk again.

"I know you don't believe in magic, Jillian, but this bird has appeared too many times for it to be a coincidence."

She thought back to the question she'd asked just before the bird's latest appearance, but she found that she didn't want to ask it again. In fact, she didn't want to ask *any* questions right now.

Fortunately, Connor didn't seem to be in the mood for conversation, either, so they continued their journey in silence, walking another hour or so before she finally said that it was time to rest. The sun had been directly overhead for some time, and the breeze had died down. She was beginning to feel almost dizzy, and the pack on her back, while far lighter than Connor's, seemed to have increased its weight twofold.

They had become more adept at finding shelter from the sun, spotting the configurations in the sand that were more than ripples and promised shade on their far sides. So before long, they had unburdened themselves of their packs, passed the bottle of warm water back and forth between them and then settled back to nap away the hottest hours in their narrow strip of shade.

Jillian dreamed frightening, strange dreams of intelligent emerald eyes and men with long white beards who wore the golden robes of the Kraaken and symbols suspended from golden chains that had the same emeralds as the Kraaken symbol, but were different. She dreamed of rocky peaks and deep valleys, of strange, rounded houses built of stone and topped with tall towers.

In these dreams, she was frightened, filled with a constant sense of dread, even though she saw no reason for it and was certain, somehow, that it wasn't her life she feared for, but something else.

When she awoke, she found Connor just awakening, too, and for a moment, they both looked uneasily around them, thinking that some sound had been responsible for waking them at the same moment. But there was nothing to be seen and no sound to break the great stillness of the desert.

"I had such strange dreams," she said, realizing that, even as she spoke, they were fading from her mind.

Connor looked at her with interest. "Tell me about them."

So, as they got up and began to reload themselves with the packs, she told him what she could recall, then muttered, more to herself than to him, "It must have been the bird—and that ridiculous talk about magic."

They trudged along for the remainder of that day and most of the night as well. When dawn came, they both narrowed their eyes at the distant horizon, willing something to appear. But the sand continued to stretch endlessly before them.

They spoke little, and Jillian, at least, did little thinking. Her entire consciousness was focused on putting one aching foot in front of the other, and the only thing she anticipated was her next meager swallow of water. Water was heavy, and there was only so much they could carry with them, even though they knew they could survive without food longer than they could without water.

Once, she was sure she saw a dark spot ahead of them, and she cried out in joy. But Connor didn't see it, and even as she tried to tell him where it was, it vanished.

At one point, she tripped, and her backpack slid from her shoulders, spilling its contents into the sand. Connor helped her gather up everything, but an hour later, when they stopped to rest, she discovered that she'd lost the cream that had been protecting her from the fierce sun and the dry air. Her lips quivered and her eyes stung, but she refused to cry. If Connor could survive this ordeal, so could she.

But by the next afternoon, her lips were cracked and her entire face was swollen. And for the first time, she saw doubt in Connor's gray eyes when he looked at her.

Before she could stop him, he'd wetted a cloth with some of their precious water and was bathing her face gently. "Keep this cloth in the pouch with your gold so it will stay damp," he said when he'd finished.

Then he took her pack and opened it, adding its contents to his own pack. She protested weakly, but he said he could manage it all now. What he *didn't* say was that they had very little left of either their water or their food.

Dusk fell and they walked on. The damp cloth

made her face feel better, but it did nothing to relieve the swelling, which was now so bad that her eyes were narrowed to mere slits. And she began to shiver as well, even though the temperature hadn't yet fallen.

Connor kept glancing her way, and she could feel his concern. He was sunburned, too, but his darker skin seemed to be protecting him better.

Her thoughts wandered—back to Talita and to a time long past when they had lived in laughter together. Small scenes she'd forgotten came back to her, clear and perfect in her mind's eye. And then she stumbled!

She scrambled to maintain her balance in the shifting sands that were finer here and less stable. Her right foot twisted painfully and she fell before Connor could grab her.

Within moments, they both knew her ankle was broken. Already, it was swelling badly. Connor knelt to examine it in the fading light, then began to rip pieces from the hem of his robe to bind it.

"It's no use," she croaked in a voice she barely recognized. "I can't walk anymore."

She began to shiver violently, and when he reached out to take her hand, his touch felt fiery next to her skin. The last thing she saw before her consciousness slipped away was the fear and pain in his eyes.

Connor moved her carefully into a more comfortable position, then sat there staring at her. Tears glistened in his eyes. He realized that he feared death far less than he feared the loss of her, and that knowledge buried itself deep in his mind.

He threw back his head and stared up at the night sky, where the last of the light was slowly being replaced by the stars. And when he saw the movement, he knew that he'd been expecting it. The bird cried out, but this time it remained high above him. It seemed to be flying among the stars themselves.

A sudden swirling wind drew his attention down again, and as he shielded his eyes from the blowing sand, he saw something very familiar in the midst of the whirlwind and knew he'd been expecting that, too.

Jillian was at Talita. She hated taking naps—especially since Connor wasn't forced to take them. She'd agreed only after gaining his promise to take her strawberry picking later. The wonderfully sweet little berries grew deep in the woods, and she wasn't allowed to go there alone.

Now Connor was teasing her awake with a peacock feather. No one at Talita really liked the beautiful but ill-tempered birds, but Jillian's father kept them because her mother had loved them, and they reminded him of her.

She felt so tired, which was strange because she hadn't been at all tired when she'd gone to bed. The feather drifted over her face again and she batted at it without opening her eyes. But it wasn't a feather, after all; her fingers encountered solid flesh and Connor grabbed both her hands in one of his as he continued to tickle her face.

Laughing now, she tried to twist her body out of his reach. Pain shot through her right ankle, and her eyes snapped open.

The clear gray eyes that stared down at her were Connor's—but the face was not. She blinked a few times, but the image refused to change. He still held her hands in one of his, but the fingertips of his other hand were covered with a white cream, and now she could feel it on her face. Why was he putting cream on her face? It had a strange but vaguely familiar smell, reminding her of something she couldn't quite grasp.

Then she saw the tears in his eyes. *Was* this Connor? She was sure it must be—but why was he so different, so big and so old? And why was he crying?

"Connor?" she asked in a hoarse, uncertain voice.

Joy shone suddenly through his tears. He reached out to touch her face again, smoothing on the cream with a gentle caress. "You've come back. I've been so—"

"Back?" she croaked, confused.

He lifted her and held a cup to her lips. "Drink slowly."

She didn't want to drink slowly. Her throat felt as though it were on fire. But he wouldn't let her have much and she was too weak to wrest the cup from him.

Where had she come back from? She was beginning to remember things, although they made little sense. The desert. A sandstorm. Her guard lying dead with a bloodstained shirt. The great bird with emerald eyes. A man with long white hair wearing a Kraaken robe. She tried to put it all together, but couldn't. The only thing she knew for certain was that she wasn't six years old anymore and she wasn't at Talita.

Connor got up from the bed and she panicked, reaching out for him. He turned back and smiled at her. "I'm not leaving. I want to get you some broth. You need to get back your strength and they said it would help."

She didn't give any thought to who they might be, or to where she was or how she had come to lose her strength. At the moment, she was concentrating solely on staying awake, because without understanding why, she knew that she feared sleep.

Connor ladled some of the warm broth into a cup and brought it back to her. Her eyes were closed again, but when he sat down on the edge of the bed, he saw her thick, black lashes flutter.

"Jillian, you must try some of this broth," he said quietly but firmly as he lifted her again into a sitting position, cradling her against himself.

Her eyes opened and she stared at him. His hopes plummeted as she frowned, obviously not recognizing him. But she obediently sipped at the broth.

For four days now, Connor had been living with the constant fear of losing her. After the first day or so, he'd stopped worrying so much that she would die, but then he realized that there could be something even worse. She might survive, but never be Jillian again. Instead, she'd be little more than a beautiful, empty shell.

During that time, she'd opened her eyes several times and looked straight at him, but always with that same puzzled frown, as though he seemed vaguely familiar, but no more than that.

She had talked, too, usually in her troubled sleep. Most of the time, he'd been unable to decipher her hoarse murmurs, but a few times, he knew she was talking about times from their childhood. She smiled then, and his heart ached watching her.

He held her and urged her to drink more of the broth, then finally gave up when she slipped away again. He sat there for a time, holding her limp hand and staring at her. The swelling was gone from her face, thanks to his constant application of the cream their hosts had given him.

Her fever seemed to be gone now as well, but for a frighteningly long time, she'd been so warm that he almost feared she would burst into flames. Hour after hour, he'd bathed her body in cool water, catching what sleep he could.

After sitting there beside her for a long time, he left the little cottage and climbed the steep hill that rose just behind it. She seemed to be sleeping comfortably, and he thought he could safely leave her for a short time.

The sun was dropping behind the highest peaks by the time he reached the top of the hill. He sank onto a rock and stared up at the jagged mountains, and for a moment he thought he saw the birds circling against the brilliant sky. But it was too far for him to be certain.

He felt the lure of those mountains. It grew stronger with each passing day. They whispered to him of great secrets, secrets he might possess if only he went up there. Powerful secrets, secrets not meant for the ears and eyes of mortal men.

If Jillian were here now and he told her what he felt, she'd be angry. He smiled at the thought. She didn't like secrets. She had to know and understand everything. Even when she'd been too young to understand some things, she'd asked questions and demanded answers—and then had gotten angry with him if he couldn't find a way to explain.

And very few things made her angrier than the suggestion that there might be forces or things in this world that simply *couldn't* be understood. Like magic, for instance.

Connor knew the reason for that—just as he knew everything else about her. For years, when she was too young to understand the concept of death, she'd been told by her father and by his mother, who'd become a surrogate mother to her, that her own mother had been carried away by fairies to an enchanted place.

It was an innocent tale, meant only to reassure her that her mother hadn't abandoned her, but when she'd finally learned the truth, she'd been very upset. And from that time on, she'd refused to listen to any stories of magic.

Connor, on the other hand, had long ago come to accept that there are many things that defy understanding and simply had to be accepted. To be sure, he had a thirst for learning, but he also knew when learning ended and faith began.

His problem now was that he was caught between those two spheres. He was just beginning to make some guesses about his strange mission, but he didn't yet have all the pieces of the puzzle. He hadn't reached the point where learning ended.

His thoughts turned back to Jillian. Communication with their hosts was very difficult, but he thought they were telling him that she had suffered from overexposure to the desert sun and might or might not become herself again.

He stood up and looked at those distant mountains one last time before starting down the hill again. He'd already made his decision. If she didn't recover, he would return to Talita with her—to stay. He couldn't become the little boy who seemed to be all she remembered now, but he could be there for her—as he hadn't been all these years.

Something drew him from his thoughts as he sat staring into the small fire he'd built to ward off the evening chill. He turned automatically toward the bed where she slept, then scrambled to his feet hurriedly.

"Jillie, don't!" he cried out as he ran to her. "Your ankle!"

But he was too late. She started to stand up, then sank down again, her face contorted in pain. He knelt before her.

"Your ankle is broken. You have to stay off it. If you want to get out of bed for a while, I'll carry you."

She frowned at him, as she'd done so frequently these past days. But he saw something different in her eyes this time, and his hopes began to soar again. Instead of merely looking confused, she seemed to be annoyed.

"Why is my ankle broken, Connor? And where are we? How did we get out of the desert? Why don't I remember that?"

All of this came rushing out in her usual rapid-fire manner, even if the voice that demanded answers was a bit weak and still slightly hoarse.

Connor sat back on his heels and began to laugh from sheer joy, ignoring her when she told him to stop.

"You've been behaving very strangely, Connor. First, you were crying and now you're laughing. Have you gone mad? Stop laughing and answer my questions."

"Yes, milady," he teased as he drank in the sight of her. She was definitely Jillian again. He would have known that even if she hadn't spoken. It was strange how her whole face seemed to have changed as she regained her mind. Always she was beautiful, but now a light shone through that beauty.

He carried her over and set her down before the fire, then urged her to take some more broth and a piece of bread. She didn't really require much urging, since she was starving. But she refused to be sidetracked and demanded again that he tell her what had happened. Her memories were confused, and some of them made no sense at all.

"We were walking across the desert—after the nomads took our camels. Do you remember that?"

"Of course," she said impatiently. She remembered what had happened before that, too, although she didn't want to remember some of it.

"You stumbled and broke your ankle. Then you passed out, and I carried you the rest of the way."

"You *carried* me?" she asked in disbelief. How could he have done that?

"It wasn't that far. We were close to the edge of the desert already. We would have seen the hills the next morning. Anyway, we didn't get very far into the hills before we were discovered by the people we're living with now. They gave us this cottage. It's just outside their village. And they've been providing food for us."

"How long have we been here?" she asked.

"A week now. You had a bad fever, Jillie. The people here have a name for it, but I don't remember what it is. It's something that can happen to people when they stay too long in the desert."

"Then why didn't it happen to you as well?"

"I don't know. I think I had it as well, but not as bad. I had chills for the first day or so, but then they went away."

"You were crying because you were worried about me," she said, making it a statement, not a question.

He nodded, his gray eyes soft and warm as he stared at her. "They told me that sometimes people recover from this fever, but lose their minds."

She shuddered. "I think I *did* lose my mind for a time. I remember thinking that I was a child again, back at Talita. I was—"

She stopped and touched her face carefully as she recalled that dream about being tickled with a peacock feather. Hadn't she awakened to find him putting cream on her face? Was she scarred? She couldn't feel anything different.

He watched her for a moment, then got up and returned with a small mirror. "I knew you'd want this. I had trouble making them understand what I needed, but they finally gave me one."

. He held it for her and she stared at herself. The mirror wasn't a very good one, but she seemed to be herself, though perhaps somewhat thinner.

"They gave me this cream for your skin. I think it's the same kind you had before we lost it in the desert. And I kept bathing you with cool water to help bring down the fever."

Another piece of the puzzle fell into place. She'd dreamed of swimming in the lake at Talita with Connor. But in the dream, she'd been naked, and she hadn't understood why she'd dream such a thing.

He'd bathed her. Unconsciously, she clutched at the long shift she wore. When he started to smile, she averted her gaze. Some other memories were coming back now, and her body flushed with a

209

sudden heat. But she didn't think it was a return of the fever.

He reached out to take her hand, which was nervously picking at the shift. "Don't be embarrassed, Jillie," he teased softly.

"I'm not embarrassed," she said quickly. "You did what you had to do to . . . save my life. Thank you."

"Thank you," he mimicked. "You talk as though I had a choice in the matter. How could I have let you die, when it is you who give my life meaning? I was just being selfish—which you've accused me of being all along."

She raised her eyes to meet his, and in that instant, she knew that something had changed for him. The knowledge made her dizzy with hope, but more than a little fearful as well.

"You're still weak," he said, his voice low and husky. "You need to eat and rest. I'll make you a crutch so that you can walk a bit as soon as you're able."

You've chosen, haven't you, Connor? The question was on her lips, but she stopped it there. She didn't trust herself yet. And she didn't want to hold him to a decision he must have made when he'd feared for her life.

And *she* was frightened as well: afraid that she would still lose him. No man could survive long when he was torn between two loyalties, two loves—unable to give himself wholly to either one.

Chapter Nine

"I think they don't *want* to talk to us," Jillian muttered to Connor, even as she continued to smile at the two men and the woman who'd come to pay them a visit.

For the past half hour, she'd been trying to find a way to communicate with their hosts. They seemed to manage well enough until she brought up the subject of the birds; then they appeared not to understand any of her gestures.

"That's possible," Connor conceded. "They may be sworn to secrecy."

Jillian shot him a disgruntled look, conceding that he just might be right. But she fully intended to go on—with or without their help—just as soon as her ankle healed. She wondered, however, about Connor's resolve. Every time she mentioned the journey into the mountains, he seemed to withdraw into himself, even though she knew he was spending time at the top of the hill behind the cottage, where he would have a clear view of those mountains. She herself was as yet unable to climb up there, and she wondered if he went there to get away from her as well.

Their visitors departed, leaving them a large basket of food. Jillian leaned on the crutch Connor had made for her, and she watched them disappear into the woods.

"Perhaps we need to offer them more gold," she suggested.

"They've refused what I offered them for the food."

"Maybe it wasn't enough," she persisted. After their treatment at the hands of the nomads, she was far less willing to trust strangers.

"If they were inclined toward greediness, they could simply have let us die and taken everything," Connor pointed out.

She had no answer to that, so she turned instead to the journey ahead of them. "My ankle is much better," she said. "I think we will be able to leave in another week or so."

"Let's go back, Jillian—not up there. If these people have been sworn to secrecy, then we're not going to be welcomed by those who have the birds."

She stared hard at him. "How can you be willing to give up now, when we've come so close and suffered so much? I don't understand you, Connor."

He said nothing and he wouldn't meet her eyes,

no matter how long she stood there staring at him. When she could stand it no longer, she clumped back inside, saying that she was going to rest. A moment later, she looked out the window to see him starting up the hill again.

Jillian didn't understand what was happening between them. In the week since she'd regained her senses, it seemed as though they'd grown farther apart than ever before. Connor was unfailingly kind to her, but his conversation often had a false ring to it, as though he would have preferred silence.

And yet the desire that had flared between them was still there. She saw it in his eyes again and again—especially when she turned suddenly to catch him staring at her. He seemed to avoid coming close to her. But when they *did* touch accidentally (or sometimes deliberately, since she'd begun to taunt him), the result was a sudden tension that she knew could not be one-sided.

She wanted to force him to talk about what was troubling him, but since she was certain she already knew what it was, she couldn't bring herself to confront him. Instead, she found herself actually flirting with him—something she'd sworn she wouldn't do and hadn't believed herself capable of doing.

Just this morning, for example, she'd followed him to the stream that ran near the cottage. She knew he'd gone there to bathe, although he'd heated water and poured it into the tub in the cottage for her.

So she'd followed him and then sat down on the bank of the stream to watch him. His back was turned to her and he was unaware of her presence until he came out of the water and began to dry himself.

She liked watching him, seeing his lean, hard body so very different from her own—a difference that made it even more exciting. She'd found herself wondering how they would have dealt with this sudden surge of desire if he'd remained at Talita. Perhaps fear of that had played a part in his decision. He'd been fourteen then, and while she certainly hadn't given any thought to such things, he might well have.

When he saw her there, he made no attempt to hide his nakedness, but his movements as he continued to dry himself became decidedly more self-conscious, adding yet another layer to the sensuality of a scene that needed nothing more.

She'd told him that turnabout was fair play, since he'd not only seen her naked, but had bathed her as well.

"Sometimes, I think you really *have* become a child again, Jillie," he said, smiling as he pulled on his clothes.

It was an acknowledgment—however subtle—that he knew she was playing games with him, though this game was far from their childhood activities.

"Now I understand why you come up here so much."

Connor roused himself from his meditations

and turned to see her standing behind him. Her crutch was nowhere in sight.

"You shouldn't have come up here," he told her. "You could have hurt your ankle again."

"I'd be more likely to do that on the way down," she responded with a shrug. "And then I'll have you to help me. Besides, my ankle is fine. Climbing up here will be—"

She stopped abruptly, staring at the distant peaks. Connor didn't have to turn to see what had caught her attention. He'd been watching them himself. They were clearly visible against the flame-colored sky.

"So many of them," she said in a hushed tone. "Surely they'll be willing to part with a few."

Then she lowered her gaze to him. "That's why you come up here, isn't it—to watch the birds? It reminds you of Talita and the keras."

He said nothing and she went on. "I suppose you thought it was wrong of me to refuse to sell any to the Kraaken, but I did it just to hurt you, Connor. It was the only way I could pay you back for hurting me by leaving."

"I know that," he admitted. He'd known it from the moment Jenner had told him about her refusal to sell them any birds. And so, of course, had Jenner. More recently, he'd realized the irony of that. If she'd continued to sell keras to the brotherhood, he might not be here.

"How long ago did the last of them die?" she asked curiously, her face once again lifted to the far mountains.

Connor wondered if there was more than mere

curiosity in her question, then decided there wasn't. "A little less than a year ago. The last two died within weeks of each other."

She lowered her gaze again, giving him a surprised look. "Then they lived much longer than they usually do."

He still heard no suspicion in her tone, although he took small comfort from that. If he couldn't persuade her to give up her quest, she would know the truth soon enough. Or what he believed was the truth, anyway.

"I've decided to make one last attempt to get our hosts to tell us about them," she announced. "Perhaps when they know we intend to go up there, they'll be willing to talk."

"Is there no way I can persuade you to give up this quest, Jillian?" he asked, not even trying to keep the note of pleading from his voice.

She stared hard at him and he met her gaze— but it wasn't easy. Perhaps, though, he could yet dissuade her without telling her what he believed. If she knew that he intended to leave the brotherhood and come back to Talita with her. . . .

No, he knew Jillian, and not even that would stop her. In fact, it would only give her more reason to go up there, because she'd say that, not only would she have him, she'd also have the birds she wanted to improve the breeding. Jillian was never one to settle for half a loaf.

"Why do you *really* want to stop me from going up there, Connor?"

She'd asked the question a moment ago, and

now he knew he had to answer her. He tried for a half-truth.

"It's too dangerous—for us both."

She folded her arms across her chest and stared at him, a small bundle of achingly desirable curves—and implacable will. It was his lot to love her for both—and more.

"I know you wouldn't actually *lie* to me, Connor, and you couldn't get away with it even if you tried. But you might see a difference between outright lying and not telling me the whole truth. Is that what you've been doing?"

"There *are* things I haven't told you. I already admitted that when you first asked me questions about the brotherhood. Don't make me tell you things I've sworn to keep secret, Jillie."

She turned away to stare at the birds again. She was silent for so long that he thought she might accept his answer. But of course, she didn't.

"Those attacks on us have something to do with your secrets, don't they?" she asked without looking at him.

"They might have. I don't really know for sure. There's a lot I don't know."

She gave him another of those Jillian looks, then turned and started back down the hill. He caught up with her quickly and took her arm, rather surprised when she didn't pull it away again.

They both spent the evening in a tense silence, with each too aware of the other—and with both knowing that it could not go on this way much longer.

*   *   *

This time, their roles were reversed. It was Connor who found Jillian at the top of the hill, her head lifted as she stared up at the mountains. The day was clear and bright and the peaks were sharply outlined against the deep blue sky, but there were no birds in sight.

Connor stopped and stared at her, wondering—not for the first time—how such unshakable bonds could have formed between them so many years ago. But there had never been a time in his life when he hadn't loved her—not since the first moment he'd been allowed to see the tiny baby with brilliant blue eyes and a nimbus of raven-black hair.

Maybe, he reflected, it had all started with the tragic loss of her mother when she was only a week old. The members of the household had been locked in their own private grief: her father, her brothers, his own mother, who'd been charged with her care.

Not that she'd been ignored. If there was one thing that could safely be said about Jillian, it was that she'd never been ignored in her life. But something in his three-year-old mind had reached out to her even though his own understanding of the concept of death was hazy at best.

And she had responded. Her first intelligible word had been his name and her first, halting step had been taken toward him.

When he thought about it now, it seemed to Connor that his years with the brotherhood had been no more than a brief excursion off the true path that his life was to follow. But at the time, it had seemed necessary for him to get away from her. Feelings he didn't understand, feelings that shamed him had started to haunt his dreams, and he feared the consequences of those feelings.

He followed her gaze up to the mountains. He knew now that they would go there, despite his deep sense of foreboding. Like Jillian herself, whatever awaited him there seemed inevitable. The lure of this woman he loved and the lure of the mountains were equal and, he feared, intertwined.

He came up behind her and encircled her waist. She didn't seem surprised, so she must have known he was there.

Jillian leaned back, resting her head against his chest as she wondered what he was thinking while he'd stood there watching her. Would he still try to persuade her to return to Talita without seeking the birds? And what was it that both fascinated and frightened him about those mountains—or the birds? After her conversation—if it could be called that—with the village elders this morning, Jillian was more than ever convinced that Connor was concealing something, and that something was what frightened him and made him want to stay away from the mountains.

"I want to leave tomorrow," she announced.

"All right."

She twisted around to stare at him. "I mean to go up there, Connor." She gestured to the mountains.

"I know."

"If our lives are in danger, I deserve to know what that danger is," she said, moving out of his arms to face him.

"What did the elders say?" He hadn't accompanied her on her walk into the village.

"Nothing—except that they never go up there. But when I told them that we were going there, they merely nodded, as though they'd expected that all along. Surely they would have tried to dissuade us if our lives are in danger."

It's not our lives that are in danger, he said to himself. *But it may be something even worse.* Aloud, he agreed with her that their kindly hosts would have warned them if such a danger existed.

She smiled that radiant smile she always got when she'd won something, then gestured down the far side of the hill. "Where does that path go?"

Connor glanced at it. He'd seen it before, but he hadn't taken it. It seemed to go nowhere. From their vantage point on this hill, he could see quite a distance, and it appeared that the path just led off deep into the woods. It wasn't much of a path, really—probably just an animal track. They'd seen a lot of deer around. He told her that.

"Let's explore it, then," she said, taking his hand and pulling him toward the edge of the hill.

He would have been perfectly content to spend their last day in this place just sitting here on the hilltop. But now that her ankle had healed, Jillian was restless, and he worried that if she went off alone, she'd get lost. She had a poor sense of direction, although she denied that.

They made their way down the slope, which was far more gradual on this side than on the cottage side. Then they plunged into the thick woods at the base. The path was very narrow and she let go of his hand to move ahead of him. He followed along, wondering when he should tell her about his decision—or if he should tell her at all before they returned to Lesai.

Maybe it would be better to wait, however much he longed to make love to her. Or maybe, he thought wryly, he was just being a coward about it. He knew that they were a man and a woman now, and not children, but that proscription remained. And furthermore, he suspected it wouldn't be easy for her, either, despite her attempts at seduction these past few days. He was sure that if he'd reacted to her flirting, she would have denied it vehemently and walked away.

Lost in thought, he nearly didn't hear that familiar cry overhead. In fact, he might not have heard it at all if she hadn't suddenly stopped and caused him to collide with her. They both craned their necks, trying to see through the trees as the bird cried out again.

Then he caught a glimpse of it, flying just above the treetops, circling. It shrieked yet again and his arm unconsciously tightened around her waist.

"What is it?" she asked, turning to frown at him.

"A warning," he said before he could stop himself.

"About what?"

He shook his head. "I don't know. It just sounded that way."

The bird disappeared and they continued along the path. But it ended just a short distance farther on at the small stream that flowed near the cottage, and they quickly realized that they had come to its source.

It was a beautiful place—and a familiar one as well. Jillian put his thoughts into words before he could.

"Doesn't this remind you of Talita—of our place?"

He nodded, smiling. Not too far into the forest that crept nearly to the rear of the manor house was a spot much like this one. They'd actually found it together when he was perhaps eight or nine and had just been given some freedom to explore. And for all the years they were together after that, it became a place for them to while away hot summer afternoons.

Like that other place, this one, too, was cooled by a spring that tumbled out of mossy rocks into a small pool from which the stream emerged. Completely overhung by huge old trees and cooled by the water, it had that same rich, damp earthy smell and the same sound of gushing water.

She smiled at him, then sat down on the thick, pale green moss along the stream's bank. He would probably laugh at her if she told him, but finding this place felt like a good omen to her.

He sat down beside her, leaned his back against a tree trunk, then slid his arm around her, drawing her close so that her head rested against his shoulder. She closed her eyes and drew in a deep breath.

"If I keep my eyes closed, I can believe that we're back at Talita again." She paused. "I've never been back there, you know."

"Never?" he asked, incredulous.

She shook her head. "It was *our* place, not just my place. I didn't want to go there without you."

He heard the slight catch in her voice and pressed his lips to her silken hair. "Then we'll go there together as soon as we get back to Talita."

She went very still. He waited, saying nothing, feeling the importance of the moment.

"You mean that you're going to visit your mother, after all?" she asked in a slightly tremulous voice.

"No, I mean that I'm coming back to stay. I'm leaving the brotherhood."

Connor had wanted to see her smile, but the face she turned to him was almost fearful. Tears were glistening in the corners of her eyes.

"You can't," she whispered in a choked voice.

"But I am."

"Was this some sort of promise you made to yourself when you thought I might die?"

He shook his head. "I *did* promise myself that, if your mind didn't come back, I would go back to Talita and take care of you."

"My mind is fine."

"I know that." He smiled. "But coming that close to losing you made me realize that I couldn't bear to lose you again when we go home." He heaved a sigh and drew her closer still.

"For all the years I was on the island, I think I always saw an end to it. And the closer I got to my thirty-fifth birthday and all that means in the brotherhood, the more I became certain that it was time to leave. Whatever it is that the Inner Circle offers, it couldn't compare to what I feel for you."

He reached out and cupped her chin to draw her face to his, and he saw that her cheeks were wet with tears. He kissed them, tasting their saltiness.

"I'm afraid, Connor—afraid that you'll regret it. I don't want you to spend your life torn between the Kraaken and me."

"I won't," he promised, kissing the dark tips of her wet lashes. "If I were at all uncertain, I wouldn't do it. I wouldn't give you only a part of me."

She straightened up and turned to stare at him; and she saw the certainty in his eyes that she'd heard in his voice. But still, she wouldn't let herself believe it.

"You were just as certain that day you told me you were leaving," she told him.

"I was fourteen years old, Jillie. I'm thirty-four now. I was scared, because I was old enough to see what was ahead for us. I thought that, if I left then, you'd be young enough to forget me in time. Fourteen's a scary age for a boy. I was just beginning to think thoughts that wouldn't enter your head for another three years."

She lowered her gaze, twisting her hands nervously in her lap. "I don't know how we would have managed that," she said softly.

He chuckled. "I'm not sure how we're going to handle it now. I don't suppose you picked up any experience along the way?"

Her blue eyes flashed anger at him until she realized he was teasing. Then she laughed, too. "And I don't suppose you were one of those brothers who sneaked off to a brothel."

A silence hung there in the cool air, heavy but not unpleasant. They both felt an eagerness, but they both felt cautious as well—conflicting emotions that sent small tremors through them.

They moved slowly, tentatively, even though their hunger threatened to devour them with its heat. They both had doubts—not about their love for each other, but about crossing that boundary that had never been noticeable before, but now loomed between them, dark and frightening. Once crossed, it would become a different kind of barrier, preventing their return to innocence.

At first, they simply held each other, lingering in that innocence, even though they both sensed the difference now, the gathering of forces within them that would not be denied. They even talked about those long-ago days, bringing them back one last time before letting them go forever.

She still feared that he would regret his decision. He worried what her family would say. Each tried to reassure the other, when they both knew that nothing could stop the onrush of passion. It began as a soft glow within them, spreading its voluptuous heat through each as one moment melted into the next.

Connor drew her across his lap, his hands falling quite naturally into the gentle curves of her body. Their lips touched softly, tentatively, then began to move with more assuredness, until they discovered the sensual pleasure of tongues as well.

It was a game, this thrusting and parrying, and for a moment they were children again, children who'd found a new and exciting way to tease each other. But there was nothing at all childlike in the sounds that welled up in them and certainly nothing childlike in the gathering tension between them.

Connor's hands began to explore her as his mind filled with the image of the body beneath his fingertips, now hidden from his gaze. He remembered bathing that fevered body, begging the gods to let her live even as he fought down the shame of his desire.

Jillian felt taut, smooth muscles tremble slightly as she touched them. Her thoughts were on his nakedness as he walked out of the stream after bathing that morning, and she too chafed at the layers of clothing that kept her from him.

But still, they were slow to remedy the situation. He slid the wide neck of her peasant blouse off one shoulder, then tasted her warm, soft skin, which still held a faint aroma of the scented soap she'd bathed with.

She unbuttoned his shirt, her fingers clumsy and uncoordinated. Her breath came more quickly, mirroring the rise and fall of his chest as she pressed her lips to its hair-roughened hardness.

He cupped a breast, liking the way its heavy fullness fit his hand; then he ran his tongue lightly over the soft swell along the neckline of her blouse. The nipple grew small and hard against his hand and he pushed the fabric away impatiently.

Jillian arched to him, then cried out as he took the nub between his teeth. He raised his head quickly, uncertainty clouding his gray eyes. "Did I hurt you?"

She couldn't speak, so she shook her head and drew him back down again, then bottled up in her throat the moan that wanted to come out. She didn't want him to stop again—ever.

His shirt and her blouse fell to their mossy bed, and once again, they simply held each other—this time flesh to flesh as they caressed each other, both of them increasingly aware of the silent cry of her femaleness to his maleness.

When he stood up to pull off his trousers, she averted her gaze quickly, suddenly shy about looking upon the naked evidence of his desire. He crouched down beside her and lifted her chin.

"I'll be careful. You know I'd never hurt you."

"I know," she replied with just a touch of her usual annoyance at any suggestion that she was less than her assured self.

"I'm a little scared, too," he admitted softly, always more honest about his feelings than she was. "But I want you so much. It feels as though I've lost control of myself."

She nodded. The throbbing deep inside her was overwhelming her own control, telling her that something had been awakened that could never be put to sleep again.

He helped her out of her remaining clothes, both of them awkward in their attempts to prove that they weren't. Then they lay down again on their mossy bed, side by side, facing each other and unabashedly trembling now at the new freedom they'd found.

For a time, they were innocents at play in a field of eroticism, learning about each other while learning about themselves. They were surprised and delighted at the power in a touch of lips or fingers to curves and hollows and skin drawn tightly over muscles and bone.

Connor dipped his tongue into the tiny hollow of her navel and drew in a breath filled with the scent of her. His hunger was raw and aching now, a thing moving out of control. But he worried that she might not yet feel what he felt. He raised his head and watched her carefully as he slid his hand down into the wiry, dark tangle of hair that was her only remaining concealment.

She could say nothing. Her throat had become so constricted that no words were possible. So she tried to tell him with her eyes that she was ready to explode and melt at the same time, that the throbbing place he touched so reverently begged to be filled with him.

His fingers slid carefully through the tangle of

hair, parting her, exploring, as he watched her. She fought the temptation to close her eyes, and then suddenly she was blinded by an explosion of sensation that sent her body into an arching invitation.

Connor was shaking now with the effort required to hold onto the last shreds of his control. A powerful and more primitive self was taking him over, urging him to plunge deeply into her and stake his claim through sheer force.

But this was Jillian and he could never hurt her or frighten her. So he managed to hold onto the fraying threads of his control. He eased himself into her, letting himself be enveloped by her moist warmth.

Jillian felt his urgency as he moved deeper and then deeper still, quickly passing the final barrier, where a brief pain dissolved immediately into pounding, driving need.

The wildness overtook them, driving them against each other and then suddenly hurling them both over the edge to the accompaniment of breathless cries of sheer joy.

Afterward, their smiles were tinged with self-consciousness and even a bit of embarrassment. Connor felt an obscure need to apologize for setting free his most primitive nature. Jillian—for what was certainly the first time in her life—wondered if she had been too assertive, too demanding.

They stared at each other silently as Connor remained propped above her, the muscles in his arms trembling slightly with the aftershocks of the cataclysm. Never tongue-tied before in each other's presence, they were stunned to realize that they had to search for words.

After a long time, she reached up to trace a finger lightly across his lips. "You're not regretting this, are you?" she asked in a hesitant voice.

He smiled and pressed a kiss against her hand. It was the first time he'd ever heard her sound hesitant about anything. He shook his head, thinking about how vulnerable she was now—how vulnerable they *both* were.

"The only regret I have is that we waited for so long," he told her, collapsing beside her and then quickly drawing her to him.

But the truth was that he *didn't* regret waiting. It seemed right that it should happen now, and in this place.

"I love you, Connor," she murmured, her voice muffled as she buried her face in his chest.

He kissed the silken top of her head. "Jillian," he whispered, pouring into her name all that it had always meant to him. "You are my soul—the other half of me."

It was true. He hadn't known what it was to be whole. They'd come as close as possible to that sense of completeness when they'd been children, but as children, they hadn't known what it meant to give themselves so completely.

Jillian's breathing slowed and Connor knew she'd fallen asleep. Holding her to him, he stared up at the small patch of sky above them. The bird had not returned. Just before he, too, drifted off to sleep, he remembered how he'd thought it was issuing a warning.

In a strange way, it seemed as though they'd regained their childhood. Lovemaking was a new and wondrous toy: endlessly fascinating and full of glorious possibilities. The faint embarrassment vanished, leaving them completely free and uninhibited with each other. For two people unschooled in the art of lovemaking, they became expert very quickly and gloried in the power they held over each other.

They did not leave for the mountains as planned. Instead, they remained in the tiny cottage for another week, completely unaware of the passage of time. Time for them was measured—when it was measured at all—by their lovemaking. Even night and day became interchangeable as they let this new dimension to their love carry them along.

They bathed each other, turning a simple act into a sensuous experience. Connor built a fire even when one wasn't necessary, because he was fascinated by the firelight that played over her naked body as he used his increasingly expert tongue and lips to drive her to shuddering ecstasy. And Jillian, who'd never paid more than the bare minimum of attention to her appearance, now exploited her body to its fullest, teasing him by wearing a long, full skirt with nothing beneath, tossing her long, black curls in what she knew was a provocative manner or allowing the wide-necked peasant blouse to slip from her shoulder.

She'd been raised in a society where women submitted to men, but she did not submit. Connor had been reared to believe that men took women for their pleasure, with little thought as to whether the woman received pleasure as well. But they ignored all that and gave to each other, and both of them submitted to the force that was far greater than either of them.

Even when they had temporarily exhausted their capacity for lovemaking—a state of affairs that came as something of a shock to both of them—they stayed close, as though physical contact had to be maintained to prevent them from losing the newly discovered magic.

Connor tried to acquire some paper and a pen from the villagers, so that he could put into words these wondrous new feelings. But after repeated unsuccessful attempts to explain, he and Jillian decided that the villagers had nothing to write on. During their infrequent trips into the village, they'd seen no evidence that the tribe had a written language.

So instead, he lay on the mossy bank with his head in her lap and composed his poetry aloud, while Jillian listened through the soft haze of her own thoughts.

"What does that mean?" she asked, breaking into his monologue.

He blinked and looked up at her questioningly.

"It sounded like hana something."

He frowned. "I guess I didn't realize what I was saying. It's a word in the Kraaken tongue. I probably used it because it doesn't really exist in

Lesai. It means"—he hesitated, then shrugged—"a separation of body and soul for a moment. Hana-shremya."

"I didn't know the Kraaken had their own language."

He nodded. "We all learn it, but it's used only for formal occasions. Most of the time we speak Lesai."

"Will they try to stop you from leaving?" she asked, her tone indicating that she still worried about that.

"No, I don't think so, and it won't matter if they do. Jenner and some of the others might be glad to see me go."

He was silent for a long time, and his eyes closed. But Jillian knew he hadn't fallen asleep. She could feel a certain tension in him, a sign of some internal struggle.

She hadn't asked him again why he didn't want to go after the birds. It was enough for her now that he'd agreed to go, and she assumed he'd tell her at some point. That willingness to wait for an explanation was perhaps the strongest evidence of how love had changed her, because she'd always demanded to know everything.

And she also hadn't told him everything that had passed between the village elders and her that day she'd gone to inform them of their journey into the mountains. At the time, she'd found it disturbing, but now it seemed unimportant—almost certainly a misunderstanding on her part.

"Your father said once that the intrigues at court were the result of too many people locked away in the palace for too long. He thought that people just naturally start to plot against each other when they haven't anything better to occupy their minds."

Jillian nodded. "That's why he so seldom went to court."

"I think the same thing happens among the brotherhood. No one would actually commit murder—or at least I don't think they would—but they still plot against each other. It often seemed very childish to me.

"The truth is, Jillie, I don't really know why I was sent on this mission. But I don't believe it was merely for the purpose of recruiting boys into the brotherhood. They knew my background and my relationship with you. I don't know if anyone other than Seka, my mentor, knew about my doubts. Conversations between mentors and students are supposed to be confidential and I've always trusted Seka, but I can't be sure.

"What I *do* know is that something happened within the Inner Circle over the past months. We could all feel it. They spent far more time in their tower than they had in the past, and they often seemed distracted at other times.

"Seka, my mentor, is a member of the Inner Circle, of course. He is considered to be our leading scholar. I would often find him in his quarters studying one of the ancient books. But in recent months he seemed almost frantic about it. Every time I'd go there, he'd be buried in one of those books, as though he was desperately seeking something in them.

"The Kraaken have a wonderful library—as complete as the great library at the palace—but the books Seka studied were kept locked up in the tower. Only the Inner Circle had access to them because they contained all the magic of the brotherhood.

"Anyway, there'd been some talk in the past about recruiting from among the Masani and possibly some other peoples, but the decision to do it came very suddenly—only days before I left. And that, too, seemed strange, because Jenner never does anything in haste.

"So when I discovered that you were to be my escort, I immediately began to suspect I hadn't been told the truth about my mission—especially in view of what Seka had said to me privately before I left." He paused and looked up at her, but his gaze seemed far away.

"He came just as I was preparing to leave. He said that he knew Jenner had given me my instructions, but that he was adding to that. He said I should follow my kraa-shaweh. It's another word that isn't easy to translate. It means destiny, but more than that, because destiny can mean something you don't truly want. Kraa-shaweh means not only the path that you're intended to take, but one that your heart and mind tell you is correct. It's the best way of all, and something that doesn't often happen."

"But you're not doing that," she pointed out after thinking about what he'd said. "You're leaving the brotherhood and you're going to the mountains. Surely Seka can't have meant for you to leave, and since you obviously don't think going up there is a good idea, you're not following your destiny there, either."

"Yes, I know," he said after a pause. "I think it *is* my destiny to go up there, although I don't know why. But I don't want to go—and I want to go even less now."

He'd told her what he could, but he hadn't told her all of it. He reached up and drew her face down to his, then kissed her with sweet fierceness.

"The only thing I'm sure of is that *you* are my kraa-shaweh: the destiny of my heart and my mind."

Chapter Ten

Connor awoke with a start, then moved carefully away from the still-sleeping Jillian, his eyes straining to see into the darkness beyond their campfire.

Something had awakened him—but what was it? He reached out for the rifle that lay just a short distance away, but felt no comfort when his hand closed over the weapon.

After a few minutes of staring into the impenetrable darkness and straining to decipher every sound of the night, he lay down again. It must have been a dream that woke him; otherwise, Jillian would surely have awakened, too. He settled down close to her and drew her into his arms. She murmured sleepily and he kissed her, gathering her as tightly to him as he could. At times like this, he had to hold her tight to convince himself that she—and what they had— was real.

Soon he was asleep again and parting from Jillian even as he continued to hold her. He was soaring high above the mountains, gliding through the night sky with the silvered heavens above and the dark, hidden land below. Only the very tops of the peaks were visible as ghostly white objects far below.

He felt exhilarated, surging with unbounded joy—alive in a way he couldn't have imagined. And although he could see no one else, he knew he wasn't alone up here, suspended between heaven and earth. He could feel the presence of the others, feel their joy, too, as they dipped and soared. But who were they? Who shared this freedom with him? He could feel the faint touch of something against his mind—whispers he couldn't quite make out though they spoke in a language that seemed familiar.

"Connor, wake up! You're hurting me!"

Down, down he came—out of that freedom. He was crying out against the loss even as he opened his eyes and felt Jillian pushing against his chest. Immediately, he relaxed his iron grip on her, but a few more seconds passed in confusion as he was caught between the dream and Jillian.

"I'm sorry," he said, drawing her to him gently and kissing her. "Was I holding you too tightly?"

"If you'd held me any tighter, I would have stopped breathing," she said, half sitting up to stare at him in the dim light of early dawn. "Were you having a bad dream?"

No, he thought, it wasn't bad. But even as he sought to capture the dream, it eluded him. He shrugged and tried to sound casual.

"I must have been, but I don't remember it now." He brushed her curls from her face. The last remnants of the dream faded and he felt that powerful surge of hunger for her, that driving need to possess her and be possessed *by* her.

"I want you, Jillie," he said huskily as his hand trailed down over her body and reached that still-mysterious female core of her that welcomed him.

The sharp fear she'd felt when she'd awakened was swept away by his touch. At times like this, when his hunger for her was greatest, Connor still tried to be gentle, and the war between those opposing forces filled her with a powerful eroticism. One look, one small movement on her part could send him over the edge, and most of the time she tried to prolong that moment. But this morning, her hunger matched his—and might even have exceeded it. Something of that fear lingered within her, and she sought to drive it away by reaching for him and guiding him into her, then arching to take all of him and hold him there, safe within herself.

And when it was over and she could no longer shelter him within her, Jillian started to worry anew.

Although she maintained an outward calm, inside Jillian was terrified. For the past two days, Connor and she had been making their way slowly along the twisting path that led up into the mountains, and it seemed to her that with each step, they grew farther apart.

Connor was so quiet that Jillian wondered if he even knew she was there. She could feel him retreating into himself, even though he still held her at night and invariably woke in the morning clutching her to him. At those times, his gray eyes seemed cloudy and even haunted, but then they'd clear and fill up with the light of love.

Twice, she'd asked him what was wrong, and both times he'd insisted that nothing was, except that he was still concerned about their reception when they reached their destination.

If his dreams were troubled, hers were as well. She would awaken in the morning crushed against him, terrified that he'd left her even when that was obviously untrue. And always there would be this vague sensation that she'd dreamed the same dream, though she didn't know what it was.

She hated the chasm that seemed to have opened between them, even though to all outward appearances they remained close. There was even a frantic quality to Connor's lovemaking, and while it aroused her even more, the aftermath left her uneasy.

Also, ever since that day they'd seen one of the birds just before finding the mossy bower where they'd made love for the first time, they'd neither seen nor heard another—and this despite the fact that they drew ever closer to the birds' aerie.

She wondered aloud to Connor if they might be

following a path that led nowhere, even though the villagers had shown it to them.

"This is the path," Connor asserted. "We're getting closer."

She stopped, having reached a decision that she'd been mulling over for some time. "We can go back," she told him. "I know you don't want to go there."

But he shook his head. "We *have* to go on, Jillie."

"Why?" she asked, but she already knew the answer before he spoke the single word.

"Kraa-shaweh," he said, his head lifted to scan the blue skies above the treetops.

They walked on in silence, then stopped as the sun vanished, leaving deep shadows that hugged the narrow path. Although it twisted and sometimes seemed to turn back upon itself, the path rarely strayed far from a small but swift-running stream and they once again made camp on its banks.

The stream was filled with more fish than either of them had ever seen, and Connor waded in and caught several with his bare hands to provide them with a tasty meal. Then, after they had eaten, they shed their clothes and bathed in the cold, clear water, washing their clothes as well and hanging them on nearby branches to dry.

Connor smiled at her—a smile she hadn't seen for days now. "Becoming Lady Jillian again will take some doing after this."

How far away all that seemed, she thought, almost as though Lady Jillian were a different person from a different lifetime. She laughed. "I was never very good at being a lady, in any event. You should know that."

Then she gave him a challenging look. "And what about you? I'm certain that my uncle will confer a title upon you. Will you like being Lord Connor?"

He laughed, and it seemed to her to be the carefree laugh of old. "I hadn't thought about that, but I suppose you're right. That would be his way of denying that his favorite niece married a peasant."

"Is *that* what's really bothering you, Connor?" she asked. It seemed so unlikely, but she suspected that such things troubled him far more than they did her.

He reached for her, drawing them both back onto the mossy bank. "No, it doesn't bother me—not anymore. We belong together, dearest, and if some people never accept that, it doesn't matter."

They began to make love slowly, their bodies still damp and cool from bathing in the stream. Even though she loved the wildness, Jillian also loved this slow building of passion. They stroked each other, warming cool flesh quickly as their lips met and their tongues intertwined in a sensual dance that left them both breathless.

The game played itself out slowly. By now, each knew exactly which erotic torment could drive the other over the edge. At first fearful of touching his hard shaft, Jillian now knew it well indeed, and she thoroughly enjoyed teasing him with her fingers and lips until her instincts told her he could take no more.

And Connor's lips and tongue had followed his fingers to that throbbing core of her womanhood, invading all her senses and driving her need to shattering spasms of ecstasy.

They both employed these torments, each bringing the other to the very brink and then drawing back, only to approach the brink all over again. Then finally, they tumbled over the edge, with Jillian astride him and Connor plunging deep into her, pouring himself into her even as she clutched him to her.

Jillian awoke in the deepest part of the night and raised her head to look at Connor. But he lay still beside her, and in the light of the fire, she could see a smile on his face.

Something had awakened her, but she didn't know what it was. The dream again? A sound in the woods? No, it was something else, she thought as she extricated herself carefully from the arm that lay curved around her.

She sat there for a moment, still listening, then got up to add some more wood to the fire. When she looked back at him, she saw Connor still lying there, smiling in his sleep.

A strange feeling crept over her—unlike anything she'd ever felt. But before she could even begin to puzzle it out, she was walking into the woods, conscious of the twigs and stones beneath her bare feet, but nothing more. Something drew her like a moth to a flame.

On and on she went into the darkness, her eyes open but unseeing, her mind blank except for the certainty that she must go this way. There was no path; she simply walked through the woods, completely naked, not even feeling the scratches acquired from blackberry bushes or the rough bark of trees.

Her legs began to ache and her feet were bruised, but still she kept going. The only effect of her various pains was to slow her down somewhat. Vague memories hovered at the edges of her mind: an apprehension, a certainty that she shouldn't be doing this. But she continued to stumble on.

Then she tripped over a tree root and fell headlong onto a bed of scratchy-soft pine needles. She started to scramble to her feet, then sank back again, frowning. What was she doing here? Where was Connor? Why were they traveling in the dark and away from the path?

She tried to fasten her mind on an image of Connor, but no sooner did she conjure it up than he began to recede again, as though pulling away from her in some unimaginably vast darkness.

"Connor!" she called, but the shout she'd intended came out as a whisper intead.

"He is gone. He belongs to us." The words that weren't words filled her mind, and she felt tears begin to slide down her cheeks. Then she got up and started to walk again.

Jillian awoke slowly as something brushed against her cheek, then against her hand. She was so tired. She felt as though she'd slept only for a few hours, but when she opened her eyes, the sun was high overhead, its light winking at her through the breeze-ruffled trees. A bright yellow butterfly fluttered away.

She sat up, frowning. Then her frown grew as she looked at herself. She was completely naked and covered with dozens of tiny scratches. Her legs ached and her feet hurt even worse. She touched the tender soles and drew her fingers away quickly.

Panic was building up in her, but she kept it down through an effort of sheer will. She didn't know where she was or why she was here, but she was sure that if she just kept herself calm, it would all come back to her.

When it didn't, she still managed to hold the fear at bay and began to search through her mind, pulling out memories and examining them as though they were ancient relics.

She knew who she was and where she lived. She could see herself at Talita with her beloved keras. As she envisioned the graceful birds, something else seemed to be trying to be remembered. But it slipped away again quickly.

She also knew that she wasn't home now, but where was she? For a long time, she sorted through those memories, trying to find one that would explain her presence here and bring it all back. But if such a memory existed, it was beyond her reach.

Finally, she looked around her at the still, deep forest, and then she could contain her terror no longer. It burst forth in a wrenching cry that shattered the stillness and seemed to echo through the ancient trees.

Another act of will brought a return of semicalm, and she decided that she couldn't be far from help. After all, she was naked, and how could she have wandered far in such a condition? Then it struck her that her clothes could be around somewhere and she got up and began to search for them, moving cautiously on her bruised feet in widening circles.

But there were no clothes to be found and a fresh wave of horror broke over her, drenching her in icy fear. She could not have gotten here on her own. Someone had brought her here, but who and why?

Those questions didn't matter, she told herself, at least not at the moment. What mattered was that she was naked and alone in the middle of the woods in some unknown place—and she had to find help.

She looked around her again, turning in a complete circle. Whoever had brought her here must have carried her. There was no path to be seen and the woods were too thick for a horse. So unless she'd been dropped from the sky, she'd been carried here.

As that thought filled her mind, she unconsciously turned her face to the heavens, seeking. Once more, something tickled her mind, but she dismissed it. There was no point in looking for her kera or for any of its kin. She wasn't at Talita; in fact, she wasn't even in Lesai. She *knew* that, and while it troubled her that she didn't understand *how* she knew it, she needed some certainty to cling to at the moment.

The forest that surrounded her seemed to be unending, but she was sure that a road or a village couldn't be far away. Not even the strongest of men could have carried her too far into the woods.

Hunger began to gnaw at her, but she ignored it as she tried to decide which way to go. Fear lent an added impetus to her desire to leave this place. Whoever had brought her here might return.

Then an old memory surfaced. Someone had told her long ago that if she were ever lost in the woods, there were certain things she could look for that might help her find her way. One was a stream. If she followed the direction the stream was flowing, sooner or later she would come to a larger stream or to civilization of some sort because people tended to build their towns and villages along the shores of lakes and streams.

But there was no stream anywhere around. She listened carefully but could hear nothing. There was no help to be had there.

The other thing she remembered was that she might be able to find her way back by looking for signs showing the way she'd come: footprints or broken branches that would have marked her passage earlier.

So she walked around the edges of the small clearing and at last found a spot where some small twigs had been broken off an unknown bush. Pleased with her success, she started off in that direction.

The undergrowth was dense, which made it easier for her to find the evidence she sought, but even so, her progress was painstakingly slow. Only after considerable time had passed—and she'd taken numerous false steps—did Jillian come to realize that whoever had brought her here had been following a more or less straight path, deviating only to avoid the thickest tangles of blackberry bushes. She gazed at those longingly. They were thick with berries, but only a few of them had even begun to ripen. And as she fought down her growing hunger, she realized that at least told her something she didn't know and hadn't even thought to question before. It must be midsummer because blackberries ripened late.

Finally, she found some blueberry bushes and stopped, then began to gather them as fast as she could and stuff them into her mouth to assuage both her hunger and her thirst. Freed for the moment from the effort required to find her way, she began to ask herself a question she'd somehow overlooked earlier.

Why was it that she didn't remember anything? If she wasn't in Lesai, why didn't she remember leaving to come to wherever she was? She sank to the ground and began a search of her memory once again, as she continued to eat the sweet, juicy berries.

She lived at Talita, where she'd always lived. Her parents were both dead and she had two brothers whose images she could conjure up easily. Her life was spent training keras, which she remembered without difficulty. Then, with more difficulty, she thought she recalled the younger of her two brothers, Timor, summoning her to Lesai City.

It felt like a recent memory, but she could recall nothing after that. She had no recollection of the journey and none of the meeting with her brother. Could she have been waylaid somewhere along the way—kidnapped?

She frowned. First of all, she would never have traveled away from Talita without guards, and secondly, such things hadn't happened for years. It was true that she could be a prime target for kidnappers, but she just didn't believe that was what had happened. In any event, why would kidnappers leave her out here alone like this? They'd want to hide her somewhere where they could keep her and not risk having her disappear.

She grew weary of asking questions that had no answers. For now, the only thing she could do was keep following the trail she'd left—or whoever had carried her had left—and hope that there would be some answers at the end.

But when she came to the end, several hours later, there were no answers to be found. Shortly before that, however, she'd become aware of a distant, welcome sound: a stream running close by. But the faint trail she was following didn't lead in that direction and, thirsty as she was, she didn't want to risk losing it to find the stream.

The sound of water receded gradually as she followed the trail, and then suddenly it was back again as she emerged into a small clearing. In the center of the clearing were the first signs she'd seen of human life: a dead campfire, some blankets and a bright woven bag with straps that was apparently a backpack.

Her spirits soared, but only for a moment. Then she stopped herself from running into the clearing and instead crouched in the bushes. Her captor could be here somewhere.

She listened and watched until finally she could stand it no longer, and then she entered the clearing, going straight to the pack that she could see was well filled.

When she had finally emptied the pack of its contents, she found rough peasants' clothing that fit her perfectly. And she found food as well: dried fruits and hard, sweet cakes aromatic with strange spices. There were several pots of a pleasant-smelling cream, too.

And there was also a knife! It was the last thing she found and the most surprising discovery of all. She picked it up carefully, staring at the sharply honed blade that gleamed in the sun. Then, with another look around the clearing, she quickly slipped the knife into the pocket of the trousers she'd already put on. It felt surprisingly good to know that she had a weapon, even though she lacked the skill to use it.

Unfortunately, there were no shoes, but when she turned her attention to the heap of blankets nearby, she discovered hidden beneath them a pair of sturdy leather shoes that also fit her well.

Were these her things? Logic told her they must

be, but what was she doing wearing peasants' clothes? She wore shirts and trousers like this at Talita quite often, but they were made for her by her dressmaker and were certainly of better quality.

She walked around the campsite for a time, chewing on the dried fruit and devouring several of the delicious little cakes while she searched for anything that might yield a clue as to her purpose here. Then, when she belatedly realized that this meager food supply might have to last for some time, she reluctantly stopped eating and thought about the stream gurgling nearby in the woods.

She started in that direction, but stopped when her attention was caught by some broken branches on a nearby bush. She'd become so attuned to such signs that spotting them had become second nature. She frowned. Was this the way she had come? She didn't think so, but she knew that her sense of direction was less than perfect.

Following the small trail of broken branches, she found herself standing on the edge of a well-marked path that ran in both directions. Finally, she saw how she must have been brought here. The path wasn't wide, but it was certainly wide enough for a horse.

She stood there staring at it, first in one direction and then in the other. To her right, the path was visible for some distance as it followed a slight downgrade. On the left, it began to climb rather steeply and curved out of sight quickly.

To the right, she told herself. Downhill. Whether

251

she chose that because it was easier or whether some instinct was responsible, she decided that was the way she should go. But first, there was the water, its sound beckoning to her from not far away. She'd found a leather water bottle in the pack as well and could fill it before she left.

But when she reached the little stream, her thirst vanished with yet another discovery. Spread out over some nearby branches was more clothing, obviously left there to dry. Some of it was quite similar to what she was wearing, but other items caught and held her attention.

The shirt and trousers she picked up were far too big for her and were obviously made for a large man. Her captor? But why would he leave his clothing behind?

Finally, she decided that he must simply have forgotten about the clothing. Obviously, he'd had other clothing with him and had just left this behind.

She drank from the cool stream, filled the bottle and then returned to the path she'd discovered, leaving the man's clothing behind, but taking the things that fit her.

When she reached the path again, she hesitated, uncertain for a moment about her decision to go downhill. But she could now see that the path followed the little stream, and remembering that advice she'd once been given, she turned right and started down the path.

"The spell will not last."
"It will last long enough, Brother."

"He has been trained—however imperfectly."

"Yes. It is gratifying to have at last the answer to an old question. But we will have many more questions for him when he awakens."

"That will be soon. We should go now. Let him find us himself."

The buzzing annoyed Connor. Some time passed before he realized that it was the sound of voices speaking in near whispers—speaking a familiar language, but not his own tongue.

Connor opened his eyes. Above him was a beamed-and-thatched roof, a familiar sight that soothed him, although he wasn't sure why he felt the need to be comforted.

Someone had been here—more than one person. He sat up, shaking his head to clear away the cobwebs. No one was there now, and he wasn't in his own home, after all. But whose house was it, and why had he fallen asleep here?

He looked around, frowning. Nothing looked familiar. After so many years on the island, he knew the homes of all the brothers, and the only thing familiar here, apart from the thatched roof, was the curved walls. And the tower, of course. He could see the open archway and the wooden stairs that spiraled up to the tower room.

He got to his feet, shaking his head again. He felt heavy and tired, as though he'd slept little. Standing now in the middle of the large room, he looked around him, seeking a clue to its owner. It was richly furnished: thick rugs, solid, well-made furniture and more books than even

Seka possessed. Connor had always believed his mentor had the largest collection on the island, save perhaps for the library used exclusively by the Inner Circle.

Drawn to the books as always, he walked over to the shelves that had been specially designed to fit into the curving walls. The books were all very old and bound in lovingly tended leather. In fact, they resembled the books he'd seen Seka poring over recently—books he knew must have been taken from the forbidden library.

He pulled one out at random and opened it carefully, not at all surprised to discover it was in Kraaken. After scanning enough of it to see that it was a philosophical rumination on the meaning of sin, he replaced it. Not that he wasn't curious enough to read on, but he was more curious about where he was.

Ignoring for the moment an appetizing meal that had been set out on the table, he pulled open the door, then walked outside. The moment he did, he knew he wasn't on the island.

The trees that grew close to the little cottage were all pine and fir; there were no such trees on the island. He took a few steps into the small yard, then turned to look back at the cottage, half expecting to find he'd been wrong about its familiarity. But it was reassuringly like the cottages on the island, including the tower with its railed balcony.

When he scanned the steep hillside behind the cottage, he could see more towers protruding through the dark evergreens, though they were some distance away. And, yes, there at the top of the steep slope was a much taller tower, exactly like the one on the island that housed the secrets of the Inner Circle.

He went back inside and sat down at the table. As he tried to think, he absently ate the meal, which he assumed had been left for him. Where was he, and how had he gotten here? He had no recollection of leaving the island—and why would he, in any event?

Gradually, an uneasiness stole over him. Was this some sort of sorcery? Had Jenner and the others decided to take action against him, fearing that, when he became a member of the Inner Circle, he would replace Jenner as high priest?

Connor decided that had to be the answer. The Inner Circle had cast a spell on him to make him believe he wasn't on the island. No doubt this was his own home, but they had contrived to make him believe otherwise. So he would simply have to wait out their game until they tired of it. It couldn't last long; others would be looking for him, and if they found him in some sort of trance, they would demand to know what had been done to him. It might last a few days if Jenner had caught him off in the woods alone, because everyone knew that Connor disappeared for a few days at a time. But sooner or later, he would be restored to himself.

He was just beginning to think uneasily about the possibility that the Inner Circle could stretch out time itself when his thoughts were interrupted by a familiar shriek from above that echoed eerily down the staircase that led to the tower.

A kera? There'd been keras on the island, but the last of them had died some months ago. Something about that thought nagged at him as he got up and walked over to the tower, then started up the stairs. He must have mistaken the sound. It was probably only a sea gull, and its cry had been distorted by the tower.

But it was no sea gull that greeted him when he reached the top and stepped into the open room beneath the roof. The bird that sat there staring at him with brilliant green eyes certainly wasn't a gull. Nor was it a kera, though it bore a strong resemblance to those birds.

.

The path wound downward, sometimes steep and other times nearly level. At a low point she reached late in the afternoon, Jillian made a discovery that further confused her already tormented mind.

It was the first soft ground she'd come upon, but instead of finding the expected horses' hoofprints, she found instead two sets of footprints. One set was hers, but the second set clearly belonged to a man. She squatted down next to them, staring at them as though they could speak to her. Obviously, she had walked along this path with someone, but why couldn't she remember? She'd been assuming that she was unconscious when she was carried up here on a horse, but now she knew she was wrong.

Something must have happened at that campsite—something that had taken away her memory of the journey. She'd heard tales of people suffering blows to the head that had left them unable to remember anything, but it seemed unlikely that had happened to her. She knew who she was. She knew all sorts of details about her life. Furthermore, there were no lumps or sore spots on her head.

She got up and walked on. Her legs and feet hurt. The cream she'd applied earlier had soothed the scratches for a time, but they were beginning to bother her again. By late day, with the path already deep in shadows, she knew she should be looking for a place to spend the night. But she kept on for a while longer, convinced that any moment she would round yet another bend in the path and come upon a village.

It was nearly dark, but she still spotted the trampled bushes along the side of the path, then saw the remains of a campfire. The path had stayed close to the stream, though not always in sight of it, and she now saw that the campsite was virtually on its banks. As she was washing herself in the stream, she saw dozens of silvery fish and wondered if she might be able to catch one or two for dinner.

It wasn't easy, because they kept slithering out of her hands, and she didn't much care for the feel of them. But she managed to catch two large ones, and, fighting down her squeamishness, cut them open with her knife and did her best to prepare them.

The results proved to be worth the effort. They were wonderfully sweet tasting and not as bony as she'd feared. She devoured them both and ate some more of the dried fruit, then built up the campfire and settled down uneasily for the night. Mindful of the state in which she'd found herself this morning, she slept in her clothes.

Dazed, Connor stumbled back down the steps from the tower to the cottage, trying to understand what had happened up there before the great bird had lifted itself from the railing and disappeared into the sky.

When he was back down in the cottage, he remembered the dreams he'd had. They seemed to have been recent dreams, although he couldn't be sure: dreams of flying through the night, soaring high up in the sky, almost among the stars.

What he felt now was similar: that sense of freedom and joy, of pure bliss combined with a certainty that great knowledge had been imparted to him—or could be imparted, if he chose to accept it. He'd looked into those emerald-green eyes and had seen eternity.

Absently, he fingered the symbol of his order that hung suspended from its gold chain. Then he became aware of what he was doing and lifted the chain over his head so he could look at the pendant more closely.

It was strange, he thought, how he'd never noticed that before. Neither had he ever heard anyone comment on it. But he could see now that it resembled a bird—not just any bird, but the great golden bird that had perched on the balcony. A bird the exact color of his Kraaken robe.

Connor found this discovery exciting, as though a veil had been lifted from his mind, showing him something that had always been there, but hadn't revealed itself until now.

It was something he had to share and he started out of the cottage, only to remember when he stepped out the door that he wasn't on the island.

Quickly, he retraced his steps, retreating to the security of the little cottage. There were others here; he was sure of that. But something was preventing him from seeking them out, a nagging thought that murmured deep in his mind.

So instead, he did what he always did when he was troubled by something: he turned to books. The remainder of the day passed as he buried himself in them, reading the thoughts of the unknown writers, who seemed to have had limitless time to ponder great questions.

Jillian continued her long trek down the mountain, praying each time she reached a blind curve in the path that she would find help just beyond it. Her feet were sore and swollen. One of the cuts had turned ugly and dark and was too painful to touch, although she continued to apply the cream. She'd torn up the extra shirt to make strips of bandage, but she couldn't bind it too thickly because then she couldn't get her shoe on.

I will survive this, she told herself. *And when I do, I will find out who did this to me and make certain he pays for it.*

To keep her mind away from questions that

had no answers, she thought about Talita and the keras, about a life that now seemed so distant in both time and place. She tried to recreate her childhood there and found that there seemed to be puzzling gaps in her memory of those days.

She remembered clambering up the cliff for the first time to the nests of the keras. It seemed that she couldn't have been more than nine or ten years old. Someone was with her. Was it Timor? But he would have been away at boarding school by then, and in any event, he'd never had all that much interest in the keras.

There were other memories, as well, of places she'd gone and things she'd done, and always she was sure that someone had been with her, even though she was certain it couldn't have been her brothers. There were too many years between them. They had no patience for her childish games.

She continued to pick at these memories, turning them over and over and examining them closely before finally discarding them in frustration. Surely it must be the result of the shock of her present situation. When she was herself again, it would all come back.

She made camp for a second night. This time, she'd been unable to find any signs of a previous camp, but wandering along in a half daze as she'd been, she knew she might have overlooked it. Her foot throbbed painfully and her scratches still bothered her and she had a rash that looked like ivy poison on the lower part of her arm.

But she slept deeply and dreamlessly before

awakening to yet another day's walk, dogged as before by a vague feeling that she'd left something important behind, up there in the mountains.

Connor raised his head and rubbed the back of his neck. The interior of the cottage was becoming shadowy. He was startled to realize that he'd allowed an entire day to pass as he lost himself in the arcane books. And he was equally amazed that no one had appeared. Wherever he was, someone knew he was here. There'd been those voices this morning and the meal left for him.

A delicious aroma wafted his way and he turned his head to see a large covered tray on the small table in the corner. He stared at it for a moment, then got up and went over to lift the lid. There was a small roasted chicken and some wonderfully fresh-looking vegetables. A bottle of wine sat beside the tray.

He thought that he'd spent the day reading, but apparently he'd fallen asleep at some point, and his unknown hosts had replenished his food supply. But who were they?

He looked toward the door, then stopped, drawn by the food smells. He would eat first, then go seek out his hosts.

When he had finished the meal, he left the cottage. It was dusk, but there was enough light for him to see the path that led toward several other lighted cottages, barely visible through the thick trees. Pausing only to reassure himself that he still had his knife, he set out. He had no reason to believe that his hosts meant to harm him, but he couldn't afford to take their benevolence for granted. Who knew what sort of torments Jenner and his crew might have conjured up?

The path wound through the trees and headed toward the distant lights. Then, after a time, he could no longer see those lights. Dusk was rapidly turning to night. He was about to give up and return to the cottage when he saw the lights again and quickened his step.

The cottage was identical to the one he'd left, but that didn't surprise him. All the cottages on the island were the same, too. Once again briefly touching his concealed knife, he walked across the clearing toward the partially open door.

Even though the door was ajar, he knocked loudly, and when there was no response, he called out, "Hello." But all was silent both inside and outside the cottage. After calling out once more, he pushed the door open.

It was the cottage he'd just left! The books he'd taken from the shelf still lay on the table next to the chair where he'd sat reading the day away. The tray with the remnants of his dinner was still there on the other table. The only thing that had changed was that the lamps had been lit.

A dizzying sense of disorientation swept over him and he went inside. Mentally, he tried to retrace his steps on the path. He had a very good sense of direction and he was sure that the path had not turned back toward the cottage.

He made a sound of disgust. More of Jenner's tricks! There was probably no one else here. But if Jenner thought that he could break him by forcing this isolation upon him, he was wrong. Connor was quite content with his own company. Even without the books, he'd be fine. He could live in his thoughts for a long period of time.

But later, as he was about to fall asleep, he found himself reaching out to the empty space beside him, and he felt something: an inchoate longing that followed him down into a dreamless sleep.

Chapter Eleven

At first, when she reached her destination, Jillian could scarcely believe it. Through the trees, she could see open land and sheep. Fearing that what she saw might be an hallucination, she kept her eyes focused ahead as she stumbled onward. And when she reached the edge of the meadow, she saw the houses.

Finally convinced that the scene before her was real, she felt in her pocket for the knife, then laughed bitterly as her fingers closed around it. What did it matter? She was too weak to fight. If these people had any part in what had happened to her, they could finish it now.

But the small crowd that quickly gathered around her seemed more curious and sympathetic than threatening. She was led into the house of an elderly woman and handed a mug of strong tea as they chattered away in their own language.

Hoping that they might have something to help her injured foot, Jillian unlaced the heavy shoes. And as she did so, she noticed that the shoes on the feet of those around her were identical in style. So, too, were their clothes, now that she forced herself to notice. This must be where she'd gotten the clothes she was wearing, which meant that she had been here before.

A woman about her own age knelt to examine the foot she uncovered, then spoke to her hostess. In short order, her feet were being bathed in a strong-smelling solution that bore a resemblance to the salve used by her own people to ward off infections.

In the corner of the little cottage, she spotted several baskets made of dyed reeds, similar in design to the backpack she'd dropped outside. It was further proof that she'd been in this place before, and her hopes rose. Surely, once she got past the language barrier, she could find out something about her purpose here—not to mention finding out exactly where here was.

But her first attempts at communication met with failure, and when food was pressed on her, she gave up. She was both hungry and tired and there would be time later to find a way to get some answers.

Most of the others left as she began to eat the delicious meal set before her. Only the young woman and the elderly one remained, talking quietly between themselves, while casting regular glances her way.

Jillian heard them use one word several times before it registered in her tired brain. Were they actually saying Kraaken? It sounded like that to her. When the young one looked over at her again, Jillian repeated the word, saying it as they had. The young woman nodded and Jillian saw a look of fear pass over her, followed by a quick exchange of glances with the older woman.

Kraaken? What could they possibly have to do with this? She knew who the Kraaken were: a secret, mystical group of priests who lived in isolation on an island off the coast of Lesai City. Their name immediately invoked a feeling of intense hatred that Jillian couldn't quite understand.

If the feeling had been contempt, she would have understood that well enough. She had no time for anyone who believed in the tales of sorcery that had always surrounded the Kraaken. But why did she loathe them so fiercely?

Then it struck her as she finished her meal. What if those tales were true and the Kraaken were responsible for what had happened to her? But why would they seek to harm her? Her dislike of them was well-known, but that scarcely seemed reason enough to kidnap her.

And she recalled now that she'd refused to sell them keras, but even that seemed a poor excuse to attack her. The Kraaken had far less need of the birds than the Lesai, since they remained on their island. And anyway, that had all happened some time ago, so why would they suddenly decide to take action against her now?

She decided that she must have misunderstood the women's words. Obviously, there was a word in their language that sounded like Kraaken. Not only did she refuse to believe that the Kraaken were sorcerers, but since she wasn't even in Lesai, how would these people know about them?

Jillian awoke late the next morning in the cottage to which she'd been taken by the young woman. Despite the lavish meal she'd eaten upon her arrival, she was famished again and was pleased to see a basket of fruit and bread and cheeses awaiting her.

She felt much better—almost herself again—and after breakfasting and then bathing in the stream near the cottage, she decided she was ready to try to gain some answers from the villagers.

The cottage to which they'd taken her was isolated from the village itself by a stretch of woods. But there was a well-marked path and Jillian soon found her way back to the village. A small market was underway in the village square. No one seemed surprised to see her, and everyone was friendly—or as friendly as their inability to communicate would permit.

She heard that word that sounded like Kraaken several times, and she began to think it might mean stranger, which would explain the young woman's nod when Jillian had spoken it the evening before.

She found that young woman seated on the ground, surrounded by woven baskets filled with herbs and several other baskets containing pots of salve and oils. Jillian decided that the young woman was apprenticed to the older woman, who was undoubtedly the village healer. She made her way through the small crowd, and the young woman smiled.

Soon, several of what were undoubtedly the village elders were gathered around her as she tried by means of gestures to find out where she was. Lesai meant nothing to them, but when she tried Masani, a few heads nodded. Hoping against hope that there might be someone here who spoke that language, she tried it out on them. But it quickly became clear that they understood it no better than they understood the Lesai tongue.

"Masani?" she asked, gesturing around her. After the elders conferred for a moment, one of the men pointed to the left, then made a series of gestures that Jillian thought meant a great distance away. Before she could pursue that, the young woman spoke, drawing her attention.

She pointed first in the same direction the man had, then stabbed a finger at the sky and drew a hand across her face. When Jillian frowned uncomprehendingly, the young woman plucked lightly at Jillian's blouse and made the same gesture again as she repeated several words over and over.

Jillian suddenly understood. The woman was trying to tell her about the desert that lay west of the Masani lands. Jillian was stunned. Could she really be that far from home?

Then she felt yet another shock. If she *was* this far from home, how was it that she couldn't even recall crossing the sea, let alone traveling through Masani lands and a desert?

Perhaps I've misunderstood, she thought and pointed to the west this time. But all she drew were shrugs and shakes of heads that seemed to indicate that the people didn't know what lay in that direction—or else that nothing lay there.

Jillian pointed to the south and got the same response, then turned to face the north, where she saw, for the first time, the high peaks that rose beyond the trees. And she belatedly realized that that was also the direction she'd come from, although she'd had no idea at the time that the mountains were so high.

She was still staring at the mountains, vaguely unsettled, when she heard that word that sounded like Kraaken again. She whirled around to face the speaker, a village elder, then pointed toward the mountains.

"Kraaken?" she asked and received nods all around.

Jillian was perplexed. If she was right that the word meant stranger, were the people simply telling her that *she'd* come from there? She pointed to herself and said it again as a question.

Several people shrank back from her, but the others shook their heads firmly, and those who'd moved away came back, smiling the smiles of people who are ashamed of having overreacted.

Jillian's confusion grew. The Kraaken lived on

an island, not in the mountains. And unless she'd completely misunderstood what had gone before, the island wasn't in that direction anyway.

She spoke the name again and finally made the people understand that she wanted information about the Kraaken. Or perhaps they *didn't* understand, since they proceeded to make a series of strange gestures she couldn't interpret, talking all the while in their own language.

Then a sudden silence fell over them and Jillian followed their gazes upward. High above them, a half-dozen birds circled in the blue sky. Jillian shaded her eyes and tried to see them better. They were much bigger than her keras, but the outlines were the same. She'd learned long ago to identify birds, even at great heights, by their silhouettes and their manner of flying.

"Kraaken," the young woman whispered, and the name was repeated by the others.

Jillian returned to the cottage and sat down beneath a tree, watching the sky as she thought. The birds had disappeared, but she hoped they might return and perhaps even fly a bit lower so that she could get a better look at them.

What was she to make of what she'd learned— if indeed she'd learned anything at all? She had to keep reminding herself that she might well have misinterpreted much—or even *all*—that she'd heard. But it *did* seem likely to her that she'd understood the part about the Masani and the desert being to the east of where she was now. And that being the case, surely she could persuade her kindly hosts to provide her with a guide back to the lands of the Masani. She had no money to offer them now, but could certainly reimburse them once she reached Trantor, where her cousin lived as wife to the Lesai ambassador.

But strangely enough, getting home was the least of her concerns at the moment—perhaps because it seemed to be the one question she'd resolved. What *really* troubled her was how she'd gotten so far from Talita in the first place, with no memory whatsoever of having left there.

She wondered where she was most likely to find the answer to that question: at home or here? It seemed likely to her that she had passed through this village before, so they must have seen her captor. All she needed was to find a way to ask about him.

It *was* possible that he was well-known to the villagers, or even that he could be one of them, but somehow, she doubted that. These were simple, primitive people, and the likelihood of any of them having traveled all the way to Talita to capture her was beyond imagining.

Unfortunately, what seemed more and more likely to be the answer was that she'd been captured by the Kraaken and subjected to their sorcery. But if that was the case, then why did they simply leave her up there in the mountains? Had they assumed she'd die there? But if they intended for her to die, then why hadn't they just captured her and killed her outright? Her head ached from all these questions. Nothing made sense.

No matter where her thoughts strayed, they kept returning to the Kraaken, even though she knew full well that she might be mistaken in her belief that they were involved. It was certainly possible for words with very different meanings to sound much the same. She could think of several words in the Masani tongue that sounded quite similar to Lesai, but had completely different meanings.

Still, she thought about the brotherhood, unconsciously clenching her fists as she did so. What did she know about them—other than that she seemed to have an irrational hatred of them?

They'd first appeared in Lesai over a hundred years ago; she remembered hearing that. And no one seemed to know their origins. It was said that the first of them were not Lesai, although she knew that since that time they'd recruited members from among her people.

Suddenly, she sat up straighter. Was it possible that *this* was where they'd come from? It seemed farfetched, but no more so than everything else at the moment. And what about those birds she'd seen, the birds that the villagers had called Kraaken? She'd seen the looks of reverence on their faces, and she recalled how they'd shrunk away from her when she'd pointed to herself and said Kraaken.

Several moments later, it all fell into place—a story so outlandish that she couldn't believe it, but couldn't disbelieve it, either.

The strange birds that were believed to have

mated with falcons to give rise to the keras had appeared at Talita just over a century ago—at the same time the Kraaken had also shown up. Now here she was, far from home, in a place where the word Kraaken seemed to be associated with strange birds and possibly with men who lived in the mountains—men who had sorcery. Now that she'd puzzled this out, the gestures she hadn't understood began to make sense.

When she'd asked about the Kraaken prior to the appearance of the birds, the villagers had made a series of strange gestures. Not one of those gestures indicated a bird, even though they'd later called the birds Kraaken. But what the gestures *could* have meant was magic.

Jillian shivered. She was certain she was right. The Kraaken *were* involved in this somehow, and so, too, were those birds. There was an irony here that she couldn't deny. She'd traveled far and wide, trying to find out about the birds that had given rise to the keras. And all the time, they'd been known to the Kraaken, to whom she'd refused to sell keras.

And yet, clearly there were still major pieces of this puzzle missing. If the Kraaken already possessed these birds, why did they want keras? And how was it that no one had ever seen them— unless, of course, they'd always been kept captive on the island?

Furthermore, fascinating as it all was, it still didn't explain how she'd gotten here.

*   *   *

He was once again soaring among the stars, riding the swift winds, his landlocked self far below somewhere. He cried out with the sheer joy of it, but the sound he made came out as a high-pitched shriek, one among many.

This time was different. This time, he'd been aware of that moment when his soul had left his flesh. For one brief second, he'd even seen himself, sleeping peacefully, one arm thrown out almost as though embracing a body that wasn't there.

That image remained with him for a few moments as he felt himself rising into the heavens. It troubled him and filled him with a vague longing, though for what he didn't know. And in any event, the feeling passed swiftly, lost in the freedom of his new state.

Far out over the desert they flew, and he stared down at the moonlit sand dunes, thinking vaguely that he had been there once, but as a man, not a bird.

Was he a bird? Connor didn't know, and somehow the question seemed irrelevant. This was not a time for thinking. This was a time for pleasure, for an incomparable freedom.

On and on they went, swooping so low over the desert that he could see the wind sculptures in the sand quite clearly now. Then they turned back, making a wide arc and flying once again into the moon. He couldn't see the others and didn't know how many of them there were, but he knew they were there because he could feel their minds touching his, sharing his exultation.

Then the desert was behind them, and the land below was dark and nearly featureless—except for a few lights close together. A village, he thought, feeling rather sorry for the earthbound humans down there.

But something was drawing him down, calling out to him. That longing unexpectedly returned, startling him. He could feel himself slipping away from the others, drifting down toward the village.

"No," whispered the soft voice in his mind. "Your place is here with us. You cannot have there what you have here."

The downward spiral stopped and he rose to join them, but a small part of that strange longing remained in Connor as they flew on toward the mountains.

Jillian rubbed her neck. It was getting stiff from all the time she spent looking up, hoping to catch another glimpse of those birds.

Since she'd first seen them two days ago, she'd become obsessed with them. She told herself that it was only because they might well be the birds she'd sought for so long—but she knew there was more to it than that. She was sure those birds were a link to her forgotten past—and probably a connection to her present situation as well.

She had spent hours with Seema, the young woman she'd met when she arrived here. Seema was bright, friendly and, perhaps more to the point, patient.

The result was a confirmation of Jillian's worst fears. The men who lived high in the mountains *were* Kraaken, and the villagers believed them to be great sorcerers, though Seema had offered no proof of that. The birds she'd seen belonged to them or lived with them and were said, in Seema's words, to be more than birds. When asked how long they'd lived in the mountains, Seema had said always.

Seema's people had seen the Kraaken occasionally over the years—or so it was claimed by some. They wore long golden robes and pendants in the shape of a bird with emeralds the color of the great birds' eyes. The birds had been seen as well, Seema said. They sometimes came to the village itself, perching on the branch of a tree. Seema had seen them twice herself.

The Kraaken were regarded by the villagers with both awe and fear, but the birds were a different matter. The villagers were certainly in awe of them, but didn't fear them. Rather, Seema said, they were considered to bring good things: a recovery from life-threatening illness, a quiet passage into death for an elder, gentle rains that ended a long drought.

Strangely enough, the villagers had no name for the birds, simply calling them by the word in their language that meant bird. Apparently, they needed no further distinction.

And after numerous frustrating conversations, Jillian learned that she had come to this village with a Kraaken. It appeared that the villagers hadn't at first known he was one of the brothers, until one of them had spotted the familiar pendant hidden beneath his desert robe.

Jillian and the man had come from the desert, their presence announced by one of the birds. The bird led them to the cottage where Jillian was staying now, unoccupied since its owner's death some months ago. Both of them appeared to be suffering from what Seema had described as desert fever, but Jillian was in far worse condition.

Seema had offered to stay and tend to Jillian, but the Kraaken had insisted that he would care for her himself. And so he had.

They'd apparently stayed in the cottage for several weeks, keeping mostly to themselves. The villagers didn't know what to make of this strange situation, since it was known that the Kraaken lived without women. Some said that despite possessing the pendant, he might not be Kraaken, but others pointed out the regular sightings of one of the birds near the cottage.

At no time, according to Seema, did anyone think that Jillian was being held against her will. Early in their stay, when Jillian's life had been hanging in the balance, the healer and two elders had arrived at the cottage to find the Kraaken in tears, obviously fearing she would die.

When Jillian had recovered from the fever and a broken ankle, the two of them had set off into the mountains. Seema assured Jillian that she'd been eager to go—perhaps more eager than the Kraaken, some had thought.

All of this took quite a while in the telling, and Jillian knew that she could have misunderstood some things, but that was the essence of the story.

Seema had also managed to convey quite clearly that the Kraaken had been young and very handsome—unlike those seen by the villagers in the past. Those Kraaken had all been old men with white beards.

Unfortunately, Seema's tale raised at least as many questions as it answered. Who was this man who'd wept at the possibility of Jillian's death? And why, if he was a Kraaken himself, was he less than eager to go to join his brethren in the mountains? Furthermore, why was *she* so eager to go there, hating the Kraaken as she did?

Jillian also explained to Seema that she would need a guide to take her back across the desert to the land of the Masani, and after conferring with the elders, Seema let her know that they would speak on her behalf to a nomad tribe they traded with on a regular basis. They were never certain just when the desert tribe would arrive, but it appeared likely that they would come soon. Her own people, Seema said, would never venture into the desert.

So Jillian was left with much time on her hands to concoct various scenarios based on the information she'd gleaned from Seema. The one that seemed most likely to her was that she'd been kidnapped and ensorcelled by the Kraaken from the island, then brought to this place by one of them.

An alternative possibility was that she *had* come willingly, because she'd been promised that she would find the birds she sought. But Jillian considered that unlikely. Given the hatred she had for the Kraaken, why would she have allowed one of them to bring her here—or anywhere, for that matter?

As to why this Kraaken should have wept at the prospect of her death, she could only assume that he'd been given the responsibility for leading her to the mountains and feared that he'd be punished if she died.

But nowhere in her many hours of speculation was Jillian able to answer the basic question of why she had been abandoned up there in the mountains.

She continued to be obsessed with thoughts of the birds, although she saw them only in her sleep. Every night her dreams were filled with them, the image conjured up from Seema's description and her memory of the keras.

But something else hovered along the dark boundaries of her dreams. At times, she thought she'd almost glimpsed it, but at other times, she only felt its presence. And she had no idea what it was, except that it was important—all important.

One morning, Jillian climbed the steep hill behind the cottage in an attempt to find something to do with her time while she waited for the nomads to arrive. When she reached the top, she drew in her breath sharply. She hadn't expected to discover an unobstructed view of the mountains, since from everywhere else they could be glimpsed only through the trees, if at all.

Her gaze was immediately drawn to the highest peaks—and then to the birds circling above them. How she wished they'd come down here again! If only she could take several of them back to Talita!

Then, abruptly, it occurred to her that the Kraaken could be deliberately showing her that which they knew she wanted, but couldn't have. Perhaps all of this was no more than a display of their power intended to force her to change her mind about them. It made sense, if one assumed that they, like so many others, believed she wielded great power over her uncle, the king.

How cruel, she thought as she continued to stare at the birds, *tormenting me with something I've wanted for so long.*

Then a strange feeling came over her, a kind of shivery sensation. "That which I want, but cannot have," she whispered, turning the phrase over and over in her mind. Why did it suddenly seem that it wasn't the birds, but something else?

She lowered her gaze and noticed a path leading off into the woods at the base of the hill. It didn't appear to go anywhere. All she could see from her vantage point was an endless stretch of pine forest, rising up and down the hills to the horizon. But once her eyes had fastened themselves onto it, they remained there, and even before she'd consciously decided to explore it, she was running down the hillside, nearly tripping in her eagerness.

A short time later, she was standing in a clearing near the stream. It was a lovely spot. The water tumbled musically over some rocks and the banks were thick with moss. But what Jillian felt as she stood there was far beyond an appreciation of the beauty of nature.

"Something happened here," she said aloud, her voice just barely audible over the rushing water. "Something very important."

She sank down onto the moss and closed her eyes, letting her other senses fill up with the place: the sound of the water, the springy feel of the moss, the smell of pine and dark, damp earth. It was there, just beyond her grasp: something good. No, more than good. Something indescribably wonderful.

She stayed there for a long time, until she was finally forced to accept that whatever it was, a formidable barrier had been erected in her mind to keep it from her.

That night, Jillian woke from her sleep to find someone staring at her. But the face faded the moment she opened her eyes, leaving only a frustrating impression of familiarity and nothing more. And the feeling that had accompanied it vanished, too—but not before she recognized it as being the same feeling she'd had at that spot in the woods.

When morning came, Jillian decided to return to the place in the woods. If one visit had triggered vague memories, perhaps a repeat visit would do more. But just as she was about to leave, Seema appeared at her door.

Through words and gestures, she let Jillian know that the nomads had arrived and were camped now at their usual spot not far from the desert's edge.

It seemed that nearly everyone in the village was hurrying along the path that led down out of the hills, most of them laden with goods to trade with the nomads. Eager as she was to get home, Jillian kept thinking about that spot by the stream and what she'd felt there.

The village elders spoke on her behalf to the nomads' chieftain, who kept staring at her curiously. When the discussion went on for longer than seemed necessary to Jillian, she began to worry that they would refuse to take her. But at long last, the elders turned to Seema, who then told her that they would take her with them to the next fazara, after which one of the youths would lead her to the lands of the Masani.

The word fazara sounded familiar to her, and a few questions of Seema elicited the information that it meant a sort of garden spot in the desert. Jillian nodded as something flashed through her mind and was gone: a pool, sparkling under the moonlight, surrounded by woods. And something else: a tall, dark-haired man.

Is it the same man? she asked herself. *And is he the Kraaken who brought me here?* The vision had been so brief, but she was sure he hadn't been wearing the robe of a Kraaken. And then she belatedly recalled what Seema had said: that they hadn't known he was a Kraaken because he wasn't wearing the golden robe.

The nomads intended to spend two days camped here before returning to the desert, so she had only a short time to try to unravel the mystery of this man and that spot in the woods—two days to find several lost weeks of her life.

She spent the remainder of the day on the mossy banks of the stream, but when hunger and the waning light drove her away, she'd learned nothing new. And that night, she was once again awakened by a dream, the same one as before: a man's face and a feeling of indescribable, sensual joy. Every fiber of her being cried out for more as the feeling faded.

Tears streamed down her face. "No," she cried. "Don't take him from me."

And then she drew in a sharp breath. What had she said? Take *whom* from her? She hugged herself miserably. What had made her say that? And what was that feeling she'd awakened with—that aching hunger? It had almost felt as if. . . . No, that was clearly impossible! She'd never made love, never had a man in her life.

She fell asleep again, tormented by memories that were fragmented, incomplete somehow, as though some all-important ingredient had been removed from them, but not so completely that she couldn't sense its absence.

When morning came, her first thought was that she had only one more day to discover what had happened to her here, and then she would be leaving this place forever.

Carrying food with her, she climbed the hill behind the cottage, determined to spend the entire day in the one place where she thought she had a chance of gaining some answers. But when she reached the top of the hill and saw once again the birds circling over the jagged peaks, she stopped for a moment.

The vision was brief, but very clear. She was standing at the base of the cliffs at Talita, where the keras nested. She was a child, and she could feel her excitement. Today, finally, she would climb up there. She turned to the boy beside her.

The vision was gone and she was staring again at the circling birds. But this time, the memory remained. The boy wasn't one of her brothers. He was tall and skinny and dark haired and several years older than she.

And then she was inundated with memories. They flooded through her mind in such rapid fashion that she sank to her knees, overwhelmed. And all of them were of that same boy: teaching her to ride her pony, teaching her to swim, sitting with her in a place much like the place down there in the woods, but not the same.

She didn't fight them, but just sat there waiting for them to run their course, making no attempt to grasp one of them and hold on to it because she knew that would be impossible.

And when she could absorb no more, one question remained unanswered. Who was he?

And in short order, another question followed the first, even though it remained unanswered: why had she forgotten him?

Or been *made* to forget him, she amended, though she was still unwilling to credit the Kraaken with having that much power.

She got slowly to her feet, her gaze once again raised to the mountains. There were fewer birds there now, or perhaps they had just become more difficult to see as the sky faded from a deep blue to a milky white.

And then she remembered her original purpose in climbing up here and looked down at the path. Somehow, she'd managed to forget the other visions—and the man.

A dark-haired boy and a dark-haired man. She tried to hold the two images in her mind, but they overlapped, and then she knew the boy and the man were one and the same.

"Connor," she whispered, as though testing the sound of it on her lips. Then she shouted it. "Connor!"

She ran headlong down the hill, tripped and fell and picked herself up and ran again, not stopping until she had reached the mossy place by the stream. She sank onto the spongy carpet and cried—tears of rage and frustration, tears of anguish and guilt.

She remembered it all now—or thought she did. Connor, her childhood soul mate who'd gone to the Kraaken, then come back, only to be taken away again.

But this time, he hadn't gone willingly. She

knew that because she now remembered what had happened in this place. Her body had remembered before her mind had.

They had made love for the first time in this spot. Jillian ran her hand over the moss, remembering how it had felt against her bare skin—and how his lips and fingers had felt and how her own fingers had sought to learn him as he was learning her. She remembered the strange mixture of emotions that had accompanied their careful passage from childhood friends to adult lovers—something that had felt almost like regret that was quickly overwhelmed by the newness and wonder of it all.

And even now, her body remembered that moment when he'd filled her with himself and driven them both to unimagined heights of pure joy.

Connor had forsworn his vows to the Kraaken. This time, he had chosen *her*. And now the Kraaken had taken him away from her again.

She was too angry to think clearly now, and the press of rediscovered memories was too strong. She lay back on the moss and let them take her. The long days and nights of lovemaking that had followed unfolded within her mind: their ease with each other, their intimate games, the shared pleasure of finding new and different ways to torment each other, the times when one or both of them tried to hold back the tide of ecstasy or to hold on to the moment when it came.

Connor. Now, at last, her past and her future had a name.

Several hours passed in a slow drift of memories that settled gently into Jillian—as gentle as Connor's touch, as relentless as their shared passion. And then she got up and went to find Seema, frightened at how close she'd come to leaving this place—and Connor.

Chapter Twelve

"The spell has been broken."

"Yes—as I feared it would. He was too deeply embedded in her mind, woven into the very fabric of her life."

"His spell still holds, though."

"Just barely—and only because we have provided distractions. We will lose him, Brother."

"Are you so certain of that? We offer him . . . *everything*."

"Everything but her."

"Can that really be so much?"

"That is a question we cannot answer, but I think his answer will be yes."

"What shall we do?"

"We can try to hold her back to give us more time to persuade him. But I think it will not work. She will not be kept from him, and he will choose her. Still, we have a chance—and we must take it."

Connor walked slowly down the hill to his cottage, his mind filled with their discussion. He had nearly forgotten by now that this was all a spell cast by Jenner and the others, and when he *did* think about it, he was no longer angry with them. In the time he'd been here— a period of time he couldn't measure—he had learned so much and learned, too, how much more there was to *be* learned.

His days were spent in long talks with the Whitebeards, which was how he privately categorized them. Not since his early years in the brotherhood had the sheer excitement of learning held him in its grip. They knew so much and somehow managed to impart that wisdom to him in ways that challenged his mind.

And then there were the nights: nights spent soaring through the heavens while his body slept—nights when the rigors of learning were replaced with the joy of simply *feeling*.

So why was there that nagging thought that something was missing in the midst of all this wonder? Was it only that he knew it wouldn't last, that he would one morning wake up back on the island, where life had indeed been pleasant, but would forevermore be a pale imitation of this?

No, Connor thought there was something else, even though he had no idea what it might be. He wanted to ask them about it, but feared that he might insult them. They offered so much. How could he question the value of such gifts?

Whatever it was might have come to him in his sleep, as such things so often did, but sleep was for his body only. His mind was flying through the night skies.

Alone in his cottage as dusk fell, Connor sat before the fire, which was necessary up here high in the mountains. It was at these rare quiet times that he felt that absence most keenly. Often, he would turn, as though expecting someone to be at his side, just as he would see his body on the bed, reaching out to someone as his spirit rose to join the others.

These were very disquieting feelings, and even if he hadn't been worried about offending his hosts, he could not have brought himself to talk about those feelings. What they suggested was a hidden desire to break his vows—vows he was sure he'd kept all these years, even though his memories seemed dim and fragmentary.

As night fell, Connor prodded at those memories, taking his mind all the way back to his childhood at the great estate of Talita, where he'd first fallen in love with the keras, bastardized offspring, he knew now, of the kraa.

They were pleasant memories, memories of a peasant boy favored by the lord of the manor. But pleasing as they were, something seemed to be missing. He was still working his way along the edges of those memories, searching for the missing pieces, when he lay down in his bed. But the moment sleep came, the memories retreated, and he felt that surge of excitement as he was separated from himself and lifted into the winds to join his brethren.

Seema did not want Jillian to return to the high mountains. When Jillian persisted, her new friend enlisted the aid of the elders, who were plainly shocked at Jillian's decision. They spoke rapidly in their own tongue, shaking their heads. The only word Jillian understood was Kraaken.

Finally, when they understood that she would go with or without their help, the elders relented and agreed to send two men with her partway. Jillian learned from Seema that the men often went some distance into the mountains on hunting expeditions, but at a certain point, they turned back. Beyond that was the forbidden land of the Kraaken sorcerers.

The next morning, as the nomads left for the desert, Jillian and her companions rode the other way, taking the trail she had followed earlier when she'd come out of the mountains without Connor and without her memories.

The sky was clear and the sun was shining, but as Jillian and the men began the steep ascent into the mountains, the mists closed around them, blotting out the sun and even the trail ahead. When she first rode into the mist, Jillian feared that it might be the work of the Kraaken. But her two companions seemed unconcerned, so she decided it must be a normal occurrence—much like the mist that often clung to the hilltop manor when the rest of Talita was bathed in sunshine.

Their first day was uneventful, and they camped

at the spot she had used before, both on her journey up here with Connor and her solitary trip back. As she lay awaiting sleep, Jillian thought about how Connor had feared coming up here—and how she'd insisted that they make the journey.

Even if I didn't love him and need him, she thought, *I would still owe it to him to rescue him from them, for I was the one who brought him to them.*

On the other hand, he hadn't been willing to tell her the source of his fears, but that had probably been because he knew well her disdain for tales of magic.

Had they cast a spell on him as well? Surely they must have, or he would have left them and returned to her. Or perhaps they were holding him captive by more conventional means.

But what was their purpose in holding him? Did they know that he'd already broken his vow many times? They must know, either through their own means or because he had told them. He would never attempt to lie about such a thing—no more than he would willingly leave her now.

A long ride the next day carried them all the way to the campsite that had marked her parting from Connor. Jillian felt the first stirrings of fear when they reached it, recalling her naked wanderings in the woods near this place.

Her companions stayed the night, but it was clear that they were uneasy now. She hadn't attempted to tell them what had happened to her here, but it seemed unnecessary. They knew somehow that they were encroaching upon the land of the sorcerers.

Leaving them to build the campfire and see to dinner, Jillian walked through the woods to the stream. A bittersweet cry poured from her when she saw Connor's clothes still spread out on the bushes as she'd found them before.

She plucked his shirt from the branches and pressed her face against it. After all this time, there was no scent of him on it, but her memory supplied it and brought back as well the lovemaking that had followed their bath in the stream.

"You will not have him!" she said aloud, still clutching the shirt to her as she turned to stare at the steep incline to her right. "Try all your tricks on me if you will—but you will still lose him."

Her two companions departed early the next morning, leaving her with the extra horse that carried their supplies and would provide transportation for Connor on the return trip. Jillian wasted no time watching their hasty departure, but instead set off up the increasingly steep trail.

From time to time, she would emerge into an open area where she could see a great vista of mountains and sky, and each time, she scanned the heavens for signs of the birds. But they were nowhere to be seen.

Jillian's determination to rescue Connor and her excitement at the prospect of seeing him again kept any fears at bay as she rode a trail that began to spiral up and around the mountains. It was wild and beautiful country, unlike anything she'd ever seen before. The trees were huge, many of them so big around that it would take three or four men to encircle their trunks.

On the forest floor, strange bushes thrived, many with striking flowers of a color and shape she'd never seen. Their scents mingled with the aroma of rich, damp earth and pine, carried to her on a cool breeze. Small birds flitted about, adding their own unusual colors to the idyllic scene.

Here and there, she came upon waterfalls, some of them only a few dozen feet high, while others roared down from great heights, splashing into frothy pools at their bases.

This was an ancient land, a land as old as time and one unchanged by the passage of the years. Jillian had never before thought of a land as being either ancient or young, but she could not escape that thought now.

And neither could she escape the feeling that she was an intruder here. She felt no malevolence issuing from this place; instead, she felt inconsequential, beneath the notice of those who claimed it.

When the shadows lengthened, she led the horses down into a narrow ravine just off the trail, a place where one of the smaller waterfalls formed a pool that in turn trickled away into a narrow, rushing stream.

Only when night fell and Jillian could postpone sleep no longer did she succumb to fear. It was during sleep that the Kraaken had cast their spell before—if indeed they *had* cast one. In the absence of any other explanation for her memory lapse, she was forced to accept sorcery, though she did so very begrudgingly.

She had not built a fire since she wanted to do nothing to draw attention to herself here. The moon hadn't yet risen and it was so dark now that she couldn't even see her own hand before her face. The horses were tethered nearby, but the only indication she had of their presence came from occasional soft whickers and their smell.

She sat there for a time, staring into blackness until her eyes hurt from the effort to see what in all likelihood wasn't there to be seen. Then she lay down and drew the blanket over herself, trying to find peace in the sounds of the water.

When she awoke, there was still no moon and the night was as black as before. She got up, letting the blanket fall away, even though the night was quite cold. Then she started to walk, following along the banks of the small stream, drawn as before by something.

But this time, she stopped. This time, she refused to give in to that invisible force. For a long while, she wavered, a picture of indecision as she took a few hesitant steps forward and then stopped. A great battle was being waged within her, though its only outward evidence was a slight tremor that passed through her.

Connor, she told herself. *Think about Connor. Remember the feel of his body against mine, the driving force of his need filling me, the sudden spasms of ecstasy that united us.*

Desperately, she conjured up the images, drawing them boldly in her mind. And then she was free! There was no slow lessening of the force that had drawn her from her sleep. Instead, it simply withdrew, leaving her trembling with cold, yet still heated by the memories of their lovemaking.

She stumbled back through the darkness, guided now by the wan light of the moon filtered through thin clouds. And when she had reached her campsite, she laughed aloud in triumph. She had won! She had beaten the accursed Kraaken. Now all that remained was to find Connor.

Above Connor, long wisps of clouds partially obscured the moon. Below, the land was in total darkness. Only the tall tower was visible, thrusting its way above the ancient trees. The scattered cottages were hidden beneath the dark canopy of the forest.

After that first great surge of excitement as he rose into the air, Connor felt something different this night. The whispers of the others as they touched his mind were louder than usual, but something else was there, something that reduced their murmurings to meaninglessness. He felt the collective will urging him in one direction even as that strangeness lured him in another.

He began a slow, downward spiral. The voices became louder, more insistent, calling to him, promising him new sights this night. A storm was brewing to the east. They could fly along its edges, perhaps even over it, and feel its awesome power that charged the very air around them.

He hesitated, still drifting downward, but slower now, torn between two destinations. Something down there in the blackness was reaching up to him, but there was the promise of the storm.

The downward spiral stopped and he flew straight up again, back into the midst of his companions and then off to the east. But he could not quite rid himself of a feeling that he'd chosen wrongly.

Jillian awoke to a misty morning and the remnants of a dream. She smiled, recognizing it even as it slipped away. For many years as a child, she'd dreamed regularly of flying—not unusual for a girl who spent her time among birds. But she hadn't dreamed of such a thing for a long time, and she wondered why it had come back now.

She washed her face and hands in the stream, then sat on its banks and ate some bread and fruit, wishing that she'd built a fire so she could have some tea.

She'd beaten the Kraaken! The triumph of last night still sang in her. And she'd beaten them in a manner that must have been humiliating to them. She'd defeated them by invoking her love for Connor—and perhaps more importantly, *his* love for *her*.

But after she'd savored her victory for a time, she began to wonder if she'd won the war—or only the first skirmish. Would they give up now—or would they simply redouble their efforts? Since she knew what *she* would do in such a situation, she had to assume that they would be no less determined.

Most people, faced with the prospect of doing battle with sorcerers, would have fled, but Jillian was nothing if not strong willed. And since her determination had invariably won the day in the past, she had no reason to doubt it now.

Moreover, acceptance of the unacceptable didn't always happen quickly—and especially to someone like Jillian. So while she was forced to admit that the Kraaken were indeed sorcerers, she was still a long way from the total acceptance that affects behavior.

Grabbing the reins of the lead horse, she started up the steep slope to the path. The fog was so thick that she could barely see the ground beneath her feet, but she knew she was retracing her path down because she could make out hoofprints.

The climb seemed longer, but then it always seemed longer when she was going uphill. So for that reason, she continued on her way for some time before the uncertainty stole over her. Even allowing for the uphill climb, it was taking far too long to reach the path.

She stopped, glancing back to be sure the second horse was still following along. Both animals whickered impatiently, as though asking why she didn't move on.

Were the Kraaken casting more spells—trying to confuse her so she would turn back and get lost? She took a few steps forward and peered at the ground, seeking more hoofprints. But even though the ground here was fairly soft, she saw no prints. And neither did she see any signs of the low bushes and weeds having been trampled.

She shivered in the cool mist, trying to decide what to do, when all she felt like doing was shaking her fist and cursing the Kraaken sorcerers. However satisfying it might be, it wasn't likely to gain her anything.

So she did what she'd done last night, except that this time she kept climbing the slope as she thought about Connor.

The mist that enveloped her became instead his body, lean and hard against her own softness as their legs and arms intertwined. She thought about the tremors that rippled along his bronzed skin as she traced tiny circles with her tongue down over his chest and his flat belly, taking her time because she knew exactly what he wanted, ignoring his groans and his hand on her head, urging her lower as he arched his long body.

She had just begun to imagine the feel of smooth-skinned hardness against her lips when the spell was broken. She couldn't have said how she knew that, since another moment passed before she realized that the steep incline had leveled off and only a short span of trampled weeds separated her from the trail. But once again, she felt that silent withdrawal.

She smiled as she led the horses out onto the path. She'd found their weakness, all right— and she suspected that it wasn't just that she thought of Connor, but rather the *contents* of those thoughts. She swung into the saddle and laughed aloud at the image of some very red-faced sorcerers.

"She dares to *mock* us, Brother."

"So she does—and for good reason. We have underestimated this woman—a mistake since we already know that however much we try to divert his attention from her, his thoughts keep trying to return to her. If she were less than she is, that would not be happening."

"What do we do now?"

"We wait for her arrival. She has found our weakness; soon, we will test *hers*."

Connor felt restless this day. He'd awakened to the memory of last night, when something had been drawing him away from his companions, and he was sure it was the same thing that had kept him from his reading this morning and continued to plague him as he sat with the Whitebeards, for once not responding to the mental challenges they hurled at him.

It had become his habit to sit beneath the trees outside his cottage and read the morning away, studying the collective wisdom of the ages as set down in the thick, leather-bound books. But this morning, he found himself continually looking up, as though expecting someone to appear.

And at one point, he'd actually seen someone, though only for a brief moment: a dark-haired woman dressed in peasant garb, standing at the edge of the clearing and staring at him. Every fiber of his being had seemed to cry out for her, almost as though she were a lost part of himself.

Had he broken his vows? Surely he wouldn't be here if he had. He would have been banished from the brotherhood, denied the powers of the Inner Circle. Or was this spell simply a prelude to that? Did Jenner hate him so much that he'd dangle before him that which he *could* have had, before sending him from the island?

The voices of the Whitebeards droned on, seemingly oblivious to his frightened and confused thoughts. But how was it that they didn't know, when it seemed that they shared each other's thoughts—especially during the nocturnal excursions?

Maybe they do know, he thought suddenly, looking around the loose circle. *Maybe I'm being given another chance. Maybe Jenner doesn't hate me, after all. But who is she—this woman for whom I have risked all I've ever wanted?*

"Do you believe in redemption, Brother Averyl?" one of the Whitebeards asked. It was Edamo, the one among them he felt closest to, and perhaps their leader as well, though they seemed not to have one.

"Yes, of course," he said quickly, responding in the Kraaken tongue.

"And how does one gain redemption?" Edamo asked in his soft voice.

"Redemption is earned," Connor stated. "It's earned by struggling to overcome one's . . . mistakes."

Then he stared directly into the pale blue eyes of his inquisitor. "But in order to overcome them, one must first know what they are."

"That is true." Edamo got to his feet, signaling that the session was over. Connor was always surprised at the youthful grace of these men. Their lined faces and white beards suggested great age—as did their wisdom—and yet they displayed none of the infirmities of the old.

Connor got up, too, and left the tower, walking slowly down the hill toward his cottage. With each step he took, he became more and more certain that his earlier speculations were true: he *had* broken his vows, and for some reason known only to Jenner, he was being given a second chance.

The closer he came to the cottage, the more sure he was that he was about to receive a revelation, and so, when he stepped off the path into the clearing in front of the cottage and saw her standing there, he wasn't really surprised.

What *did* surprise him and cause him to stumble to a halt was the sheer force of the feelings that engulfed him. Whoever she was, she had been no casual encounter. What he felt again was that sense that a missing part of him stood there.

Jillian had prepared herself for this encounter. She knew that she might find a Connor who wasn't really Connor. She'd come upon the little cottage nearly an hour ago, and she'd known from the moment she first saw it that this was where she'd find him. So she'd simply waited for him to return.

And she remembered the dream she'd had of this place: the little round cottages with thatched roofs and the tall tower atop a hill. This was where she'd find Connor, and it was here that she would defeat the Kraaken once and for all.

She made no move toward him as he stood there on the far side of the clearing, staring at her. Just seeing him sent shivers of happiness through her. Tiny coils of sensuous heat unfolded themselves, filling her with a hunger not just for his body, but for all that was Connor. She wanted this to be a joyous reunion. She wanted him to run across the clearing and sweep her into his arms and tell her that it would be all right, that they'd be together forever. But she knew it wouldn't be that easy.

He began to walk slowly toward her. She took a few steps away from the door of the cottage, her eyes searching his face as he came closer. And even though she'd done her best to prepare herself for this, she still felt a terrible sense of betrayal when she saw the puzzlement in his face, then uncertainty in his gray eyes.

He stopped, finally, about six feet away. Confusion continued to cloud his eyes. She closed the gap between them and reached up to touch his cheek, overcome with an urge to make contact— even with this stranger. She realized that he seemed even more a stranger to her now than he had when they'd met aboard ship.

He made no attempt to prevent her from touching him, although she could feel him stiffen slightly as his eyes continued to search her face.

Jillian would never again claim that she couldn't understand what drove some people to violence, because in that moment, she wanted to kill those who'd done this to him—to them.

"Connor," she said softly, her fingers still resting lightly against his cheek. "They're trying to take you away from me, but I won't let them. They tried to keep me away from here, but I beat them. You can beat them, too. They can't stand to know that we love each other—that we've made love."

At her final words, he suddenly turned his face away from her and stumbled back a few steps. But Jillian knew somehow that physical contact was important, so she reached out and seized his hand instead. Once again, he made no effort to stop her, but once again, she felt him stiffen.

"Who are you?" he asked, speaking for the first time in a voice that started out harshly, but ended on a note of pain.

"I'm Jillian. We grew up together on Talita, Connor. Then you left to join *them*." She nearly spat out the final word.

He was silent for a long time and she couldn't tell if he believed her or not. His gaze had turned inward, and she could only hope that he was now beginning to remember, as she had.

"I left Talita when I was fourteen," he said after a long silence. "We couldn't have—" He stopped, frowning.

"We loved each other then, Connor, but we didn't make love until we found each other again, on our way here."

He pulled his hand from her grasp and ran it

through his hair. She could see it trembling. "My vows," he said. "I *did* break them."

Suddenly, it was all too much for her. There remained in her enough guilt over his broken vows that her tone became harsh. "You *chose* to break your vows, Connor. I didn't seduce you, if that's what you're thinking."

She paused, wincing inwardly at the acrimony in her voice. She must remember that he was as confused now as she'd been. She couldn't blame him for his failure to remember her.

"They've cast a spell on you, Connor. I don't know why, but I know that's what they've done. They took away my memory of you for a while, too."

To her surprise, he nodded, though he didn't look any less confused.

"I know that," he said, his voice and face registering his shame. "I broke my vows, and Jenner is giving me a second chance—a chance to redeem myself. They've brought you here to tempt me again—to see if I can withstand the temptation this time."

Jillian simply stared at him, speechless for a moment as she tried to think of how she could counter his words. He was wrong; she was sure of that. The high priest wasn't giving him a second chance; he'd tried to kill them both. And Jenner certainly wasn't responsible for her coming here now. But the Kraaken here had convinced him of that.

"That's not true," she stated succinctly. "I came here to find you and rescue you. And Jenner has no intention of giving you a second chance. He tried to kill us both on our way here. You can't trust them, Connor. They're lying to you."

He merely stared at her. His confusion was painful to watch. Then he abruptly turned away from her and walked across the small yard to sit down beneath a tree. She followed him, sitting down beside him and once again taking his hand.

"What do you remember?" she asked gently. For the moment, the pain she felt for him outweighed her anger with the accursed priests.

He didn't look at her, but after a moment, his chest rose and fell in a long, ragged sigh. "I remember Talita and the keras."

He stopped and raised his head to search the small patch of sky visible above the clearing. She looked, too, but there were no birds in sight.

"Kraa mated with falcons long ago. That's how the keras came into being."

"Yes, I guessed that," she said, wondering how long he'd known that. Had he known all along? Was that the real reason he'd come here? She hated not having the answers. If she was going to get them out of this place, she needed to know *everything*, and she was unhappily aware of just how little she knew for certain at this point.

"But the keras inherited only a little of the kraa's talents," he said.

When he said nothing after that, she asked what talents the kraa had. Something in his tone had filled her with a deep sense of foreboding.

His head was still raised to stare at the sky,

and when he spoke, his voice was low and almost dreamy. "Every night, they come for us and take us with them. We fly through the night, while our bodies rest here. The freedom. . . ."

His voice trailed off into silence as she stared at him. She thought about her own dream of flying and swallowed hard. If they could really do that—No, she refused to accept such a thing. It must be merely a part of the spell they had cast upon him.

Connor frowned, remembering those times when something had seemed to be drawing him down, away from that incomparable joy. He slanted a glance at the woman beside him. It was she who had been pulling him back to earth. Why did she have such power over him?

Jillian. The name seemed to whisper down the long corridors of his mind, echoing softly but insistently. He looked at her again as he felt the soft warmth of her hand in his. Jillian. Words and phrases floated up from the depths of his memories: the poetry he'd started writing years ago. He'd forgotten about that, but now he could see himself, sitting along the shore on the island, putting onto paper feelings and memories.

Memories of a little girl. He turned his head now and stared into the blue eyes that were watching him warily. And he saw those same bright blue eyes in his memories: laughing, challenging, sometimes flashing with anger but always shining with love. Jillian. Little Jillie, who'd roamed the paths of his childhood with him—the sister he'd never had.

He looked away again, overcome with shame. She was saying that they were more than brother and sister—that they'd become lovers. He turned that thought over and over in his mind. It felt wrong—not just that he'd broken his vows, but that he'd made love with a woman who'd been like a sister to him. Could she be lying?

And then, suddenly, he knew she wasn't. He caught another faint memory that grew sharper as he reached out to grasp it—a memory of arguments he'd had with himself, of a moment when he'd been poised between the innocence of their shared childhood and a recognition of very adult hungers.

The image flooded him: naked bodies entwined on a mossy riverbank, a place like Talita but not Talita, sunlight filtering down through the trees to set her pale skin aglow and cast soft shadows on the curves and hollows of her body.

The image vanished, but the hunger remained. He felt himself grow stiff and hard, and he quickly let go of her hand and drew up one leg so she couldn't see what was happening to him. But the throbbing need persisted, hammering at him painfully. He wanted her again, and he knew it could never be enough.

He tried to fix his mind on the Whitebeards and on the nocturnal flights. He sought to recapture that wondrous, glorious freedom, but his mind kept going back to her and to their lovemaking: her soft warmth surrounding him as he thrust into her and poured his life-force into her, their bodies shuddering in ecstasy as they reached that ultimate union.

He scrambled to his feet and turned away from her, but it did no good. She was still there, and she would always be there—if not in the flesh, then in his mind and his soul.

There was a sudden fluttering of great wings, and the kraa that was Connor's special companion, his summoner each night, settled down on a nearby branch.

Its green eyes flashed at him, momentarily distracting him from thoughts of her. He saw their night flights, felt the energy as they flew along the edges of a storm and the freedom of the long, slow glides as they swooped down into the desert that glowed in the moonlight.

And then Jillian was there, standing beside him. He could feel her presence, even though he kept his gaze on the kraa.

Next to Connor, Jillian stared at the bird. It continued to ignore her, its startling green eyes fastened instead on Connor. She recalled that in the desert, she'd been irritated because it had seemed to favor him over her. Now she understood. The kraa were a part of all this— perhaps even the source of the Kraaken's powers. She had believed that it was the priests she must defeat, but now she began to wonder if her true enemy might not be the great birds she'd sought all her life.

She walked closer to the bird, deliberately putting herself between Connor and the bird until it was finally forced to turn those emerald eyes on her. And the moment it did, she felt the force of its anger swarming over her.

She staggered backward as heat chased chills through her. She was stunned not only by the fact that it hated her, but also because it could project that hatred in such a powerful manner. She had only a moment to think about those vicious talons and that powerful beak before she felt Connor's arm encircle her waist and draw her back.

He thrust her behind him and at the same time spoke sharply to the bird in what she assumed must be the Kraaken tongue. She took a step sideways, peering out from behind Connor's wide shoulders.

The bird was staring at Connor with an intensity that felt like a physical force and she could sense the rigidity in Connor's body. He spoke again, his voice low but firm. And then the bird unfolded its great wings and took off, disappearing quickly over the treetops.

"It wanted to *kill* me!" she said, still nearly unable to believe what had just happened. A lifetime of devotion to her keras had left her unwilling to accept that such a thing could happen.

Connor turned slowly to face her, nodding, and she could see her own shock mirrored in his eyes.

"Wh-what did you say to it?"

"I just told it to leave," he said. But his eyes wouldn't meet hers and she was sure there'd been more to it than that.

"Connor," she said, reaching out to touch his

arm. But he shrank away from her as though her touch was fire. She dropped her hand.

"Why do they want you?" she asked. "You told me they would let you go—that Jenner would be happy to see you leave the brotherhood."

His frown told her that while he had remembered some things, he hadn't yet gotten back all of his memories. So she told him the rest of it: the report she'd received from the sea captain about the birds, Jenner's request to her uncle for an escort so that one of their brothers could recruit in other lands, their meeting aboard ship and the subsequent attacks upon them.

"The only part I still don't remember," she said, "is the last part of the trip from the desert. The villagers told me that they found us in that cottage and that I nearly died, but you nursed me back to health. Then we started up here."

She finished by telling him about waking that morning, naked and alone in the woods, with no knowledge of where she was or why she was there—and no memory of him. As she spoke, she saw the pain in his eyes. Once, he even moved slightly, as though about to take her into his arms.

"I went back to the village and I was about to leave, to return home. But then my memory came back at that spot in the woods where we first made love. Do you remember that now?" she asked him softly, wishing fervently that they could be back there now.

His gaze had been fixed on some distant spot,

but now his eyes met hers. "Yes, I remember— all of it."

For a long moment, neither of them moved or spoke. The invisible threads of desire encircled them, binding them even as they remained apart. She felt his hunger, and her own that matched it. Then, just when that need had built to explosive force, Connor abruptly moved away from her— only a few steps in reality, but a very great distance nonetheless.

"Edamo came to us in the desert," he said in a clipped tone. "I couldn't have carried you because I was suffering from the fever, too. First, the kraa came, and then Edamo followed. He . . . brought us to the cottage."

"Who is Edamo?" she asked in confusion as she tried to quell the lingering heat of desire.

"He's one of them." Connor gestured toward the tower that loomed above the trees. "He used his powers to get us out of the desert."

"But who are they, Connor? Are they Kraaken, too?"

And if they were, why had they saved *her*? If they wanted Connor, it made no sense at all that they'd saved her life. They knew what a threat she represented to their plans. But what, exactly, *were* their plans? Connor had believed that they would let him go, that they might even be happy to see him leave the brotherhood.

There was simply too much that she didn't know, and not knowing was very dangerous for them both.

Connor didn't answer her. He was busy thinking about everything she'd said, and he was also beginning to regain his own memories. But of course he hadn't known what had happened to her when he'd been brought up here.

He clenched his fists as anger surged through him. They'd left her to die alone in the woods!

And then, belatedly, he realized something else as well. "This isn't a spell," he said aloud, but more to himself than to her. "Jenner has nothing to do with this."

"What do you mean?" she asked, frowning. "Are you saying that these men *aren't* Kraaken?"

Connor jerked his attention back to her. "There are questions I never thought to ask—but I will now!"

Chapter Thirteen

Jillian had to run to catch up with Connor as he walked swiftly up the path toward the tower. *Did* he remember all of it now? He'd said he did, but if that was true, why hadn't he told her that he still loved her?

Fear clutched at her as she remembered his dreamy tone when he'd talked about flying with the kraa. Had that actually happened? She shuddered as she thought about the bird. Priests she could fight, even if they did possess magic. But the kraa? How could she fight them if they offered Connor that which no man had ever had?

"What questions didn't you ask, Connor? And what did you mean when you said that Jenner had nothing to do with this? Who *are* these men?"

She had barely finished her rapid-fire questions when she realized how typically Jillian she

314

sounded. And that was confirmed by Connor, who turned to her with a brief smile. In that moment—*just* for that moment—everything seemed to be the same and she knew that he *had* remembered all of it.

But the smile vanished quickly and his expression once again became grim. "I thought all of this was a spell Jenner had cast over me—perhaps a part of the initiation ritual into the Inner Circle or perhaps a punishment for breaking my vows."

She was confused again. "Then you already knew that you'd . . . broken your vows?" What she'd wanted to say was that he knew he'd made love to her, but those words wouldn't come out.

He kept his eyes forward, deliberately avoiding hers. "I suspected that I might have." He paused, then went on in a rush of words.

"But now that I know this is *real*, and not just a spell, I want to know who the Whitebeards really are and why I'm here."

The Whitebeards, she thought, had to be the men from her dreams.

"I know who they are," she told him. "But I don't know why they've brought you here."

He stopped—and this time, he *did* turn to her. She shrugged.

"I've had time to figure it out, although I still don't understand all of it. I think this was the Kraaken's original home. Nobody really knew where they came from when they showed up in Lesai. And they appeared in Lesai about the same time as the keras. I think they came from here, and the kraa came with them."

But the problem with that theory, she thought, was that it didn't explain why the kraa had disappeared from the island. Or *had* they disappeared? Had Connor kept that fact from her—and had his real purpose in coming on this journey been to prevent her from finding out about them?

It seemed that, each time she thought she had found answers, more questions arose. She would grasp a thought, only to have it slither away again into uncertainty. She wanted so desperately to believe that Connor was being honest with her, and yet some doubts remained. Was it possible that he believed himself to be truthful, but that he was in fact still under an evil enchantment?

For someone who had previously refused to believe in sorcery, Jillian had become a believer in a very short time—perhaps too much of a believer, she thought disgustedly.

Connor seemed to consider her explanation of the origin of the brotherhood, but she couldn't tell if he accepted it or not. He resumed the journey up the steep path to the tower and once again she had to run to keep up with him.

"Were there kraa on the island, Connor?" she demanded.

He shook his head. "Of course not. If there had been, I would have told you."

Unless you were under a spell to keep them secret, she said silently, still hurrying to keep up with his long strides.

They passed by other cottages, but saw no one. Connor remained silent, distant. Jillian told herself that she must be patient—never one of her strengths.

Finally, they reached the base of the tower, where an ornately carved wooden door stood open. Connor seemed unfazed, but Jillian felt the icy fingers of fear begin to play their staccato tune along her spine. She had deliberately taunted these men, and she was the only obstacle in the path of their plans for Connor—whatever those plans might be.

He started into the tower, but she hung back. He turned to her questioningly.

"They hate me, Connor—just as the kraa hate me."

Before Connor could reply, a tall, white-bearded man in the golden robes of the Kraaken appeared in the doorway. His pale eyes pierced her.

"We do not hate you, Jillian. We hate no one. And the kraa, wondrous as they are, are still only birds. They do not hate, either; they only fear. I am Edamo. I cannot invite you into the tower because this is a sacred place open only to the brotherhood. The others await us at my home."

He strode past them and started down the path. Jillian and Connor followed. She stared at Edamo's straight back, fascinated. She felt a power emanating from this man, but there seemed to be no evil in him. In fact, he made her feel so insignificant as to be nearly invisible, of no more importance to him than a stone or a blade of grass.

Except that I know that isn't true, she thought. *I am important to them because Connor is important to them.*

She wondered how old Edamo was. His wispy white hair and the lines in his long face suggested a very great age, but he walked swiftly and with the grace of a much younger man. Uneasily, she thought about those tales of Kraaken immortality—tales she'd discounted so thoroughly that, even when she'd been forced to accept the truth of their sorcery, she still hadn't considered the other part of the legend.

Connor had said nothing since Edamo's appearance. Jillian reached out to take his hand. He didn't draw away, but she received no answering pressure as she slipped her hand into his. Instead, she could feel a great tension in him.

Edamo turned into one of the cottages and Connor and Jillian followed him. The main room was very much like the cottage Connor was using: comfortably furnished and filled with books. It was also filled at the moment with more golden-robed, white-haired men.

There appeared to be about a dozen of them, and all seemed to be about the same age as Edamo—whatever that age might be. Some were seated and some were standing, but not one of them showed any signs of the frailties one would expect at their advanced ages.

"You have questions, Brother Averyl," Edamo said, gesturing for them to take seats near the hearth. Jillian did so, but Connor remained standing.

"Yes. They are questions I didn't ask before because I believed myself to be under a spell cast by High Priest Jenner."

Edamo and the others merely nodded, indicating that they had known this. And undoubtedly used it to their benefit, Jillian thought, then widened her eyes in surprise when she saw a smile flicker briefly across Edamo's face. Was he reading her mind?

"Now I know that wasn't true," Connor went on in a voice that sounded like the Connor she knew and loved. "I *was* under a spell, but it was *your* spell, not Jenner's. I want to know why you brought me here." He paused, then went on in a very different tone of voice—one of barely controlled anger.

"And I also want to know why you left Jillian to die in the mountains."

"Those are fair questions," Edamo said, nodding. Then he turned to Jillian. "But first, Jillian, you should understand that I am not the leader here. We are all equals. I have been chosen to speak for all of us because I am the one most fluent in the Lesai tongue. We have learned all the world's languages over the years, but for the most part, we have studied the written language only. The Lesai have always been of particular interest to me, so I chose to learn to speak your language as well."

Jillian was shocked again—and again saw that slight smile on Edamo's face. It simply hadn't occurred to her to question how he knew her language and spoke it so well. He inclined his head slightly, as though acknowledging the compliment she hadn't spoken aloud. She quickly shifted her gaze to the others, wondering if they understood any of this.

"My brothers understand because we have another means of communication," Edamo said. "They are reading my thoughts."

"And you're reading mine as well," she said, too shocked at the moment to summon up any anger.

"Yes. There are no secrets here—or there will be none." He turned back to Connor.

"Allow me to answer your last question first, Brother Averyl, since it is plain that this troubles you greatly, as well it should. We did not leave Jillian to die, as you put it. No harm would have come to her, save for some temporary discomfort. We wanted her to leave here and to fear coming back. It was our hope that she would return to Lesai, and that the memories we had taken from her would never return. But of course, they did."

He paused briefly and smiled at Jillian, who was still in a state of shock over his revelation that he and the others could read her mind. But strangely enough, she found herself believing his words—or was he casting yet another spell?

"Now, as to why you were brought here, Brother Averyl. We had nothing to do with the decision to send you on this journey. Those answers can come only from your High Priest Jenner.

"We discovered you in the desert one night

and a kraa confirmed that you were one of us. It is impossible for me to make you understand the excitement we felt at this discovery, though perhaps you will understand better when I have finished. So, of course, we helped you to get here. And it was, after all, your destination, even though your purpose was not ours.

"Some years ago—more than a century—there was discord among us. There were many wars taking place then in the world beyond our home. Some of our brothers felt we should intervene, while others believed that we should let things run their course, unimpeded by us. It is a very old argument, as old as warring among humankind.

"The difference this time was that those who favored intervention refused to surrender to the will of the majority. Instead, they left. We knew that they crossed the sea, but we lost track of them after that—deliberately, I might add. A decision had been made to sever all ties with them.

"This, of course, is the group to which you belong, Brother Averyl. We knew that the moment we discovered you in the desert. I may have been the only one not surprised to discover that the rebels had fled to the land of the Lesai. I'd always suspected that they'd thrown in their lot with the Lesai. That was the reason for my interest in them.

"Naturally, we were very curious about how your group had fared over the years." He paused and frowned. "From what we have gleaned from your mind, they have not fared well, although we cannot be certain of that, since you have yet to be admitted to the Inner Circle."

"What do you mean?" Connor asked.

Edamo shrugged. "It is possible, of course, that they have found some way to compensate for the loss of the kraa, but we do not see how that could be. Our powers derive directly from our relationship to the kraa—and you apparently no longer have any of them."

"We had keras," Connor said, "at least until recently."

Edamo's gaze swung to Jillian. "Ah, yes, the bastard offspring raised by the Lady Jillian's family. Are they all gone as well now?"

"No," Connor replied before Jillian could speak. "But Jillian refused to sell more of them to the brotherhood, and the last of them died some months ago."

Edamo's pale eyes actually twinkled with mirth. "I see. This is in retribution for the Kraaken having taken Brother Averyl—Connor, that is—from you."

"Yes." Jillian lifted her chin defiantly.

"Tell me about your keras, Lady Jillian," Edamo requested.

She did so, explaining how she trained them and for what purposes they were used. "I have always hoped to find the birds from which they were descended," she finished.

"So when you heard about the kraa, you came here hoping to obtain some of them."

"That was my hope, yes," Jillian admitted.

"Well, I regret to tell you that that will be impossible—unless, of course, they choose to go.

And if they did, it would surely be to join Brother Averyl's group on the island."

Connor and Jillian exchanged glances, and for the first time since she'd come to this place, she saw him smile—a smile that told her he fully appreciated the irony of Edamo's words. But his smile drained away quickly as he turned back to the white-bearded priest.

"There is more, Brother," Connor stated firmly. "If all you wanted from me was information, there would have been no need to separate me from Jillian."

Jillian was startled to realize that she hadn't thought about that, and she was equally surprised when Connor reached out to take her hand, holding it firmly as he faced Edamo and the others. All traces of the confusion and tentativeness she'd seen in him were gone now, and the liquid warmth of his love flowed through their linked hands.

"That is true," Edamo nodded, and Jillian could feel a tension growing in the room. She'd nearly forgotten the others, but now she saw them all leaning forward expectantly.

"We grow old and tired," Edamo said, his voice much softer than before. "All of us foresee a time not far in the future when we will want to leave this world. We need . . . replacements. When we found you, we knew you would be perfect. You have a fine mind and a strong sense of justice, and you share our love of learning. That may or may not be true of your brothers on the island. From your mind, we have gotten troubling impressions of some of them."

"I have broken my vows," Connor stated. "And more than once."

"Yes, we know that. But we are prepared to overlook it—if you are prepared to renew those vows."

Jillian gripped Connor's hand tightly as she glared at Edamo. "No! You cannot have him! We belong together! Don't you dare cast any more of your spells on him!"

"There will be no more spells," Edamo assured her. "Brother Averyl must make this decision for himself. But you, Lady Jillian, must understand—as he already does—what it is that we offer him.

"If he remains with us, he will spend his life in the manner he loves best: studying and learning from all the collected wisdom of the ages. And he will spend his nights with the kraa, soaring through the heavens, experiencing a freedom not possible for mortals. And, of course, he won't *be* mortal."

Jillian chose to focus on his final words, since fear clutched at her as she thought about the rest of what they were offering Connor. "You're not immortal! You just said that you're growing old and tired and will die soon."

Edamo smiled gently at her. "After so many centuries, it is understandable that we grow tired, is it not? And the true gift of immortality is to be able to choose the time of one's death and to live a full life until that moment."

Jillian swallowed hard. "How . . . how old are you?"

His smile remained. "I came into this world more than a thousand years ago, child. We all did. We were chosen by the old gods and brought with the kraa to this place when the rest of mankind was not yet civilized.

"Connor must choose. Either he can stay with you and have a normal human lifetime with all its distractions and uncertainties—or he can join us here."

Jillian turned to stare at Connor, whose gaze was fixed upon Edamo. The silence in the room was absolute. It seemed that everyone there was holding his breath. Connor never even glanced her way.

And finally, in that silence, Jillian had her answer. She withdrew her hand from his, hoping against hope that he would reach out to her. When he didn't, she got up from her seat and walked away—out the door and downhill to Connor's cottage, scarcely aware of what she was doing.

The world she had always accepted had just shifted beneath her feet. She felt disoriented, with nothing to cling to as her mind spun about wildly. The rock-solid strength of Connor's love was now gone forever, leaving her adrift in a place without meaning.

When she reached the cottage, she went directly to the horses and climbed into the saddle. She was still only barely conscious of what she was doing. All she knew was that she had to leave here.

She had left the cottages of the Kraaken far

behind before she began to shake off the sense of unreality that surrounded her. Then she stared at the ancient forest surrounding her and silent tears began to flow down her cheeks.

She had truly lost Connor now; she knew she had to accept the fact. And strangely enough, she no longer hated the Kraaken. If she was beneath their notice, they were beyond her hating. They lived in a world she simply could not imagine, and now they had gathered Connor into that world with them.

He hadn't made a choice this time; there was no choice to be made. She had nothing to offer him, while they had everything.

Connor watched as Jillian left the cottage. He put out a hand and started to call out to her, then stopped as Edamo spoke in a kindly tone.

"The pain will go away in time, Brother Averyl. I speak as one who knows well the effects of time."

Connor thought about his words and about what Edamo had said earlier. He could have years, decades, centuries, to explore all knowledge, to see all the changes. He could have countless nights to soar in the dreamworld of the heavens.

Then slowly, he shook his head—knowing what he was refusing and knowing, too, what he must have.

"Perhaps you are right," he told Edamo. "Perhaps the pain *would* go away in time—but the memory of her would not."

He saw himself sitting in his cottage, surrounded by his books, remembering a woman long dead—and a love long lost.

"I cannot stay," he told Edamo.

"Do not make this decision so hastily," Edamo replied. "And remember that, in any event, you have unfinished business. There is much to concern us all about some of your brethren on the island, and we will need your help. Stay with us for a time, while we decide what must be done. Then, if you must go to her, we will understand."

Jillian stopped as the shadows deepened into night. She made camp in the spot where the Kraaken had come to claim Connor. She would have preferred to have gone farther—away from the Kraaken lands—but the trail was too treacherous in the dark. In any event, she knew she was safe now. The Kraaken had no further need to bother her now.

She built a campfire, moving slowly, like a sleepwalker. She was numb, almost beyond feeling, but she knew that the worst was yet to come. At some point, whether on her journey home or after her return to Talita, the pain would come.

I was happy enough before, she told herself as she sat before the fire, forcing herself to eat some bread and dried fruit. *I have Talita and the keras and the life I've always had. He wasn't a part of that, but still I was happy.*

Then she remembered when she met Connor on the boat that he had said he was content, and she realized painfully the difference between contentment and happiness. Hadn't she always, deep down inside, believed that Connor would return one day? Wasn't that the *real* reason she'd been content?

Darkness fell, closing in around the campfire. Overhead, the stars pierced the blackness. Was Connor up there somewhere, gliding far above her? Had he already begun to forget about her?

Then she wondered if she would ever be able to work with the keras again, and a fresh wave of pain engulfed her. She knew she would never see a kera again without being reminded of the kraa—and of a man who soared the heavens with them.

She had fallen into a sort of trance, sitting there before the fire, when she suddenly heard a familiar rustling sound. When she opened her eyes and looked up, she saw that the moon had risen and was directly overhead. And in its silvery, ghostly light, she saw Connor and the kraa.

The great bird was perched on a nearby branch, its emerald eyes dark in the color-draining moonlight, its head tilted slightly as it stared at her. And Connor stood near it, perhaps twenty feet from her, motionless but staring at her as well.

"Connor!" she cried, getting quickly to her feet, and a hope that she'd thought gone surged anew. He'd come back, after all! He'd chosen her!

But she had taken only a few steps toward him before hope drained away into a chilled anger. It was Connor, but it wasn't Connor. His face was devoid of expression, and it was as still as his body. And there was an insubstantial quality to him, a blurring of that familiar form.

Rage poured through her as she shifted her gaze to the kraa. "Go away! Leave me alone! You've won. He belongs to you now."

For one long moment, Jillian and the bird faced each other, filling the still night with a tension that seemed to quiver in the cool air. Her hand slid down to touch the small knife she still carried with her. Such was her anger that she gave no thought to the sharp talons and the vicious beak. She took a step forward.

The bird issued a single shriek that in its echoes rang mockingly in her ears—and then it was gone, lifting off quickly into the darkness. She stared after it, then slowly shifted her gaze to the spot where Connor had stood. Still, that foolish, doomed hope remained, and even when she saw that she was now alone in the clearing, she continued to stare at the spot where she'd seen him.

Moments later, she heard the faint cries of the kraa—many of them somewhere overhead among the stars. She withdrew the knife from her pocket and thrust the blade upward. Moonlight glinted off it as she brandished it.

"If you come back, I will kill you!" she cried as tears streamed down her cheeks once again.

Then finally, she stumbled back to the campfire and sank into the welcome oblivion of sleep.

Each step down from the mountains carried Jillian farther from Connor and deeper into an abyss. The kraa did not visit her again, and she took some small satisfaction in that. When she reached the village, she felt drained of all emotion.

Jillian remained in the village for five days, waiting for another nomadic tribe willing to provide transport for her across the desert. The villagers told her it was likely that another tribe would be visiting soon, but she hoped that it wouldn't be too soon, because she couldn't yet quell the last tiny hope that Connor would appear.

She saw no sign of the kraa and didn't hear their shrill cries at night, either. Now that she was out of the land of the sorcerers, they had apparently forgotten about her. In that primeval land, she had probably become nothing more than a minor memory rapidly dwindling away to nothingness. How did one measure time when one was unaffected by its passage?

The nomads came and arrangements were made for her to go with them. When the time came for her to leave, Jillian climbed one last time to the top of the hill behind the cottage. The sky was a brilliant blue, and as she stared at the distant peaks, she saw several specks circling and gliding above the home of the Kraaken.

She lowered her gaze to the path that led into the woods, then started toward the edge of the hill. But she stopped before she could begin her descent. She could not go back to that mossy spot on the stream's bank any more than she would ever be able to visit the place like it at Talita. To do so would be torture beyond endurance.

A short time later, she was once again mounted on a camel, riding in the midst of the nomads as they left behind the green hills and set out into the desert.

This time, Jillian seemed almost impervious to the heat of the desert and the glaring sun. The nomads were kind, but since they shared no common language, she was left to her thoughts, and those thoughts slowly veered from past and present to the future.

Jillian realized that one issue had remained unresolved: those attempts on their lives. If Jenner was behind it, would he continue to try? Or had it really been only Connor he had sought to kill? The tale told to her by Edamo suggested that the brotherhood on the island could no longer possess any magic, if indeed they ever had. But that didn't necessarily mean that she was safe. Her unknown enemies could still come after her with hired assassins.

And what should she do about the brotherhood when she returned to Lesai? Anger burned in her once more. She would destroy them! They were fakes—frauds who'd lured Connor and countless other young boys into their clutches with false promises of magic and immortality.

Already, by refusing to sell them keras, she had unwittingly taken from them any opportunity to regain their powers; now she would complete their humiliation by exposing them and forcing her uncle to drive them from their island.

As she rode on through the desert heat, Jillian's

thoughts remained focused on their treachery. How dare they lie like that? How must those boys feel when they discovered that they'd been tricked? Or had they become so thoroughly under the sway of the brotherhood by then that they'd simply accepted it?

And those thoughts led her to an answer. Now she knew why Jenner had tried to have Connor killed. In a few months, Connor would have been admitted to the Inner Circle, and the pretense of sorcery could no longer be maintained. Connor would never have accepted the lies, let alone have agreed to their continuation. Connor had simply become too grave a threat to be allowed to live.

Her anger boiled up again. Jenner would pay now by losing everything. And she knew he could not run to the Whitebeards. They'd never accept the likes of him.

The travelers reached a fazara early the following evening. The nomads had already explained to Jillian through the villagers that, from this point on, she would be accompanied only by two youths, who would see her safely to the garrison at Shereva while the rest of the tribe turned south.

That night, for the first time since leaving the land of the Kraaken, Jillian heard the cries of the kraa. She awoke from a deep, dreamless sleep to the sounds, which were distant but clear in the cool night. She sat up and scanned the starry heavens, but saw nothing, and after a time their cries ended. Was Connor's spirit with them? And if it was, did he know she was down here?

* * *

The desert was one of their favorite haunts. At night, as the burning sands gave up heat, the air was turbulent, providing a challenge to their soaring and dipping and gliding.

Connor was with them, his pain temporarily held in abeyance as he reveled in the freedom. And as always, there were the whispers in his mind, the murmurings of the kraa, who communicated with their chosen companions not in words but in soft brushes of mind against mind.

They whispered of an eternity of nights, of ever more distant places, of times when he could join them not just for the hours of darkness, but beneath the sun as well—soaring to distant lands, places Connor didn't yet know about. And in time, he would be able to pick up the thoughts of people in those lands and add still more to his knowledge.

But then, even as he listened to the mute voices of the kraa, Connor felt a tug, a drawing away. Beneath him was a fazara, its campfires twinkling in the darkness of the desert floor. Jillian. She was down there. His weightless self began to drift lower, yielding to temptation, ignoring the ever more insistent cries of his companions.

The cries of the kraa died away slowly and Jillian drifted down into sleep once again, seeking that welcome respite from her pain. But then she began to dream.

She didn't see Connor, but he was there. She

was floating in the blackest of abysses, but he was with her. His body was entwined with hers, solid and hard and yet somehow ethereal, light as the touch of a feather. Lips brushed against hers; fingers traced the gentle curves of her body. Her nipples grew taut from the erotic torment of a tongue. Ghostly fingers probed, seeking her warm, moist feminine core.

She moaned and the sound echoed, then trailed away into the abyss. He called her name softly, and that sound whispered along the corridors of her mind.

When she reached for him and tried to draw him closer, to fill herself with him, he became insubstantial: there but not there. She protested and arched her body, seeking contact with solid flesh. But even as she did so, she could feel him withdrawing, pulling away, vanishing into the all-encompassing darkness.

"No!" Her own cry woke her. No one was there. She strained to hear the sounds of the night, and for one brief moment thought she heard again the distant cries of the kraa. But she wasn't sure, and the tears began to roll down her cheeks, continuing their silent glide as she fell again into a dreamless sleep.

Jillian awoke to a bright day and the cacophony of the nomads' camp. A smiling woman brought her a cup of strong tea and she sat there sipping it and thinking about her dream.

Was it a dream or something more? She was sure she'd awakened to hear the kraa. Had they pursued her even into the desert to torment her?

Was Connor with them? Would he permit such a thing? It had seemed to her that he controlled the kraa who'd accompanied him that time, but perhaps he hadn't.

If the kraa had brought her the dream, surely the birds would cease at some point. They'd grow tired of their cruel game and forget about her. But even as she thought about the dreams, a part of her wondered if she really wanted them to vanish. The dreams were all she had left of Connor—a final, tenuous link.

Reluctantly, she got up and went to share the bathing pool with the other women and the young children. Not even their laughter and happy chatter could drive out the pain, though she managed to smile in return. Her body felt . . . different—the way it had after she and Connor had first made love. She had a heightened awareness, a sense of belonging to someone other than herself. But the feeling faded as she bathed in the pool.

After sharing a meal with the nomads, she mounted her camel and set off with the two young men who were leading her back to Shereva. They talked and laughed between themselves, leaving her to her thoughts.

She began to wonder if she would ever again feel at home in her other life. It all seemed so far in the past now, as though she'd traveled through time itself—or perhaps as though she'd stepped out of time. Was that what Connor felt? Or would time simply cease to have any meaning for him?

After the long day's trek across the sands, they

camped that night in the dunes. After her guides had fallen asleep, Jillian sat staring up at the night sky, a blanket wrapped around her to ward off the chill. But the kraa did not appear, either that night or the one that followed. Neither did the dream of Connor.

The next day was her last in the desert; by nightfall, they would reach the low hills that separated the desert from the Masani outpost of Shereva. The return trip had been much shorter than her earlier journey because there had been no sandstorms to contend with.

As she lapsed into a sort of daze under the hot sun, lulled by the rhythms of the camel's tireless loping, Jillian found herself regretting that the journey was at an end, however uncomfortable it had been. Although she would still have a long way to go before she was home at Talita, by day's end, she would be back among people whose language and customs she understood.

By late afternoon, they could see the dark hills ahead that marked the boundary of the desert. Remembering her other journey across the sands, when she and Connor had strained their eyes to catch a glimpse of the desert's end, she now found herself fighting a nearly overwhelming urge to turn around and go back across the desert to find Connor again.

She shouldn't have given up so easily. She should have fought the Kraaken for him. But what did she have to offer that could compare to their plans for him? Nothing more than love and a lifetime spent at her beloved Talita. It wasn't enough. She knew that—and so, apparently, did he.

As the sun sank toward the distant horizon behind them, Jillian signaled to her companions that she wished to stop for a time. They agreed, though it was clear that they were puzzled. She turned around in her saddle and tried, through a variety of gestures, to make them understand that she wanted, one last time, to see the sun set on the desert. She wasn't sure they understood, though. After a lifetime spent wandering in this magical place, they were not as awed by it as she was.

She drew in a ragged breath as the sun dropped from view in a final, brilliant burst of color, setting fire to the sands and turning the heavens into a palette of reds and golds and green and purple.

"Good-bye, Connor," she whispered as the tears streaked down her cheeks. "Be happy." Even now, in the pain of her loss, she took some comfort in the knowledge that he *would* be happy, and not just content.

When the colors drained away, leaving only lengthening shadows, Jillian urged her camel forward and rode out of the desert, trailed by her two companions, who continued to give each other puzzled looks and shrugs.

The land into which they rode was largely uninhabited, a barren borderland between the fertile hills and plains of the Masani lands and the desert of the nomads. It was nearly dusk when they passed through a small, poor village. Few people were about, and those who were peered at them indifferently from gaunt faces.

They rode on through the hills into a steadily encroaching night. Jillian assumed that they would camp somewhere, rather than try to reach Shereva this night, since that would mean at least three or four more hours of riding, but she was still surprised when her companions turned off the narrow road onto a barely discernible path that led upward into dark hills.

She was about to try to question them when they came to a halt and she was able to make out a campsite that bore traces of much use. Apparently, this was a regular stopping place for nomads who made the journey to Shereva. There was even a small stream nearby, making it a perfect stopover.

After the camels had been fed and the three travelers had eaten as well, Jillian sat apart from the youths, once again staring up at the heavens. But her mind was resolutely turned to the future. She longed for Talita, yet feared that it would no longer welcome her. Over the years, Connor had become no more than a distant memory, a soft touch against her mind, tinged with bitterness and sadness. But now, when she saw all those familiar places, she would see him as well—not as the boy she had remembered so wistfully, but as the man whose love she had known.

Her companions had stopped talking and settled down for the night, and Jillian prepared to do likewise. Not far away in the darkness, one of the camels made a snorting, chuffing sound. She turned toward it, wondering what was disturbing it and hearing the other camels stir as well.

Was there an animal nearby—something that posed a danger to them? She glanced back at her companions, wondering if she should awaken them. And as she turned, she saw several shadows suddenly detach themselves from the darkness!

For a brief instant, the two dark-clad men were silhouetted sharply against the light of the campfire. Jillian screamed, but her warning came too late. She caught the flash of knives arcing toward the bodies of the sleeping youths, and then she scrambled to her feet and began to run.

She ran as fast as she could, down the path toward the road. But she was no match for them. Before she had even reached the road, one of the intruders caught her from behind and threw her to the ground.

The wind was knocked out of her and she barely managed to hang on to consciousness as they twisted her arms painfully behind her and tied them roughly. Then one of them lifted her up and slung her across his shoulders and began to talk excitedly to his companion—in the Masani tongue.

"We've got her!" he exulted.

"But where is he? They wanted them both. Will they pay us for just her?"

Jillian didn't hear the other one's muffled reply. She was having trouble understanding their heavily accented speech—an accent she recognized as being that of the rural people she and her companions had met on their way to the desert.

Who was paying for her? She knew they must have expected to get Connor as well. Was it Jenner? Who else could it be? Did these men intend to kill her—or would they turn her over to some accomplice of the high priest?

She was dumped unceremoniously across a saddle as the two men argued about the camels. One said they should take them, but the other said they were worthless, and if they were caught with them, they risked the wrath of the nomads. In the end, the second man prevailed and they rode back to the road, where they turned toward Shereva.

Jillian thought fast. She had one advantage at the moment, and that was the fact that they probably didn't know she could speak their tongue. Neither would they be expecting any resistance from a woman; they hadn't even bothered to search her for a weapon and she still had her knife. If she remained docile, perhaps they would untie her.

She was glad they appeared to be heading toward Shereva because there, at the garrison, lay the only help she could expect. Did they intend to sneak her into the town under cover of darkness and then hide her somewhere until they made contact with whoever had hired them? She hoped that was their plan, because it might afford her the opportunity to escape.

She was certain that Jenner must be behind this. Having failed to kill Connor and Jillian before they had crossed the desert, he had concocted another plan to capture them on their return trip. No doubt these two men were from that village she and the two nomads had passed through, and they'd been paid to keep an eye out for their return.

She thought about her erstwhile companions, young men with long lives ahead of them—lives that had been brutally snuffed out because of the Kraaken priest. Jenner would pay for their deaths and for the other deaths he'd caused. If she'd felt that her life had no purpose, she knew she'd found one now.

The two men slowed their horses. Given the darkness and her face-down position across the saddle, Jillian could see little, but she knew they were still on the road to Shereva. The men had by now slowed to a walk, and this time, she couldn't understand their words. But a moment later, they turned on to what looked to her like little more than a narrow track, and her hopes of getting to Shereva fell.

She had no idea how long they rode over the hills and down into narrow ravines, but she saw no signs of any dwellings. Then they turned again, this time onto another path that led steeply upward. And a few minutes later, they came to a stop.

She was lifted roughly from the saddle and carried along in the darkness, fearing even more that they'd merely been seeking some isolated place in which to kill her. But if killing her was their intention, surely they could have done that back at the campsite. She clung desperately to that thought.

Slung over the shoulder of the one man, she

didn't see the tiny cottage until they were inside
its dank confines. The man dropped her onto
a dirt floor, not hard enough to do her any
harm, but not exactly with gentleness, either.
She started to struggle into a sitting position,
but it was impossible with her hands tied behind
her back. Besides, she reminded herself that she
should remain passive and bide her time.

So she lay on the cold, dirt floor and watched
as they jabbered away and built a fire in the
crude stone fireplace. She caught only a few
words, but it was enough to make her decide
that they intended to leave her here while they
went to meet whoever had hired them. Would
they both go, or would one of them stay here to
guard her?

Her question wasn't answered for some time,
as they ignored her and brought out a bottle
of wine, talking now about what they would
do with the money that had been promised to
them. Listening to them, Jillian found it hard to
hate them. She'd seen the poverty in that village
and she knew that kidnapping her was bound to
bring them more money than they could ever
have hoped to gain in a lifetime of hard work.
That didn't make their crime acceptable, but it
did make it understandable. She only wished that
they'd simply captured the nomad youths as well,
instead of killing them.

Frightened and angry as she was, Jillian still
drifted off into a light doze. She realized that
she'd slept only when one of the men knelt beside
her and began to tug at the ropes that bound her

wrists. At first, when she saw the knife in his hand, she thought he was going to kill her, and she was prepared to offer him double whatever price had been offered for her capture. But then she realized that he was cutting her bonds.

She sat up the moment she was freed, rubbing her wrists and waiting to see what would happen next. But nothing at all happened. They simply left the cottage, slamming the door behind them. She was still staring in disbelief when she heard a loud clunk outside that rattled the wooden door; then she realized that they must have barred it from the outside.

For a moment, she heard voices and the sound of horses' hooves, and then she was left alone in the quiet night. She struggled to her feet and stared around the fire-lit cottage. There were no windows and only the one door. She walked over to it and pushed at it as hard as she could. It budged only a few inches, then held.

How long would they be gone? They must be going into Shereva, so she had to assume it could be a while. That gave her some time—but how was she going to get out of here?

Connor felt the excitement the moment he entered the tower. The very air seemed almost to quiver with it. The base of the tower was one large round room, open clear to the top. It was built of a mellow golden stone, with curved stone steps carved into the walls in a spiral that ended at the open balcony many feet above.

The only furnishings were comfortable, padded

benches lining the curved walls and several large braziers that provided heat when needed. There were no tapestries, no golden adornments, no trappings of power, even though surely there could not be a place in the world that held more power than the ancient stronghold of the Kraaken.

The Whitebeards were all gathered, waiting for him with a barely concealed excitement. Connor had to suppress a smile when he saw them, forgetting at the moment that he couldn't really conceal anything from them.

"We have reason to be excited," said Edamo, proving that he could carry on a conversation and still manage to eavesdrop on Connor's thoughts. "After all, we are about to attempt something we've never done before."

And realizing that before for them meant a thousand years, Connor smiled. Whatever they were about to do was indeed reason to be excited.

Connor took his place in the very center of the circular room and the Whitebeards moved into their places, surrounding him. Even they didn't know if what they were attempting could actually be done, though they were inclined to think it could. Connor hoped they were right.

They began their chant, their voices rising and falling in a lilting manner that was almost hypnotic. After a time, Connor's mind began to drift. He wasn't expected to take part in the chanting; rather, he was the object of their chants.

He knew he should be focusing on what lay

ahead, but an image of Jillian crept into his mind and refused to go away. An inner smile warmed him. He'd found her in the desert last night and been drawn to her presence like a moth to a flame. He'd intended only to swoop down and look at her, but when he saw her, he forgot completely that he was without body, no more than a spirit.

Even so, she'd known he was there. She'd felt his touch and arched to his lips and tongue and fingers that weren't really there, opening to him, welcoming him with her moist warmth. And he'd felt her as well, though perhaps it was only a tactile memory of her.

He sensed himself growing hard, hot with desire even now, as the blood coursed through him, carrying the memory, carrying a pounding need, driving—

"Brother Averyl!"

Connor blinked away the images with difficulty as he met Edamo's eyes. The old man shook his head.

"You must focus on your goal, Brother Averyl: the reason we are here. The Lady Jillian plays no part in this."

Connor apologized, just as he had after his slip last night, when he'd let himself be drawn by her. He *was* sincerely sorry for upsetting Edamo and the other Whitebeards, even though he wasn't sorry about his thoughts. It was, he supposed, a good thing that the others were so patient with him and his imperfections.

Casting Jillian from his mind, he concentrated

instead on his home: not the small cottage in which he'd lived, but a spot along the shore of the island where he often sat and read. It was no coincidence that the spot also afforded a distant view of the hills beyond which lay Talita.

Talita. His mind began to slip again. Images of the aeries came into his mind—and of a boy and girl climbing up the rocky cliffs. Then he felt himself being jerked back to the moment, but whether by his own subconscious prodding or through some intervention on Edamo's part, he didn't know.

The chanting continued. Voices wove words in the air, as they rose and fell in a steadily increasing rhythm. He let the sounds take him this time, all thoughts of Jillian now buried deep in his memory.

Chapter Fourteen

It took Jillian what seemed to be forever to drag and push the heavy table over to the door of the cottage. She had examined the door very carefully and knew it wasn't that sturdy, although, of course, she had no idea just how strong the bar was that held it from the outside.

The narrow end of the table was only slightly smaller than the width of the door, which meant it should be perfect to use as a sort of battering ram. She pushed it up against the door, then sat down on the dirty, smelly cot for a moment to rest.

She wished she knew how much time had passed since her captors had left—and how much time she had remaining before their return. If they were meeting those who'd hired them in Shereva, she should still have several hours. But she was uneasily aware of the possibility that they could return at any moment.

She'd also given little thought to what she would do if she succeeded in breaking down the door and escaping. She would be on foot in a very isolated area, probably more than a day's walk from Shereva even if she kept to the road, which would be risky. But doing nothing was unacceptable to her, alien to her nature.

She got up and walked over to the table, stopping at the end away from the door. The table was certainly heavy enough to break down the door—if she had the strength to push it that hard. She began to push at it. The door obligingly moved, but no more than a few inches before the bar stopped it.

After pushing again and again as hard as she could, she backed up and ran at the table, her arms braced to push it again. The old wood in the door groaned in protest, but continued to hold. Before long, *she* was the one who was groaning in protest at the pain of abused muscles.

Jillian stopped and put her brain to work instead of her muscles, which were clearly not up to the task at hand. It occurred to her that the table might be the same height as the bar, and therefore she was pushing not only at the door, but at the bar itself. She dragged the table back a few inches and pushed lightly at the door, trying to determine just where the bar was. Her suspicions were confirmed. What she needed was something lower—something that might break through the door below the bar.

There were several chairs in the cottage, but

they weren't particularly sturdy. That left the narrow cot, which upon examination appeared to be just as sturdy as the table. So she dragged the table out of the way and then tore the foul-smelling mattress off the cot.

After forcing herself to rest for a few moments, she dragged the cot over to the door. Its heavy oak frame was definitely lower than the table, and it touched the door in a spot where she could already see evidence of some splintering. Encouraged by that weakness, she backed off and ran at the cot, shoving it as hard as she could against the door.

After many tries, she was rewarded by the shrieking sound of splintering wood. The door was composed of four panels. One had given way completely and another was badly cracked.

She backed up and ran at it again, slowed down now by her weariness. But another panel gave way. Now there was a gaping hole in the lower part of the door, but was it wide enough for her to crawl through?

It was—just barely. She gathered up her cloak and pushed it out through the hole, then slithered through sideways herself. She was free!

But she knew she didn't dare stop to savor her victory. The first tentative light of dawn was softening the darkness. She had to get away from this place quickly. So, wrapping herself in her cloak to ward off the early morning chill, she hurried down the narrow track that led back to the main road.

Once she reached the road, she turned toward

Shereva. But she soon realized that she was very exposed and that leaving the road would offer her no protection, either. There were brief stretches of woods, but most of the land here was open.

She stayed on the road, praying that someone other than her captors would find her. She still had the small bag of gold coins that she'd kept with her—and she had her knife. Tired and hungry and aching in places where she'd never ached before, Jillian continued to walk toward Shereva. And with every step she took, she became angrier and angrier at Jenner and his unholy brotherhood.

The sun was well above the horizon when she had her first encounter with a possible source of rescue. She'd been turning around regularly to see if anyone might be coming up behind her, and as she rounded a bend in the road, she suddenly caught a glimpse of movement through the trees. Grateful that those who approached were coming upon her in a spot that afforded her some protection, she scrambled off the road and hid herself behind the trees and shrubs as she watched the cart.

She was reasonably certain it couldn't be her captors, since they should be coming from the other direction. But as the travelers drew closer, she could see that they looked much the same: roughly dressed, gaunt-looking men driving an old, sagging cart. The two horses that pulled the cart looked as worn out as the cart itself.

Jillian gnawed at her lower lip, thinking. No doubt these men were from the same village as the ones who'd captured her—and just as poor. They would certainly be tempted by her gold, but what was to prevent them from simply taking it and leaving her there—or killing her? There were two of them, and she certainly couldn't hope to subdue them both with her small knife.

So she lay there motionlessly and let them pass by; then she rose and trudged on. By now, she was very hungry and wished that she'd had the presence of mind to have taken the loaf of bread her captors had left her.

She was surprised at the lack of traffic on the road. The sun was high in the sky before she saw riders approaching from Shereva. This time, unfortunately, there was no place to hide. On both sides of the road, broad, open plains stretched away for more than a mile.

She scanned the area desperately seeking anything that would offer a place of concealment. It was possible that the men hadn't seen her yet. She'd only glimpsed them briefly as they descended into a dip in the road. If she could be hidden before they came up the other side. . . .

The field to her left wasn't totally flat and some of the weeds were quite tall. She took off at a run and headed toward a low spot in the field. If she flung herself to the ground and covered herself with her cloak, they might not spot her.

Just as she reached the low spot, she thought she heard a shout, but she flung herself onto the ground and threw the cloak over her, praying that she was wrong. With her heart pounding in her chest and her breathing loud and ragged in her ears, she lay there. Her hand went to her small knife. She waited.

"Hello there! Come out where we can see you!"

The command was issued in the Masani tongue, but it took her a few seconds to realize that it didn't sound like the voices of either of her captors. That heavy accent was missing. Still, she ignored the command, hoping the riders didn't really know where she was and would lose interest before finding her.

But they persisted, and each time she heard the voice, it was closer. She had no doubt now that they would soon find her. But were they friend or foe?

She drew out the knife, knowing it was probably useless, but hoping that the riders might be unarmed and unwilling to risk trying to take her.

"There!" one voice shouted. "Stand up! We see you now!"

Since she had no doubt that he spoke the truth, Jillian got to her feet, the knife clutched in her hand. And the moment she saw the riders, she nearly fell over again in relief. When she'd seen them before, she hadn't gotten a good enough look at them to see that they were wearing uniforms: the uniforms of the Masani army.

The two men brought their horses to a halt some ten feet from her. She saw their gazes go to the knife she still held, so she put it away quickly. The men stared at her. One of them looked vaguely familiar and it seemed likely that he was thinking the same of her, because his frown deepened.

"I'm Lady Jillian from Lesai," she prompted him, though she didn't need to look at herself to know just how absurd that sounded.

Both men dismounted, and now both of them were wearing frowns. Then one of them laughed. "If you're a lady *anything*, I'm His Majesty, the King."

But the other one—the one who looked familiar—was still staring hard at her. "No, she speaks the truth, Tolva. I saw her when she was at the garrison. She was with that Kraaken priest. They were crossing the desert."

Jillian nodded gratefully. "He . . . stayed behind." Then she explained about the attack and the deaths of her nomad companions and her escape from the cottage.

"Who were these men?" the soldier asked her.

"I don't know, but I think they came from that village near the edge of the desert. They attacked not long after we had passed through there."

Both men nodded grimly. "A bad lot they are. It wouldn't have taken much gold to persuade them to do something like this. But who paid them?"

"I don't know for certain, but I have my ideas," Jillian said.

The soldier who'd recognized her helped her into the saddle in front of him and they set out to the camp where the nomads had been killed. Along the way, both men plied her with questions and she told them an abbreviated version of the truth, stating that she had enemies in Lesai who she suspected were behind this. The other soldier turned to her with a frown.

"Now that you mention it, milady, there were two men from Lesai staying at the inn just the other day. Noblemen, I thought. A bit arrogant, if you know what I mean—and well dressed, too."

Two Kraaken brothers, Jillian thought, but didn't say. None of the priests were of the nobility, but they could easily make one believe they were. And they weren't likely to be wearing Kraaken robes while they were on such a mission.

"Do you know if they're still there?" she asked, hoping they could be caught. That way she'd have her proof that the brotherhood was behind all this.

"I don't know, but you can be sure we'll find out as soon as we get back to Shereva."

They reached the camp, which the soldiers knew well as a site regularly used by the nomads who traveled to Shereva. Jillian exclaimed in surprise. The bodies were gone, and so too were the camels.

"Not surprising," the soldier told her as he examined the ground. "Word probably spread in the village about what those two were up to, and some others came out here to take what they could."

"But the bodies?" she asked. "What would they have done with them?"

The man looked around. "They probably stripped them and buried them somewhere."

They found the shallow graves a few minutes later. Some attempt had been made to conceal them, but it was obvious the nomads had been buried in haste. The soldiers piled up some stones to mark the graves and said that they would get word to the tribes so the families could come to claim the youths' bodies.

Jillian stared silently at the graves, thinking about the lives lost because of Jenner's evil. She *had* to find a way to have him punished for this. She found herself almost regretting her uncle's penchant for meting out justice fairly. She *knew* Jenner was behind this, but if she couldn't *prove* it, he would go unpunished.

"They probably took the camels to the village," the soldier said as they mounted again. "By now, they've probably been slaughtered for their meat, because the villagers know the nomads could identify them. Did you have any valuables on them, milady?"

"Some gold," Jillian told him. "But if you find that, just see that it's distributed fairly."

He nodded. "They're about as poor as can be, but they're not all bad. Chances are that your gold has already been distributed among them. The only ones we'll be after are the ones who killed the nomads."

Jillian dozed off on the long ride to Shereva, waking only when she and her escorts came in sight of the garrison. She was still far from home, but the bustling town and the great stone garrison ahead signaled her return to a familiar world. And as they rode into the garrison, her thoughts turned once again to how she could see to it that Jenner was punished.

Saranne Dawson

*   *   *

Connor awoke slowly, sluggishly, feeling as though he'd been drugged. Turbulent dreams swirled about in his befogged brain: dreams of flying, dreams of a circle of white-bearded old men in Kraaken robes, dreams of singsong chanting, dreams of himself dissolving, disintegrating.

He shook his head to clear away the cobwebs and his surroundings came slowly into focus, hazy at first and then gradually clearing. The familiarity of the place was soothing to him, and yet it troubled him as well, for reasons he only very slowly understood.

"Jillian," he whispered. She had been part of the dream, too. His gaze went to the land across the water, where a succession of green hills rose toward dark mountains—toward Talita. "Jillian," he said again, his voice strange in his own ears.

He looked around him, frowning. It was strange that he'd come here without a book or his journal in which he wrote his poetry. This was his special place, the place where he studied and thought and struggled to put words onto paper. He always brought something with him when he came here.

The dreams nagged at him, circling in his mind. Images appeared and then dissolved only to reappear a moment later. A sea voyage, a desert, great birds similar to keras but far more majestic, a green, mossy bower like his and Jillian's favorite place at Talita, bodies entwined, naked skin dappled by sunlight and shadow. *Their* bodies: Jillian's and his.

He sat up quickly, his eyes wide, but now staring unseeing at the distant hills. It wasn't a dream! All of it had actually happened! He whispered her name for a third time and sank back to let the memories take him: memories of their lovemaking, memories of other times together when they'd picked up the threads of the past and had woven them into something new and even more wonderful.

But even as he began to lose himself in these memories, something else—something dark—was whispering in his mind. With a great effort of will, he set aside thoughts of Jillian and let the rest of it come flooding back, until he understood why he was here and what he must do.

He got to his feet. The sun was setting. Already, the dark hills of Talita were nearly invisible. He started back, staying in the woods instead of walking along the shore, where he might be seen from one of the towers. The spot he'd chosen long ago was very isolated, far from the compound that hugged one corner of the island.

By the time he saw the Great Tower through the trees, it was full dark. He circled the cluster of cottages carefully, keeping himself hidden in the woods as he sought the cottage of his mentor, Seka. He'd told the Whitebeards that he could trust Seka, and now he hoped he was right.

A lamp burned in the window of Seka's cottage and Connor crept up to it. The man he'd grown to love as a father sat in his comfortable chair, his gray head bent as he read a book he'd probably read many times before. Seka had told Connor that one read the first time for the flavor, then again and again for the essence.

Seka's head lifted suddenly, then began to turn slowly toward the window. Connor nearly withdrew, but stayed where he was. His mentor rose from his chair.

"Brother Averyl! You've returned!"

In the older man's joy, Connor let go of his doubts and walked to the cottage door, reaching it just as Seka flung it open and quickly drew him inside. Then he stepped out and scanned the area before retreating back inside and closing the door. He cupped both hands around Connor's shoulders. There were tears in his eyes.

"I thought I'd never see you again in this world," Seka said, his dark eyes shining. Then his gaze went to the door. "Do the others know that you've returned?"

Connor shook his head and a long look passed between them. "Did you know that Jenner was plotting to have me killed?"

Seka recoiled as though he'd been struck, then raised a hand and let it fall slowly in a gesture of regret. "I didn't know, but I feared. I tried to warn you, but it was all I could do in the absence of any proof."

"Why, Seka? Why does Jenner fear me so much that he would have me killed?"

Seka gestured Connor to a chair, then poured him a glass of the Kraaken's golden wine and refilled his own glass as well before taking a seat. It seemed to Connor that the lines were etched more deeply into the old man's face than before, as though he'd aged years in just weeks.

"Tell me first what happened," Seka said, then leaned forward with unconcealed interest. "Did you find the birds?"

"Yes, and much more."

For the next hour, Connor spoke, telling him everything. Seka stopped him a few times with questions, but for the most part let him tell it in his own fashion. And by the time he had finished, Seka was nodding.

"So I was right. At least there is pleasure in that."

"Right about Jenner? Tell me what's going on, Seka."

His mentor waved a hand in dismissal. "Apparently, I was correct about Jenner and the others as well, but I was referring to the existence of the men you call the Whitebeards and of the kraa.

"As you know, I have always been fascinated by our origins—far more than the others. No one else has studied our most ancient books as much as I have.

"Over the years, small pieces of information came to me from them. Nothing was clear. Always, the writings were couched in subtleties. Many of them were the personal journals of long-dead brothers. But they all seemed to hint at the story you've just confirmed: that our true home was far away and that our powers were linked to those of the birds. How I envy you the pleasure of knowing the Whitebeards."

Seka paused, seeming to drift off into his thoughts for a long moment. Connor was eager to hear the rest of what he had to say and Seka must have finally realized that, because he suddenly focused on Connor again.

"We have lived a lie, Averyl. Of course, you must know that by now. If one is inclined to be charitable, one could say that it was a partial lie, but that makes it no less reprehensible.

"It worked well enough, though. The brotherhood always selected very bright young men who had no future because of their low birth. Men like us. Here they were fed and clothed well— better than most of them had ever been before. And they were encouraged to use their minds and given self-esteem. The result was that, by the time they entered the Inner Circle and learned the truth, they were willing to maintain the lie.

"I, like all the others, convinced myself that it didn't matter, that what we were doing was good, even if we had been lied to. But the fact that the lie existed was the reason I have studied our origins all these years. Even in the worst of lies, there is often a small kernel of truth, and that was what I sought.

"The Inner Circle *was* capable of producing some magic: small, meaningless things. But then, some months ago, it stopped. No matter how hard we tried, nothing happened."

"This happened when the last of the keras died?" Connor asked.

Seka nodded. "I made that connection immediately because I'd discovered veiled references to the kraa in the old writings, and by then, I'd learned from you about the mysterious origins of the keras. In fact, your connection to Talita and the keras was one of the reasons I'd chosen you to be my pupil.

"I told Jenner of my theory that our magic derived from the keras, but he rejected it— outwardly, at any rate. He blamed our failure to produce magic on distractions and simple laziness on the part of some of us.

"But I know now that he must have believed me, because when his spies told him of the sea captain's tale and of Lady Jillian's quest, he immediately decided to send you with her.

"I still do not know for certain what was in his mind, but what I believe is this. Jenner was facing several problems. First, there was the question of the birds. I'd always kept him apprised of my studies and he knew the direction of my thoughts. I think he very much feared that I might be right—that the men you call the Whitebeards did in fact exist, together with the kraa."

"But why should he have *feared* that?" Connor asked, confused.

"He feared it because he feared losing his own power. He has plans, Averyl—plans he's been working on for years. And I suspect that he knew those plans could and would be thwarted by any contact with the Whitebeards. But more of that later.

"The second problem Jenner faced was *you*. In only a few months, you would be eligible to enter the Inner Circle. As you know, a mentor can prevent that, by stating that the pupil is not yet ready. But try as he did, he couldn't get me to say that about you.

"Jenner believed, and in this I agreed with him, that you would never accept the lies. And then, of course, there was your past. Like the rest of us, you came from peasant stock. But *unlike* us, you were reared in a great house and treated like the son of a powerful lord. Your strong connections to the nobility could have easily become a threat. If another had tried to expose us, he would not have been believed. This I know because it has happened on a few occasions in the past. Always, such rebels have been cast out and tales have been circulated that they broke their vows and were therefore untrustworthy.

"But you might well have been believed—especially if the Lady Jillian took up your cause, as we feared she would. We knew she never forgave us for taking you from her.

"And of course, there were your own lingering doubts about committing yourself fully to the brotherhood. These doubts, too, would have made you more willing to leave and to expose us."

"But if you knew I still had doubts, then why were you willing to vouch for me to become a member of the Inner Circle?" Connor asked.

Seka smiled sadly. "Because I hoped that you would do what I'd never had the courage to do myself. It was long past time for a breath of honesty to blow through the brotherhood. We are not all bad, Averyl. We allow talented young men to pursue lives they could never have pursued otherwise. We don't need the magic to do that.

"But here is where Jenner's plans enter the picture. I have never been one of his confidants, so it took quite a while for me to learn about them, and when I *did* learn about them, it was only because a few of those around him began to have doubts.

"For years now, Jenner has been busy cultivating the Lesai priests. You know that. His stated reason was to ensure peace between us and to enlist their aid in finding suitable recruits. But he had a much darker purpose.

"The Lesai priests still hold great sway over the peasants, and Jenner's goal was to build up an army—an army he could call forth to conquer the Lesai nobility and seize their power for himself. Or for the brotherhood, as I'm sure he would say."

"But the army—the Lesai army, I mean?"

Seka waved a hand dismissively. "He has worked among them as well. Don't forget that they, too, draw upon the peasantry for all but the very top officers. Some elements in the army have been discontent for years, anyway. Warriors like to make war, and Lesai has been a peaceful place.

"From what I've been told, vast caches of weapons have been smuggled out of garrisons over the years and stockpiled in various churches belonging to trusted priests. These priests await only a word from Jenner, and the rebellion will begin."

Connor was appalled. This was worse than hearing the confirmation that the high priest had indeed intended to kill him.

"When will this happen?" he asked, choking down his anger.

"Soon, I fear—perhaps very soon if Jenner discovers that you've returned. Where is the Lady Jillian now?"

Connor was startled at the question, since his own thoughts had just turned to her safety. "She's on her way back here, but the trip will take weeks."

"So she is safe for now." Seka nodded, but he sounded less than certain.

Connor followed the direction of his thoughts. "Do you think that Jenner might still try to kill her?" he asked with mounting alarm.

"It's possible. If he knows that you've escaped, holding her captive might be the only way he could prevent you from exposing him."

Connor flung himself out of his chair and began to pace about the room. "I have to go back—to find her."

Seka shook his head. "If Jenner intended to capture her, he would already have done so. And I do not think he will kill her. If she were dead, it would only add to your rage. Alive, he can use her to control you."

Connor nodded, acknowledging the truth of that. Then he shot a glance at Seka. "I failed to tell you everything that . . . happened."

Seka smiled gently. "I am quite capable of hearing what isn't being said, as well as what is. I know you broke your vows, and I have to assume that the Whitebeards knew it as well. And yet they still accepted you."

"What can we do?" Connor asked. "I must save Jillian, and we have to prevent this rebellion."

Seka got up to pour some more wine. "We must put our heads together and try to come up with something. If only the kraa had accompanied you. . . ."

Chapter Fifteen

"They have been found, milady!" the garrison commander said.

Jillian cleared the remnants of sleep from her brain quickly. A maid had summoned her from sleep to announce that the garrison commander had important news for her.

"Who has been found?" she asked. "The two men who attacked the nomads and me?"

"They were caught several hours ago, and now we've captured the two Lesai who hired them. They were about to leave—rather hastily, in fact. They'd probably learned about your escape."

"Who are they?" she asked eagerly.

"They claim to be Lesai noblemen simply traveling for pleasure. But they won't give their names and they pretend not to understand us."

"Take me to them," Jillian said. "If they are who

they say they are, I will know them."

"Exactly my thoughts, milady." The commander nodded.

The two men were being detained in a small room in the garrison. When their gazes fell on Jillian, all traces of arrogance vanished from their faces. Jillian stared hard at them, then turned to the commander.

"They have lied to you. They are not Lesai nobility."

The commander nodded. "Very well. Since the men they hired have already confessed, they will all be put to death. If they were who they said, I would have been forced to send them back to the court, but since they're not. . . ." He shrugged, and signaled to a guard to take them away.

"No!" one of them cried, turning from the commander to Jillian. "Milady, we are Kraaken brothers! If our lives are spared, we can tell you important things!"

The other man began to shout at him in what Jillian now recognized as the Kraaken tongue. She couldn't understand the words, but it was obvious that he preferred death to the truth.

"Can you prove that you're Kraaken?" she demanded, turning back to the one who'd spoken first.

In response, the man tore open his shirt, exposing the gold chain and the familiar symbol of the brotherhood. Jillian stared at it, momentarily paralyzed by her memories of Connor. How distant he seemed now, more a dream than a reality. But the pain was real enough. It sliced through her, making her catch her breath sharply. The commander looked at her.

"I would like to hear what he has to say," she told him.

And the Kraaken had a great deal to say, even though it soon became obvious that he didn't know the whole story. But between his confessions and her own suspicions and knowledge, Jillian was able to piece what had happened together.

"So Jenner feared Connor and wanted him killed," she said when the Kraaken had finished. "But what about me? What threat am I to him?"

"We were told to kill you both," the man admitted. "And our instructions were that, if Brother Averyl somehow escaped, we should hold you."

Why? she wondered. The only thing that made sense was that Jenner intended to use her to bend Connor to his will and keep him from exposing the brotherhood's lies.

"There is more to this," she said, as much to herself as to the two priests.

Then she saw something flicker in the eyes of the man who hadn't spoken. She stared at him. "You know more, don't you?"

He was silent for a long moment, then shrugged. "I've heard things," he admitted finally.

Jillian turned to the garrison commander. "If he tells me all that he knows, can you spare their lives?"

"Since they are Kraaken, that decision must, I think, rest with the king."

"Very well. Then we must return to Trantor

as soon as possible. I will have my cousin and her husband speak to the king on their behalf—providing, of course, that they tell me all they know."

Jillian decided that the journey to Trantor should provide plenty of opportunity for the two priests to decide to cooperate. She knew, but they probably didn't, that the Masani king would never refuse a petition for clemency from the Lesai ambassador, and in any event, he would be reluctant to put to death a pair of priests.

They probably deserved to die, she thought, given the number of deaths they'd ordered. But she was willing to forgo the taste of revenge if they could incriminate Jenner still further. And she had a strong suspicion that something else was afoot here. She only hoped that whatever it was, it would not only destroy Jenner, but the whole brotherhood as well.

One week later, Jillian set sail for Lesai. The journey was a painful one, particularly because she was sailing on the same ship that had carried Connor and her to Trantor. The ship had been repaired and, with a new crew sent from Lesai, was the first one to be sailing for her home. Despite the urgency she felt to get home, she had very nearly waited to seek passage on another vessel.

Memories assaulted her at every turn. She could not walk upon the deck without thinking about her meeting there with Connor, and one question continued to torment her—as unanswerable questions so often do. Would it have been better never to have seen him again, never to have known the transformation of childhood friendship into adult love? She knew she did not want to give up those memories, and yet she knew as well that they would haunt her for the rest of her life.

But Jillian had another matter to occupy her thoughts during the long voyage. Thanks to the intervention of Trevor, her cousin's husband and the Lesai ambassador to the Masani court, clemency had been granted to the two Kraaken brothers in return for their story—a story that was responsible for her hurried departure for Lesai. That she was not the only one who accepted the story was attested to by Trevor himself in a letter she would carry to her uncle, the king. As Trevor had pointed out, Jillian's dislike of the Kraaken was well-known, and if the court should doubt her word, she would also have his affirmation.

As for the two priests, they were being detained in Trantor for the time being, to ensure that they had no opportunity to get word back to the island.

The story they told had been pieced together over time by them both from hints and overheard conversations. Although both were members of the Inner Circle, both also claimed that they were not part of the small cabal surrounding High Priest Jenner. Instead, both had been recruited for their deadly mission because they were considered to be resourceful and also because they spoke the Masani tongue.

What they told Jillian and Trevor was that Jenner had apparently decided long ago that true power for the brotherhood lay not in magic, but in the conquest of the Lesai. Toward that end, he had enlisted the aid of various sympathetic priests. They had covertly gathered an army of peasants who awaited only the word from the island in order to take up arms. Additionally, the Lesai army had been infiltrated, including even the Royal Guard—a fact Jillian could not dispute, since she'd seen evidence of that firsthand.

The captured priests told her that vast quantities of arms had been stolen over the years from various garrisons and stored up around the country, often in the churches of rebel priests. Unfortunately, they didn't know which priests had joined with Jenner or where these arms were stored.

Neither did they know exactly when the rebellion was to take place, but both agreed that it would likely be soon. In fact, their detention was likely to precipitate the war, since Jenner would soon guess that they'd been captured.

Horrified as she was by this tale, Jillian was not surprised; she even felt some satisfaction at having been right all along in her belief that the Kraaken were up to no good.

As she wandered the deck, she thought about the Whitebeards and their possible role in all this. Were they unaware of the Kraakens' plans? They'd professed to have had no contact with the renegade group on the island since the Kraaken established themselves there, but could she believe them? The farther she got from those ancient mountain forests, the less she was inclined to trust the Whitebeards. She couldn't deny that they possessed magic or that they might easily have used it to convince her of their goodness.

And, sadly, they might have convinced Connor as well. Jillian knew that Connor could not have had any advance knowledge of Jenner's scheme, and she knew, too, that the Whitebeards might well be keeping him in the dark even now.

And finally, in the middle of the night, when her most horrible thoughts tend to creep forth, Jillian wondered if Connor would really care. With his newfound powers and immortality, was he above such things—as removed from such considerations as he now was from her?

One starry night, Jillian was standing at the rail, her thoughts veering between Connor and the dangers that lay ahead. Every night since they'd set sail, she'd found herself listening for the cries of the kraa because she recalled what Edamo had said about the possibility that the birds might choose to come to the island. Lesai—and the island—were only a day away.

Still, when she heard the first faint cries, she didn't believe her ears. Then she listened more carefully, while at the same time searching the dark heavens for any shapes. She saw nothing, but as she stood there, her head raised into the night wind, the cries seemed to grow more distinct.

Then she had a sudden sense of a presence and turned sharply. Connor! For one brief moment—

hardly more than the blink of an eye—she saw him standing there only a few feet away. He wore the long gold robe of the order, and the gold chain and emblem of the Kraaken gleamed on his chest.

And then he was gone! She'd had only a moment to register his expression and couldn't be certain what she'd seen. Had he been smiling that gentle smile he'd given her so often?

The distinctive cries of the kraa faded away quickly, leaving her uncertain that she'd ever heard them in the first place. Perhaps the whole thing had merely been a waking dream—or perhaps the kraa hadn't yet given up tormenting her.

Late the next morning, Jillian was again on deck when the ship came at last into sight of Lesai—and the island. She'd spent a nearly sleepless night in torment, seeing in her dreams not the Connor she loved, but the gold-robed Brother Averyl, a Kraaken priest.

Even before setting sail, Jillian had decided that it would not be wise for her arrival in Lesai to be observed. The ship on which she sailed belonged to her disliked cousin, and the captain had assured her that the crew could be trusted to keep her presence secret.

So she retreated to her cabin long before they reached port and remained there, awaiting nightfall. The captain himself would inform her brother, Timor, of her arrival, and Timor would send his men to meet her at the ship—men she knew could be trusted, since they had been in the employ of her family all their lives.

Unfortunately, the porthole in her cabin looked out toward the island, and no matter how she tried to ignore it, Jillian found herself staring at it. Only the Great Tower was visible above the trees on the thickly forested island, and the sight of it reminded her of the tower in the mountains where she'd seen Connor for the last time.

When this is over, she thought, *I will personally see to it that that tower is destroyed.* The thought gave her more pleasure than it should have.

Timor's men came for her just before midnight, when the busy docks were deserted. Jillian had borrowed rough seamen's clothing, and Timor's men were similarly dressed, forsaking their usual livery with her family's crest boldly emblazoned on the chest. She knew them all, so she felt safe in their company as they made their way on foot through the quiet streets.

No sooner had they entered her brother's walled compound than Timor himself rushed forth to greet her, embracing her only briefly before ushering her out of the compound again.

"Where are we going?" she asked, noting that her brother, too, had eschewed his usual finery.

"To the palace. The others await us there. We'll use the servants' entrance, in case anyone is watching."

She stared at him in surprise. "Who would be watching and why are the others there?"

Timor drew closer to her, wrapping his arm around her waist as though they were lovers hurrying home to bed. His men followed after them at a discreet distance.

"There are stories, Jillian—rumors of rebellion. When the captain came to me and said you feared for your life and had important news, I had to assume you'd uncovered something as well—though I'm hard pressed to understand how, since you were far away. I know that it was Connor who accompanied you. Did he give you this information? And where is he?"

She sighed. "It's a long story, Timor, and one I would prefer to tell only once. Connor isn't with me because he made a choice, and he didn't choose me."

Timor's arm tightened around her. "You aren't to be blamed if the child in you blinded you to the man he's become. Even I find it nearly impossible to believe that Connor could betray us."

"How do you know that he *has* betrayed us?" she asked fearfully.

"He's a Kraaken," Timor said ominously, just as they reached the rear entrance to the palace grounds.

They were quickly waved through by the guards and then ushered along back corridors and up a narrow stairway, emerging into the private family quarters of the palace. A dozen or so men were gathered in the royal sitting room, all of them in nondescript clothes that belied their noble birth. Only the king was attired in his customary splendor, and as he rose from his seat to greet her, Jillian thought he looked very tired and sad.

"Jillian, my dear! Timor's news of your safe

return was the best news I've had in a long time. And he tells me that you have important news that might have a bearing on this rebellion."

Jillian embraced her uncle and nodded. "I do. Has it started, then? Am I too late? I came as quickly as I could."

"Some peasants have taken up arms in the northern provinces, and they're very well armed, too," the king told her. "There are rumors of more arming themselves elsewhere, though not at Talita, I should hasten to add."

Naturally, she thought—but didn't say. Unlike so many of the estates, the people at Talita were well treated and therefore loyal to her family.

Jillian told her story, ignoring the skeptical looks on the faces of some when she described the Whitebeards and their sorcery.

"According to the two Kraakens, some priests are involved, and they're providing storage for arms that have been stolen over the years from various garrisons. As I said, Jenner has apparently been planning for this day for a very long time."

She turned to the commander of the Lesai army. "I must say, Uncle Jobe, that you obviously haven't been very good at keeping track of your weapons." She'd never liked him and couldn't resist the dig.

"Now, Jillian," the king said soothingly. "Please try to control your well-known sharp tongue. If, as you say, these weapons have been stolen over a long period of time, it would have been impossible to keep track of them."

Since Jobe was the king's favorite brother,

Jillian knew better than to continue the argument. Instead, she reminded them that the priests and the others had probably been persuaded by tales of Kraaken magic, and once they saw that no such magic existed, they might change their minds.

"I think you should invade the island immediately," she stated firmly. "When the others find out that the brotherhood cannot even defend their own home, they will give up the rebellion."

"And you're quite certain that they have no magic?" the king asked.

"I'm as certain as I can be. That's why Jenner was so eager to get rid of Connor—Brother Averyl. He knew that Connor would never be willing to go along with such lies."

"I remember Connor," the king said musingly. "A fine lad. Your father had plans for him, you know—until he chose the brotherhood."

"He did?" Jillian asked, surprised.

The king nodded, glancing at his brother, the general. "He'd already spoken to Jobe about placement in the military school. He remarked to me at the time that, in view of your feelings for each other, he'd better get him set in a respectable career."

Jillian swallowed hard. "You mean he wouldn't have objected if we'd married?"

"No, I think he'd already accepted the inevitable. He said that the two of you reminded him of himself and your dear mother. They'd known each other from childhood, too, and neither of them ever looked at anyone else."

Jillian said nothing. A whole different life

opened before her—a life that would never be, thanks to the accursed Kraaken.

The general spoke up. "I have already proposed just what you suggested, Jillian, and that was before we knew they had no magic. We should attack the island immediately. I have troops ready to board ship the moment the order is given."

"I suppose we really have no choice," the king admitted. "But I am troubled by one part of your story, Jillian. You said that the powers of the Kraaken derive from their bonds with these birds—the kraa—and we've had reports of strange birds above the island."

"You have?" Jillian stared at him, recalling that night on the ship when she'd heard them and had that vision of Connor. She'd convinced herself that it was merely her imagination, but now she wondered.

"If kraa *have* come to the island, doesn't that mean that the Kraaken would now possess magic?" the king asked her.

Jillian thought about it. "They could, but I had the impression that it doesn't happen that quickly, that they have to bond with the men. How long have they been there?"

"They were first sighted only a few days ago," the general told her.

Then she might very well have heard them en route, she thought. But what about that vision of Connor? Had they created that—or could he be there?

No, that was impossible. He couldn't have gotten here before her. They'd only been tormenting her. Connor was safe in the mountains.

* * *

Jillian returned to Timor's house, tired but elated. The Lesai army would advance upon the island at first light, and before the day was over, Jenner would be exposed for the fraud he was and made to pay for his crimes.

But for all the deaths Jenner had caused, what she hated him for the most was the death of a life she might have had with Connor. Jillian was still stunned to think that her father would have accepted Connor into the family—a fact that was confirmed by Timor, to whom he'd also spoken about it.

Still, she knew that Connor would never have been happy as a warrior, and she knew he *was* happy now.

Jillian and Timor were back at the palace shortly after dawn—in time to see the ships carrying the Lesai army making their way through the gold-tinged waters of the harbor toward the island. The palace stood on the highest ground in the city and afforded a perfect view of the operation.

Several of those gathered there on the parapets were watching through telescopes, and at one point, someone cried out that a figure could be seen on the narrow balcony surrounding the top of the Great Tower.

"It must be Jenner," Timor remarked, peering through his scope.

"Doesn't look like him to me," another said. "He's not that tall."

Timor was silent as he continued to peer

through the glass. Then he drew in a sharp breath. "It looks like. . . ."

His sentence was left unfinished as a collective gasp of astonishment arose from the group— including Jillian. The island had vanished! One moment, it was clearly etched against the sky and water; the next, it had simply ceased to exist!

They stared at the empty sea and at each other. Jillian hugged herself miserably. She'd been wrong! The kraa had bequeathed their magic to Jenner and his group. What would happen now?

Others were asking the same question as they saw the ships stop, now deprived of a destination. Then, after a time, a small boat was lowered from one ship and it began to proceed toward the spot where the island had been. They all held their breaths, waiting. And then it, too, vanished.

"They must turn back!" the king said. "Jobe won't risk all those men." He laid a hand on Jillian's arm. "I must confess, my dear, that I doubted your tales of sorcery until now."

His gaze went to the sea and Jillian followed, barely able to suppress a shiver. The evidence of sorcery that she'd seen paled by comparison with this. An entire island had disappeared, and a boat as well!

She was thinking about what that meant when the king's voice drew her attention as he addressed Timor. "You started to say something, Timor— something about that figure on the tower, I believe?"

Timor frowned, then said nothing for a moment as they all watched the ships begin to turn and head back to port. Then, before responding to the king, Timor glanced at Jillian.

"I would swear that the man I saw looked like Connor," he said at last. "It's been many years, of course—but still. . . .".

His voice trailed off as he saw the look on Jillian's face. The king turned to her. "Could it be Connor?"

"No!" she stated emphatically. "Connor would never make war! He hates war. That's why he never wanted to enter the military."

Then, in a softer tone, she went on. "Besides, there is no way he could have gotten back here before me. I came on the first ship that sailed from Trantor in a week's time. It's impossible. Timor hasn't seen Connor since he was a child. He's mistaken."

But in her head, the questions buzzed like so many annoying flies. Could Connor have gotten here by means of sorcery? And why would she think that Timor wouldn't recognize him, when she herself had had no doubts?

"We have already seen evidence of very powerful magic, Jillian. Is it not possible that Connor utilized that magic to bring himself here—perhaps with the aid of the Whitebeards?"

Jillian turned away from the king's question, unable to acknowledge that he could be right. She so desperately wanted to believe that Connor was back in the mountains, sitting beneath a tree with one of his books, living the life he'd chosen over her. She couldn't bear thinking that he might be a pawn of the Whitebeards—or even that they had lied to her, given her a false impression of themselves while all the time they'd been plotting against her people.

The possibility that Connor could have acquiesced in all this did not enter her mind. In a world that was shifting beneath her feet, she clung resolutely to a belief in him and his goodness.

The others left the parapets and returned to the king's quarters to await the return of the military commander. Jillian went with them, unable to bear being alone with her thoughts.

The general returned. He and a number of his men had seen the tall man in Kraaken robes on the tower just before the island vanished. He, too, recalled Connor from his visits to Talita and admitted that the man he'd seen bore a strong resemblance to the boy he remembered.

Reports began to filter in from the countryside. The rebellion was still going on in the far north, but everywhere else there was quiet. Several of the hidden caches of arms had been discovered by the army. Two priests were known to have fled, and in one case, there was a puzzling report that villagers had seen a Kraaken brother talking to a priest who had subsequently disappeared.

There was much discussion. No one understood what was going on. If the Kraaken were fomenting a rebellion, then why had the priest fled without raising up his peasant flock in revolt?

Jillian remained apart from the lengthy discussions, paying attention only when new reports came in. Several times, she got up and went to a window to stare out at the empty place where the island had been.

Then suddenly, she felt a tingling awareness she couldn't quite understand. And as she looked up, she realized that she wasn't the only one feeling something. Voices in the room died away as men looked uneasily at each other and then into the corners.

He appeared in front of the closed doors. One moment, there was only the richly carved wood with gold inlays; and the next, Connor stood there, tall and powerful in his Kraaken robes. The others stared. Jillian cried out and stood up slowly on shaking legs.

Connor's gaze swept the room and finally came to rest on her. He crossed the room in swift, long strides and reached out to her. She hesitated, certain he couldn't be real. But the hand that grasped hers was solid and warm and the eyes that met hers glowed with desire.

Still holding her hand, he turned to the others, then bowed slightly to the king, who had risen from his chair.

"Forgive my intrusion, Your Majesty, but there was no other way for me to come here. My name is Connor—formerly Brother Averyl. I was born and raised on—"

"I know who you are, Connor," the king said. Given the circumstances, his tone was surprisingly mild.

"Then Jillian has told you about our journey," Connor said, his eyes flicking back to her for confirmation.

"I've told them all of it," Jillian confirmed, still clinging tightly to his hand. Through her mind ran his words: *formerly Brother Averyl.* What could he mean? He was more Kraaken than ever.

"Connor, are you responsible for . . . for what happened?" Timor asked.

Connor smiled. "Yes, Timor, I am. Or perhaps I should say that the kraa and I are responsible."

"Connor!" Jillian withdrew her hand, even though she felt bereft without it. "You can't mean this! They've got you under a spell!"

"No one has me under a spell, Jilly. I am acting of my own will, with the aid of the kraa, of course. I did what I believe must be done."

"And what is that?" the king inquired.

"Your majesty, not all of the brothers are evil. In fact, most of them are good men. Only Jenner and a few others conceived this plot. If I had permitted your army to attack the island, innocent men would have died."

"So you don't deny that Jenner was behind the rebellion?"

Connor shook his head. "He was behind it. He wanted power—the power he couldn't get through magic. But I've put a stop to it, except for the northern province. I'm afraid that the army will have to take care of them. I have no taste for using my powers in war."

He paused, then strode to the window and raised his hand. Jillian and the others watched as he traced something in the air, then turned back to them.

"The island, as you can see, is back where it belongs. Jenner and those who plotted with him are dead. They took their own lives rather than let me deliver them into your hands. Some others have already gone to the mountains to join the Whitebeards. Others, with your permission, wish to remain—as teachers. They have no sorcery and no desire to cause harm to anyone."

As Connor spoke, Jillian and the others all moved toward the windows. When she saw the island, Jillian felt cold. *He* had done this: Connor, the man she loved. Unconsciously, she moved away from him, avoiding his gaze even though she could feel him staring at her.

"I found a list of the places where the weapons were stored among Jenner's things," Connor said, handing it over to the general.

A silence fell on the assembly. Lost in her private pain, Jillian failed to notice that everyone was staring at her as she continued to stand at the window.

Surely, she thought as she stared at the island, *I can take some satisfaction in the knowledge that Brother Averyl the powerful sorcerer did not betray the Connor I love.* But try as she might, she couldn't summon up any pleasure over that. What she wanted now was for him to be gone—back to the Whitebeards, back to the life he'd chosen. Each moment he remained here was a torment.

"Connor," the king said, breaking the silence.

"We are in your debt. You have prevented a war that would have cost many lives."

Unseen by Jillian as she continued to look at the island, Connor inclined his head. "There are two favors I would ask in return, Your Majesty."

"Name them and they are yours," the king replied.

"I would like your agreement that the brotherhood can remain on the island and continue to recruit young men to be educated by them. I give my personal guarantee that there will be no more plots."

"Of course," the king agreed quickly. "And what is your second request?"

Still unseen by Jillian, Connor glanced at her and smiled. "I am requesting your permission to marry the Lady Jillian."

A stunned silence followed that statement. Jillian whirled around to face Connor, as confused as the others.

"I don't understand, Connor," the king said. "Your vows. The powers you have."

"I have no more powers. I forswore them back in the mountains. But the Whitebeards persuaded me of the necessity of setting things here right. They knew something was about to happen."

He smiled again, his gaze going from the king to Jillian. "As of this moment, I am no longer a sorcerer—only a man who very much wants to spend the rest of his days with the woman he loves."

The king beamed at both of them in turn. "You

not only have my permission, Connor, but my blessing as well."

Jillian crossed the room to him, though she was scarcely aware of doing so. The hand that took hers was warm and solid and real. But the magic—their special magic—was still there.

Epilogue

"Daddy, look!"

But Connor had already spotted the great bird as it spiraled down from the blue skies.

"What is it?"

"It's called a kraa," he said, taking his son's hand as he waited for the bird to land. "They live in a place very far away. Your mother and I saw them long ago—before you were born."

"Daddy! What is that bird? It's so big!"

Connor smiled down at his daughter as she came running to him and took his other hand. At six, she was a perfect replica of her mother in every way.

"It's called a kraa," he told her. "And I think it has a message for me."

"But it *can't* have a message," she protested. "It's not wearing a pouch."

The great bird had settled gracefully to earth about twenty feet away, its brilliant emerald eyes sweeping over the children before coming to rest on Connor. Then it suddenly shifted its gaze to a point behind him and Connor turned to see Jillian running toward them.

"Why has it come?" she demanded, glaring at the bird.

"It has brought a message," Connor told her, smiling because he knew her anger was born of fear—even after all these years.

The bird stared at him for a long moment, then rose once again into the heavens and was gone from sight quickly.

Connor continued to stare after it, and Jillian waited patiently for him to explain. She'd managed to learn some patience over the past twelve years, though only with considerable effort.

Finally, he turned to her and she saw the unshed tears in his eyes. "Edamo and the others have died of their own choice. He sent the kraa to tell us that he wishes us a life as joyous as his was. And Seka and the others send their greetings as well. They are the Whitebeards now."

The children began to pelt their parents with questions, but Connor told them to return to the house and he would tell them the story later. They both ran off and Connor wrapped his arms around Jillian, then kissed the top of her head. Suddenly, he drew back, laughing.

"Do you know you have some gray hairs?"

"Of course. Not all of us have been given the

opportunity to become immortal."

"Oh?" He arched a dark brow. "And if you had the choice?"

She laughed. "Ask me in another twenty years or so."

Futuristic Romance

Journey to the distant future where love rules and passion is the lifeblood of every man and woman.

Heart's Lair by Kathleen Morgan. Although Karic is the finest male specimen Liane has ever seen, her job is not to admire his nude body, but to discover the lair where his rebellious followers hide. Never does Liane imagine that when the Cat Man escapes he will take her as his hostage—or that she will fulfill her wildest desires in his arms.
__3549-9 $4.50 US/$5.50 CAN

The Knowing Crystal by Kathleen Morgan. On a seemingly hopeless search for the Knowing Crystal, sheltered Alia has desperate need of help. Teran, with his warrior skills and raw strength, seems to be the answer to her prayers, but his rugged masculinity threatens Alia. Even though Teran is only a slave, Alia will learn in his powerful arms that love can break all bonds.
__3548-0 $4.50 US/$5.50 CAN

LEISURE BOOKS
ATTN: Order Department
276 5th Avenue, New York, NY 10001

Please add $1.50 for shipping and handling for the first book and $.35 for each book thereafter. PA., N.Y.S. and N.Y.C. residents, please add appropriate sales tax. No cash, stamps, or C.O.D.s. All orders shipped within 6 weeks via postal service book rate. Canadian orders require $2.00 extra postage and must be paid in U.S. dollars through a U.S. banking facility.

Name _____

Address _____

City _____ State _____ Zip _____

I have enclosed $_____ in payment for the checked book(s).
Payment <u>must</u> accompany all orders.☐ Please send a free catalog.